"*A comparatively new writer of science fiction, Robert Carr is a welcome one. . . . The four stories in this volume evidence his humor, his absorption with human values, and his writing skill.*"

— **New York Times**

"*Four beautifully written stories. . . . Crackling dialogue and complete freshness of phrase.*"

— **Theodore Sturgeon**

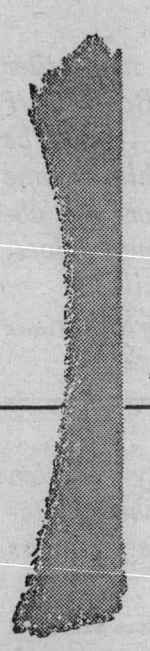

Author of:

THE RAMPANT AGE

THE ROOM BEYOND

BEYOND

INFINITY

**ROBERT
SPENCER
CARR**

A DELL BOOK

Published by
DELL PUBLISHING COMPANY, INC.
261 Fifth Avenue
New York 16, New York

Copyright, MCML, MCMLI,
by Robert Spencer Carr.

Copyright, MCMXLVII, MCMXLIX,
by The Curtis Publishing Company.

Reprinted by arrangement with
Fantasy Press,
Reading, Pennsylvania.

Designed and produced by
Western Printing & Lithographing Company

Cover painting by Richard Powers

Printed in U. S. A.

TO TIMOTHY,

for whom these stories may come true.

■

CONTENTS

Beyond Infinity 11

Morning Star. 87

Those Men From Mars 131

Mutation 209

CONTENTS

Beyond Infinity 19

Morning Star ....

Time Will Tell Over 131

Afterlife 205

BEYOND INFINITY

It MADE HIM FEEL LIKE a beachcomber, to stroll back to his office after a long, late, leisurely lunch, wondering what rare and curious new business matters the tides in the affairs of men had cast upon the small shore of his desk in the hours he had been gone.

He rode up in the elevator full of warm well-being, sirloin steak, and an affable readiness to be entertained. Perhaps the murmuring gray city had washed up a pearl, or fragrant ambergris, among the driftwood of the day. There might even be some money in the afternoon mail, he thought hopefully, and smiled.

He ambled down the corridor until he came upon his name, in small black letters on the frosted glass. It always surprised him a little, to find it still intact.

Don Brook. Room 79. No occupation stated. The door to his modest two-room suite gave no clue to what went on inside. It was difficult to state his business in words that would not prey upon the minds of other tenants. Don didn't like to worry people. He didn't worry himself.

As he did from force of habit before he entered any room, he paused at his own door and listened. He could hear his secretary, Miss Mosely, enjoying a personal telephone call. It was mostly shrieks and giggles. Don smiled indulgently. So spring had come again. He hoped she would be happy. Perhaps her punctuation would improve.

Rather than inhibit her, he stepped around the corner of the hall and quietly unlocked the side door to his private office. He crossed catfooted to his high, old-fashioned desk and leafed through the telephone-message slips that had accumulated in his absence. Some were funny. Some were going to be sad, for somebody. A few were cryptic utterances no sane mortal could have made; but Miss Mosely would die gamely at the stake insisting that was what the Voice had told her. The oddest things happened to Miss Mosely. People said peculiar things to her, and to no one else. She paid receipted bills a second time, and saw bluebirds out of season. Don Brook would not have traded her for the sharpest secretary on Sunset Strip. Miss Mosely kept him on his toes, a quality essential to his profession.

When Miss Mosely finally signed off, with a singing commercial, Don coughed apologetically. There was a scurry in the outer office. She came in contritely with the afternoon mail, unopened. She was a small, plump person with an earnest red apple of a face that looked as if it wanted to be picked.

After throwing the advertisements and bills into the wastebasket, Don was left with one envelope that looked like it might be a letter. "Can that be all, Miss Mosely?" he asked, disappointed.

"It can," she said. "All except a woman who keeps calling."

"Did she leave her name?"

"You know they never do. These dames—"

"What does she seem to want?"

"Same thing I always want. To know when you'll be in."

"And what did you tell her?"

"Expected momentarily."

"Did she laugh?"

"Not a snicker."

"Must be serious. Let her in, when she comes."

"Ohh kay," sighed Miss Mosely, and trudged out.

Don examined the envelope. It was postmarked *Pasadena, 7 a.m.*, that day. Plain white envelope. Address typewritten on a new machine. No return address. Stamp upside down.

Don reached for his letter opener, had a hunch, snapped on his lamp instead, and held the envelope against the strong white light. Inside, dimly outlined, he could see a folded triangle of darker paper. He worked open one of the seams at the side of the envelope, leaving the closure intact, and drew out a square of violet paper folded once diagonally. On it was typed, by a very old machine, in quavering queer letters like a cracked, mad voice:

My friend, prepare yourself for the inevitable dawning of the golden day of which the bravest hearts and noblest minds of every generation since the world began have always dreamed: The day when we shall know the Answer to what lies

The message ended in mid-air, without punctuation or signature. The paper had been torn straight across.

Don sighed. Another screwball. He brushed the message off into the wastebasket. Living in Los Angeles, you learned to take these things in your stride. The parks were full of them. They rang your doorbell, phoned you, mailed you the mimeographed secrets of the universe, postage due. In the City of the Angels, the beat of mighty wings was not far overhead.

His buzzer buzzed. "Lady to see you, Mr. Brook." It was Miss Mosely's favorably-impressed voice.

"The one who phoned so many times and wouldn't laugh?"

"I'll ask her." The circuit clicked into silence. When Miss Mosely's voice returned, it had suffered a spiritual defeat. "She wants to know what blessed difference that could possibly make."

Don chuckled. "Send her in." Miss Mosely having promoted her from woman to lady, Don emptied the ash tray in her honor. Then he lay back in his swivel chair, relaxed, and made his mind a neutral blank. First impressions of clients could be as useful as a wax imprint of a key. Sometimes in the first few seconds you sensed situations that took weeks of outside work to prove.

The door was opening. A cool, tall girl entered with an easy stride. She wore a straight white dress so smartly simple that Don had to look a second time to convince himself that it was not a nurse's uniform. Her dress had tiny, triangular black buttons and a long, long zipper down the front, from throat to hem. He liked that; but he did not like the little smile of scornful amusement she wore upon a pale, fine-featured face. She glanced around his office with delicate disdain.

Slumming, Don decided. *She's more amused by her surroundings than by her errand. And that is bad for me.* He stood up. "Good afternoon. Won't you sit down?"

"Not yet," said the tall girl, and turned her back. She had found his bookcase. She went to it, bent close, and read the rows of scientific titles to herself.

"Hmm," she said to the books. Presently she straightened up and took a new look at their owner. Her smile of amusement was still there, but the scorn was fading from it. "Aren't these books rather unusual reading for a detective?" she observed. *"Our Expanding Universe. Our Shrinking Solar System.* How did you get interested in such deep subjects?"

"From reading the comic books," said Don.

She tried to stare him down, and permanently failed. He held out the chair for her in silence. She surrendered, conditionally, and sat down, curling herself in a way that made her look much smaller than she really was.

She made a move to open her handbag. Don parried with a cigarette. She nodded, and he lit it for her, observing that she wore no rings. She could scarcely be looking for an absconding husband, he decided. Even from a cursory examination, Don doubted that missing mates would ever be a problem in her life.

He put on his professional manner. "What's your trouble?"

"Haven't any." She crossed her ankles. "I am representing someone. Under protest." She watched closely for the effect of her next words, as if much depended on it. "Doctor Burgess Wood."

Don nodded. "The great astronomer. Retired last year as president emeritus of the Astro-Physical Institute."

Her look of amusement went the way of her scorn, leaving an unalloyed smile of frank approval and surprise. "Imagine a policeman knowing that. Or even pronouncing it."

"I'm not a policeman," Don said patiently. "I do not take criminal cases."

"What, no murder mysteries?" She summoned her amused smile to return to her defense. She was fighting against a favorable impression.

Don looked down at the soles of her outthrust, tilted sport shoes. "Murder is no mystery," he said, patting in a yawn. "Killing is the commonest thing in life. What is more obvious and unmistakable than death?" (She had stepped recently in red clay, he noted.) "But the inexplicable, uncanny disappearance of a responsible adult is different," he went on. *(Wonder where she found red clay to step in?)* "It may mean anything from amnesia to espionage. More disappearances remain unsolved than murders. That's because there's no law against taking a powder, if you don't take anything else. And that's why I specialize in missing persons who've done nothing but disappear."

"Another specialist," she said. "Aren't there any general practitioners any more?"

"Your Doctor Wood was something of a specialist himself," said Don, trying hard to find common ground with her elusive smile. "His life work, as I recall, was combating the dangerous theories of Professor Pritchard Leigh. The rocketeer who killed so many volunteers in his experiments, some years ago."

"You needn't use the past tense," she said quickly. "Gramps is still very much alive, at home in Pasadena." She sensed his scrutiny of her shoes, and tucked her feet back underneath her chair, self-consciously.

Don raised his eyebrows. "I read in the Astronaut that

Doctor Wood was a confirmed bachelor."

"He is. Oh, don't look so conventional. Gramps is my pet name for him," the girl explained. "I've been his confidential secretary for a long time now. Since I was eight. Titles wear off, around the house. He's such a grand old party, I just call him Gramps. Think nothing of it."

"I don't. What did he send you to see me about?"

"To ask," she said with disapproval, "how much you would charge to find a woman. A distinguished female scientist whom Doctor Wood has been in love with all his life—and lost. She's dropped completely out of sight, and yet he knows she isn't dead."

Don studied the zipper. "Isn't Gramps getting on a bit for such research?"

"He's only eighty," she said maternally. "Is that too old?"

"I wouldn't know," said Don. Her proposition sounded as wacky as the one in the wastebasket. There seemed to be a bumper crop of nuts, this season. He decided not to bite. He said, "Since you're here under protest, I think you'd better go somewhere else."

"Oh, I intend to," she said. "This call is a mere formality, to humor Gramps. Some colleague told him that you are the top man in your field. Some absent-minded professor."

"Investigations are expensive," Don warned her. "Astronomers haven't much money, as a rule."

"Not as a rule," she agreed. "However, Doctor Wood has just won the Pelton Prize in Science, as, of course, you wouldn't know—"

"For his remeasurement of all interplanetary distances," Don went on modestly.

"Oh, stop showing off," she said. "Just tell me how much you'd charge for wasting your time and our money, and I'll leave. And you can stop staring at my zipper. It doesn't work. It's stuck."

Don could feel his neck growing red. He found himself disliking her intensely. He tried to fight it off, for she was as inviting as a long slim glass of iced champagne. She had a tall girl's lonely look underneath her clever air. And still the price was set too high. Needling. Badgering. Condescension. He decided not to take the case. He would get rid of her immediately; but it would have to be done with finesse. The best technique, safer than a blunt refusal, was now to say something so preposterous and alarming that the client would voluntarily withdraw, never to return.

Don thought quickly while he lit a second pair of cigarettes for both of them. In her case it should be easy to drive her away at once. Her employer was notably conservative, even among the high academic brass. For half a century, through his telescopes and in the science journals, Burgess Wood had fought the fantastic in every form. This girl's weak spot—no doubt her only weakness—was her loyalty to Doctor Wood. He began obliquely.

"My fee depends upon the type of disappearance I am asked to solve. The other-man and other-woman runaways are fairly easy to trace, as a rule. Love is not only blind, but careless with clues. Did Gramps's lady scientist run off with another man?"

The girl nodded. "Yes, but she married him first. Gramps was best man at their wedding. Broke his heart, poor dear."

Don blinked. "When was this, please?"

"Long before you or I were born."

He scratched his head. "I don't understand the time element in this case."

"Don't try to. Astronomers think in closed, curved space time. The Einstein Theory. That lets you out."

Don knew the time had come to scare her off. Lowering his eyes, he said mysteriously, "I think it's only fair to warn you there is one common type of disappearance I have found impossible to solve. I never take those cases."

"What on earth is that?"

"That's just the trouble," he said darkly, unable to look her in the face for fear he would laugh out loud. "It is not entirely of this earth, I fear. After investigating many inexplicable disappearances, it is my considered judgment that certain selected human beings, usually persons of talent, are deliberately plucked off this planet by unseen hands that reach in from the Outside!" He kept his eyes fixed on the floor and braced his pride against the coming of her scornful laughter. She would rise and leave in indignation, freeing him from the disturbing sense of stimulation he had experienced since the moment she came in. His life would be simple again. But a little lonely, ever after.

He waited. Nothing happened. He looked up. She was nodding gravely. "Yes," she said, "you are definitely the right man for this case."

Don sat up in alarm. "Now wait a minute—"

"Yes," she went on thoughtfully, "nothing will bring Gramps to his senses more quickly than to have a lunatic like you around. Then he'll drop this quixotic notion, and save his money for his old age."

Don stood up smiling. He was definitely angry now; and when his temper rose, his mind grew clearer, calmer, more controlled.

"That will be all, thank you," he said quietly. "Good afternoon."

She crushed out her cigarette. He did not offer her another. She opened her handbag and began to rummage. "Why don't you like me?" she said in a smaller voice.

"How could I?"

She found a cigarette and tapped it on the corner of his desk. "Please understand that I have nothing against you personally, Mr. Brook. You're passably good-looking in a battered sort of way. You're no midget. You have a beautiful bright red neck. Under different circumstances— Never mind." She waited for a match. No light came. She delved in her purse again. "But under the present impossible circumstances, we'll just let the whole thing go." She broke off, stared into the clutter of her purse, and gingerly removed a triangle of violet paper.

Don watched narrowly while she unfolded it into a square and read it through. It seemed to him that her surprise was genuine. There was so little of it. An actress would have given the part more emotion than she did. This girl was trying *not* to seem surprised at what she had found in her purse.

She finished reading the few typewritten lines and looked at Don resentfully. "Veddy, veddy funny," she said. "How did you manage to slip this into my purse without my knowing?"

Don took a quick look into his wastebasket. His violet message was still there. He held out his hand to her. "Let me see that, please."

She drew away. "No, I'll save this for evidence at your sanity trial."

"I didn't write it or put it there. Give it to me, I said."

"But it fits in exactly with that rubbish you were talking a moment ago," she insisted. "Listen, in case you've forgotten your own prosody." She read aloud, in a taunting voice of mock grandiloquence:

"... *beyond the skies; but when the cosmic promise is revealed, then strengthen your soul, O little men, for the great surprises of the spirit. What man in his earth-blindness seeks upon the luminous high seas of space may not*"

She put it down impatiently. "Torn off, top and bottom. You should learn to finish sentences, Mr. Brook." She arose with a gesture of dismissal. "This is too much. I'll go back and tell Gramps to forget it. You said you hadn't accepted the case. Well, you needn't—now. Good afternoon." She replaced the violet paper in her purse, and started toward the door.

The moment her back was turned Don stooped and snatched the first part of the message from his wastebasket. He put it in his pocket, took his hat, and beat her to the door by one long stride.

To his bewilderment she raised her face gratefully to

him. "Thank you very much," she said with sincere simplicity. "I really wanted you to come with me all the time, you know."

"You conceal your desires well," said Don dryly.

"I'm no good at crawling," she confessed. "Especially when it's something I want very much. I always kick it in the shins."

As if embarrassed by having said too much, she veered away from him, circled back to his bookcase, and drew out a volume bound in purple. "You'll need this," she said, "where we are going."

They were in the elevator before he got a clear look at the title of the book she had selected. It was *The Sublime Adventure,* by Pritchard Leigh. It had been written years ago, before Leigh's billions were cut off by an outraged Congress and his whole project discredited by the orthodox astronomers, led by Burgess Wood, marching as to war. The book's jacket showed stars and skyrockets; but Leigh's fireworks had fizzled out long ago.

Answering Don's puzzled frown, the girl explained, "I brought this book along because I want you to get off on the right foot with Pritch. Since his fall from grace he's hard to know. Suspicious of strangers."

"Pritch," said Don. "I thought we were going to Pasadena."

She led him toward a parking-lot on Olive Street. "We are. Right up the speedway."

"But it says in the Astronaut that Professor Pritchard Leigh never, never leaves that desert hideaway of his out in New Mexico."

She laughed. "The Astronaut should have said, 'Well, hardly ever.' Pritch has been our house guest one week a month all year."

While Don pondered on this, a panhandler with the face of a tragic poet crossed the busy sidewalk, cut Don out of the crowd, and asked him for a dime, in cultured accents.

Don gave him a quarter. The beggar bowed silently

and dropped astern.

"Always impress females with your generosity," the girl teased. "It helps fool them. Leave big tips on restaurant tables. You'll be eating off the ironing-board soon enough, honey."

"But I didn't have a dime," said Don mildly.

"You could have asked him to change it."

In front of the interurban station, a little old lady stood tremulous and lost. She had a furled umbrella, a straw suitcase, and an air of bewilderment. The passing throng ignored her, but when she saw Don Brook, yards away, she brightened and signaled to him with her umbrella.

Don sighed and went to her assistance. The tall girl followed curiously. "Are these characters your confederates?"

"Yes," said Don. "Yes, ma'am?"

"Young man, how do I get to the LaBrea Pits?"

Don told her. It took quite a while. When they walked on, the girl asked, "How long does this go on?"

"All day," said Don.

"What happens if you take your hat off in a department store?" she asked thoughtfully.

Don grimaced. "You tell me."

"Which counter has stylish stouts, and where do I open a charge account?"

He nodded sheepishly. "Also, on what floor are girdles?"

"That's bad." She stopped and took his chin briefly in her cupped hand. "Let me look." She looked and let go. "Yes, you've really got one." She turned into the parking-lot and handed the white-robed attendant a claim check. "They're fairly rare, too. Those nondescript, good-natured faces that simply look like whatever kind of man a body happens to be waiting for. A laundryman, a doctor, a kindly janitor. I assume you've been mistaken for long-lost relatives, and soundly bussed?"

Don nodded grimly. "And old school chums. On buses."

A large open roadster, shimmering in two tones of pastel blue, lurched up in front of them and skidded to a stop

21

with the angry violence by which parking-lot attendants avenge themselves for having to fetch other people's cars. The girl slipped in on the right side and curled up on the canary-colored leather. "You drive," she said.

Don flashed her a warm look of appreciation. "How did you know that about me?"

"I don't know anything about you, personally," she replied, "but I know a little bit about men. They love to be fed regularly, have their backs scratched, and hate sitting idly by while a mere miss enjoys driving a high-powered car. But if this was a vacuum cleaner, you wouldn't mind my driving it."

He swung into traffic with a grin. "You know everything you need to know, miss."

"You don't, mister. Take the emergency brake off, please. It's under there."

He flushed and drove north in silence. The girl lay back in the warm breeze and closed her eyes. At traffic lights, he studied her. In repose, her face revealed that she was younger than she acted. He wondered what her name was. The California registration certificate on the steering-column caught his eye. He turned the big card in its leather holder and read aloud. " 'Holly Summers, age 23, eyes blue, hair brown, sex female, height five-ten, weight two-twelve' —they must mean one-twelve, Holly— 'valid only while wearing glasses.' "

"Oh, shut up," she said sleepily, and turned her back.

Far out on Colorado Boulevard he slowed down and debated how best to wake her. He ruled against anything sensational, although she did look quite appealing, asleep with her face against the yellow cushions. Deciding upon a policy of slow but sure, he tapped her formally on the shoulder.

"Pardon me, Miss Summers, but how do we get where we're going?"

She woke up quickly and took her bearings. "I'll drive now," she said. She stood up against the windshield, and held the wheel. They changed seats without stopping.

She turned off Colorado and took him careening up into the hills. He closed his eyes and hung on as she barreled into the corkscrew curves. He remembered questions he had wanted to ask while she was asleep. "In the Astronaut," he shouted, against the rushing wind, "it always says that Doctor Burgess Wood and Professor Pritchard Leigh stand at opposite poles of the scientific world, and are bitter enemies."

She turned off toward thin air and parked on a narrow ledge. When she replied her voice was low as if they might be overheard. "Pritch held out the olive branch some years ago. Gramps took it; Gramps would. They're both getting to the age when a good tangible cigar and a game of chess are more important than abstract theories no one has ever proved, and probably never will. Too bad all men can't live that long! Besides, Pritch has got Gramps working hard on some kind of super-dooper calculations, for him. Says he'll recant, if Gramps proves him wrong." She guided Don to a narrow flagstone walk that curved around the hilltop like an encircling arm.

"That doesn't sound like Leigh to me," Don said softly, keeping close behind her. How convenient it was, he found, not to have to stoop to whisper into a girl's ear. She was right there.

"I told you Gramps is a gullible old dear," she whispered. They turned a rocky corner and came upon a hilltop house, rambling and low, with more ups and downs to it than an author's life. A taffy-colored cocker spaniel bustled up to Don, sniffed his credentials, woofed cordial greetings.

Directly below them, in a tiled patio on the edge of a sheer precipice, two old men sat eating in the sun. One was long and thin, with a feathery white plume of hair; an egret of a man. The other was short and round, with a large sun-bronzed bald head like a cannon ball.

Don gripped Holly's arm. "Why, that stocky man is really Leigh!" he whispered. "I thought you were kidding!"

23

"It could be a fatal mistake," she said, under her breath, "to think I'm kidding. When I'm not, that is. Or, if I *am,* to think I'm *not* kidding." She handed Don the book that she had carried from the car. "Be very boyish about asking Leigh for his autograph. It's the only way of disarming a misanthropic author. Now with Gramps you'll have to smile expressively and make eloquent gestures. Gramps goes by people's expressions and behavior, more than by what they say. Usually he doesn't even listen to what they say. He just watches their hands— Now be still. Here are the stairs."

She stepped down first into the patio, and introduced them with the easy air of a veteran hostess. Wood's hand-shake was dry and cool, his voice deep and slow. Leigh's palm was moist and warm, his voice high-pitched and rapid. The three men stood waiting for Holly to sit down. "Don't mind me," she said. "When I'm starved, I eat standing up." She went to a portable steam table and began to fill her plate.

"My grandniece has an appalling appetite," said the old astronomer. "I can't see where she puts it all."

"She transforms mass directly into energy," said Leigh. He pushed aside his empty plate and stood up patting his solid midriff with satisfaction. Then he saw the purple cover in Don's hand, and gave a sickly smile. "Well, now," he said. "It's been a long time since I saw one of those. Don't tell me I have a reader, after all these years."

"Yes, and I'd like your autograph," said Don, opening the book at the flyleaf and holding it out.

"Why, I'd be delighted," said Professor Leigh, his nervousness disappearing. Then he stiffened and scowled. "But who told you I'd be here? Who are you, anyway? You look like a reporter to me!"

Don concentrated upon unscrewing his fountain pen. Holly came to the table with a steaming, heaped-up plate. Leigh turned to her. "I begged you not to tell anybody where I am. My visits here are top secret."

Holly said, with a pacifying sweetness Don found quite

surprising, "It happens that this young man carries your book around with him wherever he goes. That's how much he admires you, Pritchard. He wouldn't be without it."

"Oh, really?" said the stout professor, growing pleased. He turned back to Don and scrawled his name in backhand loops like whiplashes. Then he said, "Excuse me, I must begin packing." He started toward the house.

Doctor Wood smiled at Don. "So you're going to find Martha Madison for me."

Leigh paused, picked up his empty plate, and went to the steam table.

Don looked at Burgess Wood. Despite his reputed sensitivity to behavior, he had noticed nothing. He turned hospitably to Don. "Help yourself to anything you see. We don't pass things here. This is Freedom House." He beamed. "I'm eating breakfast, my guest is eating lunch, while my ravenous niece is eating the first of a series of dinners. So we never know. Which will you have? Cereal, or lobster?"

"I'll settle for black coffee," said Don. He went to the electric hot plate, and poured. Professor Leigh was taking a long time selecting second helpings of everything, in homeopathic portions. One olive. Two mushrooms. Three peas. He kept his face averted, toying with the curried lobster. The peas shook on his plate. One rolled off, and fell into the sautéed kidneys with a tiny splash that could be heard in the silence that had descended.

Don carried his coffee back across the patio and sat down beside Doctor Wood. He remembered to smile encouragingly. He made risky gestures with his brimming cup.

"Ah, yes," said the old man. "Let's get under way. How much has my niece told you?"

Don looked to Holly for his cue. She minutely shook her head.

"She didn't tell me anything," Don said promptly.

"Excellent," said the old astronomer. "I always prefer to present the original formulation myself. Briefly, these are the factors: The girl married my best friend, instead of me. Oh, there wasn't any ugliness." His keen eyes took on a far-off, starry look. "Martha made her choice openly, honestly, and calmly, in front of both of us, one moonlit night. She said that since she loved us both, and knew we were both destined to become great men, it was for her a question of deciding which man needed her the most in his life's work.

"I was bound to be a scientist, an astronomer. I already had a respectable, well-paid appointment at the Yale Observatory. But Martha was smart. She knew intuitively that stargazers need less from their wives than almost any other men. They sit up with their telescopes all night, and sleep all day. Their minds are apt to be light-years away from home. That's where Martin had it over me. He had just been ordained a minister of some peculiarly penniless sect. A medical missionary, if you please, bound for no less than the Cannibal Isles, where he would put pants on the pagans while they took his off and put him in the stewpot. Martin Madison would need a good woman's love, to say the least; not to mention a few regiments of Marines.

"Martha's heart being what it was, big and brave as all humanity, she kissed me good-by—and married him. That was fifty years ago this month." He paused and looked questioningly at Professor Pritchard Leigh. "Is anything wrong, my friend? I thought you were going to pack."

The stout, bald-headed man was standing in a cramped position, looking pale. "My sacroiliac is out again," he groaned. "Give me a hand, somebody."

Don rose and helped Leigh to a chaise longue. His hands had turned quite cold. He lay down at full length, and closed his eyes. "I'll be all right if I don't have to move," he said weakly. "Carry on. Just ignore me."

While he was up, Don filled his coffee cup again. "Yes, Doctor Wood?" he prompted, expressionless and still.

On her way back for second helpings, Holly kicked him lightly on the shin. He turned on her in exasperation. She showed him in swift pantomime how he looked, and how he ought to look, to keep her uncle's attention.

Don turned back to Doctor Wood with an engaging smile, and waved his free arm with animation.

"Oh, yes!" The old man brightened and resumed his tale, puffing on a long, pale cigar.

"I prayed that after a few years of malaria and jungle rot, Martha would have enough religion, and come back to civilization. Meaning me. I was then a full professor. I measured the distance to Saturn; but I misjudged Martha's courage. She went with Martin Madison from triumph to new triumph, through every hellhole on this pestilential planet. Madison became a scientist, of sorts. Obviously to compete with me. For I was growing famous, too. The deeper they went into the jungles, the higher I went into the skies. And then Martin Madison began to develop his obscene obsession." The old man chomped angrily on his cigar.

Leigh opened his eyes a slit. They were guarded, veiled. "You shouldn't say that, Burgess. There is nothing obscene about the major promise of all the higher religions. You're blasphemous!"

Wood pounded his cane on the flagstones. "I say it's blasphemous, and obscene, for anyone to want eternal life—literally, in the crumbling prison of the flesh. Nothing in Nature lives forever. Stars are God's grandest creations, but even they don't live forever. Old stars burn out, like altar candles, and have to be replaced by novae." The old man turned to Don. "Do you know what that crazy sky pilot did to my Martha?"

"I'm afraid I don't," said Don, uneasily.

"Why, he dragged her up and down the boondocks, looking for a source of everlasting youth, to prove the Bible's promise. They went into the Florida Everglades, ostensibly as missionaries to the Seminoles. Actually he was hunting for Ponce de Leon's fountain of eternal youth. All he got was amoebic dysentery, the same as Ponce de Leon. Then he took her to Tibet, presumably to convert the Dalai Lama, but in reality to study the secrets of longevity those old buzzards up there claim to know. All that he acquired in High Asia was altitude sickness, and pinworms. The last I heard, he was trying to break into Russia the back way to try some weird new long-life serum they claim to have developed. I can't imagine why." His voice sank. "That's where their trail faded out, ten years ago. That's where you come in, young man. Somewhere in the Gobi Desert."

Don stirred his coffee industriously. He had a feeling he was falling into the black whirlpool in his cup. Off at one side he heard Leigh saying to Holly, in the plaintive voice of an invalid, "Bring me a cup of coffee, too. That's a good girl. Oh, my aching back."

"That, Mr. Brook, is my problem," Doctor Wood said. "Any questions?"

"Yes," Don said. "Why do you want to find Martha Madison?"

The old astronomer waved his arms. "All kinds of obvious reasons. She may be alone, and in poverty. They were the kind who donate their book royalties and their lecture fees to charity. For the first time in my life I've got some money. I'd like to bring her here and make her comfortable for the first time in her life. We could sit here on the patio side by side, enjoy a good long rest, and watch the sun go down together, thinking of all that might have been."

Don observed a minute of respectful silence, to let the picture fade. Then he asked gently, "Where do their children live?"

"They never had any children. Now, if she had married me—"

"Do you have any pictures of her? Any records or mementos—"

It was Wood's turn to interrupt. "Have I!" He laughed. "You come with me." He arose and hobbled down a walk toward a concrete vault with barred windows. At the threshold he pulled out a jingling key ring and unlocked a fireproof door. "Step in here," he said, and smiled.

Don entered a dark room. A switch clicked behind him, and a light came on. He saw a shelf of books. All were by Martin and Martha Madison. He saw two enlarged photographs of a strikingly beautiful woman. In one she wore Arctic furs. In the other she wore a sun helmet. She looked at home in both. Near the door stood a small motion-picture projector. Don saw the white rectangle of a screen in the shadows at the far end of the room. Flat tins of movie film were ranged in metal racks. On long library tables lay huge scrapbooks fat with yellowed clippings. There were bound volumes of geographic magazines, and stacks of illustrated poster cards heralding transcontinental lecture tours, in the quaint type faces of decades ago. Don picked up one and read at random:

. . . not only missionaries extraordinary, but also the most famous man-and-wife team of writers, photographers, and explorers in history. Their daring expeditions carry not only the Bible and the Flag, but also the microscope and the movie camera into the last blind spots on earth. These copilots are also the world's greatest celestial navigators. Their bold discoveries make history in a dozen branches of science. They introduce new food crops wherever they go. She carries seeds from land to land like the goddess Ceres herself. . . .

Don dropped it. "Who was their lecture manager?"

"Don't think they had one," said Wood, taking down a can of film.

"I think they did," said Don. "The Madisons wouldn't write such stuff about themselves."

The old man was happily threading up his projection machine. "Mr. Brook, no pilot taking off upon a distant mission was ever so well briefed as you are going to be in the next few days. First I'll show you ninety reels—"

"Home movies hurt my eyes," said Don. He fled to the books. "Who was their publisher?"

"Bother their publisher," said the old man testily.

"These films of theirs are full of clues. I've collected them from visual education libraries in schools and churches all over the world."

Don took down the Madisons' complete works one by one. He glanced briefly at each colophon. They had stuck to the same minor publisher all their lives—the same fantasy publisher who put out Professor Leigh's visionary works.

Don turned to leave. The lights went out. He collided with someone very solid and very close behind him. The movie projector began to buzz. A bright scene struck the beaded screen. In the reflected light, Don recognized Professor Leigh standing beside him.

"Back better?" Don said pleasantly.

"The sacroiliac," said the professor, "slips in, as well as out. Shall we sit down? I'd like to see these pictures, too. Surely you weren't leaving?"

"I wouldn't think of it," said Don. They sat down warily on bitter little folding chairs.

The film was of an African expedition, in color, sound, and not a little fury. There were some embarrassing sequences of baptizing seven-foot sepia buckaroos, and some fair shots of the Madisons' famous houseboat floating down a muddy river. In it they had reached many an otherwise inaccessible shore. As the prow passed the camera Don saw that the boat was called *The Question Mark*. He was wondering about that when suddenly there shone out a scene of breath-taking beauty, one of those happy flukes the worst photographer will sometimes hit upon. An old-fashioned airplane taxied in and stopped, its fuselage filling the screen. The cabin door opened and Martha Madison climbed out on the wing. Unaware of the camera, she looked about and smiled as if she were glad to be alive, and back on terra firma. She wore tropical shorts and a low-necked sports blouse. Don began to see her husband's side of it; why he kept her in inaccessible localities, and searched for the fountain of youth.

"Nice looking woman," said Leigh casually. "Sorry I

never got to meet her."

Wood sat entranced some feet ahead of them, closer to the screen. The old man's Celluloid dream spun on, evoking colored shadows from the sleeping past. Now Martha was climbing down a swinging ladder from the high old airplane. Her movements were graceful, lithe, and wonderfully natural. Her hair was an exciting shade of reddish gold. Not too red, and not too golden. She was heaven and she was earth in a unity of opposites.

Halfway down the ladder, Martha Madison paused. She must have heard the camera behind her on that long-gone day. She glanced over her shoulder and saw the photographer. Her perfect naturalness remained unchanged. She swung around lithely on the ladder, waved, and smiled a smile of love so boundless that it leaped across time, space, and reason to include everyone who ever would see the film. She called in a lively voice whose warmth some sound recorder long gone to rust had captured perfectly.

"Oh, hel-*lo* there, everybody! This *is* a surprise!" She added something pleasant in Zulu.

Don felt a poignant nostalgia. What a girl she must have been.

Suddenly there was a ripping sound in the projector. A jagged sheet of light flamed across the screen. There was a frantic flapping as of frightened birds. Doctor Wood hastily shut off the projector, turned on the light, and sadly surveyed the broken film. "Getting mighty old and brittle," he mused. "Like me." He looked up sharply. "You men aren't leaving? My show has just begun. Ninety reels—"

"I've got to go to Hollywood," said Don.

"And we've got to get back to work, my friend," said Leigh to Wood. "If we go to your study now, and buckle down, we can be finished by midnight. We're nearly through."

Holly appeared in the door and hung listening.

The old astronomer stood mournfully holding his torn

ribbon of frail Celluloid. "Confound you, Pritchard," he said. "Why are you so anxious to get those quadratures computed? You're not going anywhere."

Leigh turned away. "Of course not," he said lightly. "As I told you, Burgess, if you will help me with these measurements, I will publish a paper formally confessing my errors of the past. And give you full credit, too. I shall beat my breast with one hand and scratch your back with the other. But how can I correct my own mistakes if you won't help me with those outer orbits? You won the Pelton Prize in this, not I. I'm an ignorant old scientific has-been who haunts the ruins of an abandoned laboratory in a Godforsaken desert, ashamed to show his face. Come on, now. Let's get to work."

"I've got to talk to my detective," said Wood firmly.

"He's leaving," said Don. "I'll think this over and phone you when I can." He hurried toward the patio to find his hat.

In a secluded corner, Leigh overtook him at a trot and drew him aside to the edge of the cliff. "I hate to butt in on a matter that's none of my business," he said apologetically, "but before you take this old man's money I think you should know that the Madisons have been dead for years."

"I don't remember reading anything about it in the papers," said Don.

"There was only a line," said Leigh. "A cabled dispatch from Outer Mongolia. Nobody noticed it. Why don't you be a sport, Brook, and drop this wild-ghost chase?"

"Why don't you be a sport and tell your host yourself his love is dead?" Don suggested. "You can see how much this means to him."

"I don't want to hurt him," said Leigh. "He's been such a help to me." He fidgeted. "Besides, he would demand all sorts of proof, and never let me go until I'd dug it up for him." He looked around uneasily, as though unseen eyes were watching him. "I've got to leave," he said half to himself, "quite punctually, this trip."

Don looked at his wrist watch and was startled. He had no idea that it had grown so late. He looked up impatiently. Leigh was plucking at his sleeve. "All right, then, I'll buy you off," Leigh said bluntly. He had a checkbook in his hands. "Rather than see this ghoulish farce go on. I'm doing this for Doctor Wood's sake, you understand."

Don smiled. "I have a funny rule. I can be corrupted by only one side at a time."

Holly was approaching, with her easy stride. Don said, over Leigh's head to her, "I've got to call a cab."

"I'll be your cab," she said. "No taxi man has ever yet found this address. This hill must be inside a time-twist or a space-warp." Noticing something about his face, she began to take longer steps. She had the motor running before he could snatch his hat off the table and jam it on his head and overtake her.

The corkscrew curves unwound. "Where to?" she asked, when they hit Colorado Boulevard, with a screech of tires.

"Hollywood and Vine," said Don. "Get there before five o'clock. That's probably when they close— No, don't ask questions. Just drive. I'll answer your questions without your asking them." He held his hat on with both hands. "We just got a break. What break? Not having to fly to New York tonight. Why not? Because the Madisons' publisher happens to be here. Why publisher? Because their books are still in print. That last edition was printed only five years ago. If anybody on this earth knows where they are, it would be their publisher."

"Couldn't we have—"

"Phoned? Not a chance. The Madisons' forwarding address, if it is known at all, is probably top secret. You'd be surprised how hard it is to find where certain authors live. And yet fan letters reach them promptly. I am now composing one to the Madisons."

His head jerked around. "Holly, you hit that man!"

"Just nicked his astral body. That's how fast he jumped. Don't watch the traffic, please. Scrunch down and contemplate my feet. Or something. And tell me why Leigh got jittery when he heard that Gramps wanted you to find Martha Madison."

"That's one of several odd angles we're going to try to figure out."

"We? Not me. I'm His Majesty's loyal opposition."

"You're certainly driving loyally and well. We may even make it, both alive."

"Oh, I just like to drive fast. You're merely my excuse for speeding. Nothing personal about it. But you'll have to keep telling me fascinating things or I will surely hit a traffic cop. How dangerous is my fat little house guest, if the chips were down?"

Don sank low in the deep upholstered seat and watched her slim shoes tread the pedals. "According to what I read in Astronaut," he said, "Professor Leigh could be about as dangerous as anybody. Because, when Congress stopped his project, they failed to dynamite his laboratories with all that heavy equipment in them. The excuse was that they could not be used for any other type of work. They were out in the middle of a howling desert. And besides, he still had powerful friends in Washington, who believed in him. Still do, in fact. The bill outlawing his activities passed by only seven votes, you may recall, if you weren't too busy dressing dolls at the time. Leigh's inventory was never checked, so he may have hidden materials in those tunnels he was always having drilled into Meteor Mountain." Don winced and stuck his head up over the edge of the door. "What happened then?"

She shoved his head down. "Don't look now. Tell on. What could Leigh do alone?"

"The joker is," said Don from below, in a muffled voice, "that Leigh is not alone. More than a hundred of his scientific staff elected to stay on in New Mexico after the government stopped their salaries. They formed a colony, and farmed and mined. They let their beards grow, wear leather britches, and shoot every head that shows among the rocks. Are they working on something *verboten*? Tut-

tut. They are retired civil servants, out there for their health." He raised his nose and sniffed. "We're in Hollywood," he said.

It was five minutes after five when the blue roadster came sizzling into North Vine Street. "You can look now," said Holly.

"I want the tall office building on the corner," Don said, tensing. "You park and—"

"Meet you in the doorway, by and by. Count nothing and pull your rip cord."

He lit running and caught the elevator's closing door with his forearm. The operator told him the proper floor. Don sprinted down the hall, skidded to a halt, and sedately entered an imposing paneled waiting-room, full of books and book displays.

The receptionist was pulling on a pair of long black gloves. "You're late," she said.

"Yes, I know," Don began humbly.

Ten minutes later he came out on the sidewalk and found Holly standing where he wanted her to be. He took her arm like a fast train taking on a mail sack. In one stride she was abreast of him.

"Get it?" she asked, opening the car door.

"Yuk."

"How?"

"I was mistaken for a literary agent's messenger boy. It seems the editors were waiting for a manuscript to publish. Then I met a stray secretary, who said the mail clerk had gone home, and for me to do the same. After a while she said all right, she'd look up the address for me, if they had it. She pulled out a drawer of filing-cards, looked under the M's, announced firmly they weren't allowed to give out that information. But I had peeked over her shoulder. The Burbank airport, please."

She nodded and flew him up Cahuenga Pass. "Which plane?"

"Anything that lets down at Albuquerque." He bent almost to the floor of the car to light two cigarettes in the gale. He passed one up to her, and asked, "You don't happen to remember Professor Leigh's New Mexico address?"

"It's the kind you can't forget. Route One, Box One—"

"Meteor Mountain, New Mexico," Don finished for her. "That is the Madisons' address, too. Their publisher's file card was smudged and worn and covered with a smear of old notations. They must have been living there for years! If they're still alive—"

Holly took the fourth groove of the eight-lane superhighway and held it against all counterattack. "Some people," she said, "think all Leigh's volunteers may not have died."

Don said, "I hope they died. I'd hate to think that any of them were still alive, after what Leigh did to them. A year out there would be bad enough. But ten years, twenty, thirty— Brr!"

She said, "Leigh may still beat us to the Madisons."

"Us," said Don. "I thought you were my opposition party."

"I am," she said. "That's why I'm going with you. I want to see exactly how you spend Gramps's money." A four-motor plane droned low across the highway, tucking up its wheels. She swung into the entrance of the huge air terminal. "Besides," she said, a little differently, "you may need my help."

"The way Martin needed Martha's in the Cannibal Isles?"

"Maybe worse. Pritchard Leigh has pressure cookers." She pulled up at the curb and handed a five-dollar bill to the dispatcher. "Keep this car in the garage until I come for it." He nodded and slipped in under the wheel as she slipped out, snatching a blue cape from the car. They ran for the steps.

How easily she kept up with him, Don noticed. "I thought women always had to go home and pack and pack," he panted.

"I can't go home. I'll have to live out of my checkbook."

"That won't help at the ticket window. I've barely enough cash for my own ticket."

They took their places in the queue. "I also have," she said on his shoulder, "a burdensome roll of bills that Gramps insisted I bring with me to your office, three hours ago, as a retainer fee. He said you'd be skeptical of checks." Don felt something large, thick, and cylindrical being slipped into his side pocket, under cover of her blue cape. "The meaning of this money has now been revealed."

"Now look," he began helplessly.

"You'd better pay for everything," she whispered, "or people will think we are married."

The line moved forward. Now they were only one thin man away. "Why can't you go home?" Don asked.

"Because Gramps would know, from looking at me, that you'd found out where Martha is. It is impossible to keep anything from him except in total darkness. He'd confide his joy to Leigh, and Leigh would murder both of us and wire ahead to his wild men to have you murdered, too. They're not working night and day on mechanical quadratures for nothing."

"What the hell are quadratures?"

"It's our turn," she said, nudging him. "I'll tell you in the plane."

The clerk had two no shows on the El Paso local, leaving in three minutes. "You see, Don," she laughed, loping along beside him on the runway, "I'm good luck."

"You'd better be," he said. They captured the last double seat and sank back to catch their breath. The plane rose into the setting sun, swung eastward toward the night. Over San Bernardino, Don drew the telegram pad from the seat pocket and handed it to Holly. "Take two telegrams," he said.

"You are confused," she said. "You are *my* employee. I am *your* employer. You take two telegrams."

"You take your salary out of mine. Now take—"

"Two telegrams," she said, pencil poised. "One to Miss Mosely, saying you'll be out of town until further notice,

37

but are expected momentarily. The other to the Albuquerque airport, ordering a rented car to meet us with its motor running."

Don looked weak. "I'm not used to such efficiency," he said. "It frightens me. Especially the rented car. I hadn't thought of that."

"Then what was your second telegram?"

"I was going to wire your uncle that I'd be delayed a few days in starting on his case."

She shook her head. "Naïve. The telegram will be date-lined Las Vegas, or wherever our first stop is. Leigh might get his hands on it and guess where we're going. We need all the head start we can get."

Don looked down. The street lights were coming on in Barstow.

"But what will your uncle think if you just vanish like this, with me? I'm supposed to solve disappearances, not cause them."

"I suppose he'll think we're, oh, you know."

"I'm afraid I don't know, Miss Summers."

"Oh, looking at the moon, or something."

"But isn't that pretty serious—for you?"

"Isn't *that*," she said, "pretty much up to me?"

They let back their seats and reclined side by side. After a while she said, "Now tell me about your life inside a barrel, Don."

"All right. Why barrel?"

"Not knowing who the Madisons were."

Don gazed at the ceiling of the plane. "Holly, when I was seven years old my parents took me to an illustrated, edifying travel lecture by certain pious missionaries at Memorial Hall, in Columbus, Ohio. I went with both feet braced together, skidding, one strong parent pulling on each long, translucent ear. Grooves can still be found on Broad Street. Two hours later I came out walking on thin air, and in love. The Madisons were both lovable, marvelous people. I went backstage after the lecture to get a closer look at these two demigods. Martha Madison patted me on the cheek, gave me a shark's tooth, and said, 'What a homely little boy.' And that's why I have remained a lovelorn bachelor all my life. Like Gramps."

"I'm glad you told me why," she said. "I was beginning to have my doubts. Well, finding her again should release that boyhood fixation, shouldn't it, according to the rules? Thereby unpenting a pent-up flood of something or other?"

"We'll have to see," said Don. "Usually the rules are lost in the exceptions. My case may be hopeless. Like Gramps's."

"Maybe I can get you on the rebound, Don," said Holly. "Martha must have been a grand old girl. In her day. Such courage. Such composure. Such a sense of humor. You should have read—"

"I have read all their books," said Don. "His as well as hers. Now go to sleep. It may be your last."

"Don't you take your hat off when you go to bed, mister?"

"If I take my hat off the passengers will just know I'm the flight steward, and ask me the altitude."

"What is our present altitude, steward?"

"Veddy, veddy high."

"They won't mistake you for flight personnel with your arm around me. Or will they?"

He handed the passing stewardess the two telegrams and two dollars.

"You win," he said. "Let's sleep." He wrenched loose his hat. A folded triangle of typewritten violet paper floated down into his lap.

They looked at the violet paper slip. It had been torn off, top and bottom. Then they looked at each other.

"How did that get out of my purse, into your hat?" said Holly.

"Look in your purse," suggested Don.

She looked. "Mine's still there. Are you reduced to writing to yourself? Although I must admit you looked convincingly stupefied, just then."

Don snapped on the little spotlight above their seat. They put their heads close together.

be of a tangible nature that moth and rust doth corrupt; but spiritual treasure that can never die. What if the Universe is not out there to be plundered by Tellurian pirates? The stars are votive candles to man's immortality. But because we have materialistic minds

They sat without speaking. Clouds scudded past the airliner's windows. The stars were coming out.

"That crack about the materialist mind was obviously aimed at me," said Don.

"The votive candles sound like Gramps," said Holly.

"Who do you think is writing us these cosmic love letters?"

"Obviously Leigh. I caught him reading science fiction one day, out behind the barn. Gramps won't allow it in the house."

"Do you know what I think?"

"*Do* you think?"

"I think you're writing these yourself, my sweet little fellow-Tellurian."

"Oh, hush," she said sleepily, and curled up with her head on his shoulder.

"Hey," he whispered. "You were going to explain mechanical quadratures to me."

"Too sleepy," she murmured. "Jus' imagine playing ticktacktoe in cubes instead of squares." She closed her eyes. "Plot curves through space that show you where you ought to be, even when you ain't." She was asleep.

Don laid his cheek against her glossy hair, and dreamed.

The mountain road was narrow, rough, and dusty. The rented car was stiff and new. The noon sun of Southern New Mexico was crystalline fire on their faces. Holly applied a Vaseline stick to her chapped lips and passed it to Don, who sat beside her with a fluttering road map open on his knee.

Presently he stood up in the car for a better view ahead. "Well, here is their mailbox. Number One. Drive around the curve, up there. We'll hide the car." He looked down at her and frowned. "That white dress of yours is going to be conspicuous here in the boondocks."

"Are you suggesting that I take it off?"

"Still a bit conspicuous," he said. "You'd get sunburned. —Run the car up this arroyo, out of sight."

They got out and walked back toward the lonely mailbox on its weather-beaten fence post. Holly carried her cape folded over her arm. The barren desert sloped away into infinity on their left. A dark mountain rose sullenly on their right.

"Now let's find a nice shady place to wait," said Don. "Someone will have to come and get the mail, eventually. Then we'll follow him in to where the Madisons are being held. Easy. Just like that."

He parted the bushes on the high side of the road, crawled up, and made a nest for them. "This will have to do," he said. "Watch out for these red ants." Holly spread out her cape and sat on it.

They settled down to wait. A black vulture circled far overhead against the burning blue. "Does he see us?" she whispered.

"Why do you think he's hanging around?"

She shifted uncomfortably. "I wish we'd brought something good to read."

"We did. Take that violet prose out of your purse and match it up with these installments." He handed her his two fragmentary messages.

She pieced them together on the sandy hillside, read them through, and sighed. "I hope it's true."

"Is this sun too hot on you?" he asked.

She cocked her head. "Sssh. I hear a car coming."

They crouched down motionless. A jeep proudly painted *U. S. MAIL,* driven by a Spanish boy in a sombrero, chugged up to the mailbox and stopped. The driver sorted out a stack of magazines and stuffed them into the box. Then he drew a yellow envelope from his shirt pocket, tossed it into the box, and drove on. In a little while the jeep reappeared higher up the road, swinging out to turn a shoulder of the mountain. Then the jeep was gone.

It grew very still. Aromatic with the tang of sage brush, the dry wind blew silently and steadily. A large rattlesnake slowly crawled across the road.

"Well, who goes and gets it?" said Holly finally. "One of us girls?"

Don shook his head. "It's against the law to monkey with anybody's mail. I don't want to lose my license."

She stood up in the bushes. "You and your license. The whole future of the human race may be at stake. It says so right here." She patted the three typed messages, stacked them in order, and handed them to Don. "Read these majestic thoughts while I scoot down and read Leigh's telegram ordering our execution."

She started to push through the chaparral. Thorns tore her skirt. Don stopped her. "All right, I'll go get it," he said. "But we can't keep it. We'll have to deliver it, no matter what it says about us." He stood up beside her in the bushes. "You wait up here, where you can see farther. If you spot anyone coming, give a bird whistle and I'll duck."

He dropped down upon the road, crossed to the mailbox, took out the telegram, and looked quickly at the other pieces of mail. They were all scientific journals, addressed simply to the box number, with no addressee named. Among them was the latest issue of the Astronaut. He was tempted to take it, too. They printed nonsense, of course, but it was good clean fun.

Suddenly he heard heavy footsteps close at hand, below him. In the next second, Holly whistled softly from the hillside up above. Don dropped silently over the edge of the road and lay flat against the sloping bank half hidden behind the thick post that supported the mailbox.

The telegram was still clutched in his hand. He pressed his cheek into the sand.

An old couple was coming up the path. At first all Don could see was the woman's beautiful white hair, and the man's iron-gray beard.

"What kind of bird was that, Martha?" rumbled an old man's voice.

"I don't think it was a bird," replied a woman's voice, soft and fine-textured as old cream-colored lace.

Don felt a shiver go through him. It was the living echo of the golden voice that he had heard on the sound film the afternoon before in Pasadena. His boyhood hero worship began to stir in his heart. Cautiously he raised his head. They were almost at the road now. He could see them clearly, at close range. Even in their rough outdoor clothes, they were a distinguished-looking couple. Bowed down with age, they bore their years with grace.

Don watched them approach. Martin Madison limped on his right leg. Don remembered reading how it had been mauled by a lion when he was on his honeymoon.

At the edge of the road they paused. With the chivalrous gesture of a bygone age, Martin Madison offered his wife his arm. She took it with a gracious nod of thanks.

Don felt moisture in his eyes. The old gentleman's little gesture of respect, intimate as only formality can be, symbolized to Don the old-fashioned and enduring love that had sustained this magnificent pair through half a century of braving the Unknown together. And as he lay there on the hillside hearing his heart thud into the sand, Don Brook experienced an unaccustomed pang to think how soon these gallant comrades, who had so loved life and so well lived it, must set sail upon their final voyage of exploration over the last horizon, from which there is no return.

Now they were directly above him, standing before the mailbox, taking out the magazines. "Well, I guess this is the last we'll be seeing of these for a while," said Martin Madison, with a chuckle.

Martha took up a bulky journal thoughtfully. "I wonder what they'll be printing—then?"

"The same self-hypnotic chants, my dear." He took an armload of magazines, and laughed. "These same issues will still be selling on the newsstands, if all goes well with us. Now let's get out of sight."

Martha lingered by the mailbox, her white hair snowy in the sunlight. She stooped and peered inside. "I wonder why we don't hear from Pritchard. The time is getting short. There ought to be a telegram."

"Yes, but we're all ready, dear," he reassured her. He took a long, deep breath of the scented breeze. "Come, let's go back underground, and get it over with."

Don Brook felt a wave of anger toward whatever evil force had thrust these serene and lovable old people, who had lived such blameless lives, into the orbit of Professor Leigh's murderous experiments. The Madisons obviously were not prisoners, but volunteers. If he could make them change their minds—

Their backs were turned. He raised up to call to them. With the words half-formed on his lips he saw, fifty paces down the trail, two bearded men with rifles. They motioned impatiently to the Madisons. Both riflemen wore faded camouflage suits, helmets, leggings, and canteens.

"We're coming," Martha called to them. Then she stopped and looked up at the hillside just above the road. "Martin," she said calmly, "a girl in a white dress is lying in those bushes. Come with me." She crossed the road and slowly climbed the slope.

Don watched tensely, feeling his plans crash about him. Then he relaxed and wryly smiled.

Holly had given a convincing groan and was sitting up holding her head. "Where am I?" she asked weakly.

Martha Madison bent down. "What's happened to you, girl?"

"I'm not sure," said Holly feebly. "Last night—a man —we parked here—"

The Madisons helped her to her feet. "We'll take care

of you, don't worry," said Martha quietly. "What's your name, child? Where do you live?"

"I can't remember." She began to sniffle.

The armed guards came running up the trail, alarmed. They were respectful toward the Madisons, but resolute. "This won't do," the first guard said. "No visitors."

"We've got to get this girl to a doctor," Martha Madison said firmly.

"That's impossible," the second guard said. "Today's the day."

"But we can't leave her on the road," Martin Madison protested.

"No, not after she's seen you," said the first guard significantly.

"We'll take her inside, Martin," said Martha eagerly. "We've got more doctors there than we've got sense."

The two guards exchanged worried glances, then grinned and shrugged. They seemed to have thought of the same thing at the same time. Don wondered what it was.

"She'd only need to stay until tomorrow," said the first, in an undertone.

"After that it wouldn't make any difference what she knew, would it?" agreed the second. He raised his voice. "All right, folks. You can bring the girl inside," he told the Madisons. "Now let's all get out of sight, please."

The five of them descended the winding trail. Holly walked between the Madisons, acting dazed and helpless. As the procession rounded the last corner below, the second guard looked back up the slope straight at Don and raised his rifle.

Don held his breath, closed his eyes.

The rifle cracked. Don felt nothing. Then he did feel something, and opened his eyes. A large rattlesnake, its head shot off, writhed across his outstretched hand, slid down the slope, and died. The guard turned his back and strode out of sight.

Don waited until the sound of their footsteps had been

gone for some minutes. Then he gingerly slid down, came out upon the dusty path, and tracked them by their footprints. The small, emphatic point of Holly's heel was clearer than the others.

The trail descended through thickets of scrub oak almost to the sparkling white gypsum sands of the desert, then turned abruptly and dipped into a narrow canyon. Don crawled to the edge and looked over. Far below, Martha and Martin Madison, with Holly still between them, were disappearing into the black maw of a tunnel. The first guard accompanied them. The second stayed outside, sat down on an acetylene tank, and rolled a cornhusk cigarette.

Don surveyed the situation. Narrow-gauge railroad tracks ran up and down the hidden canyon between great heaps of furnace slag. Glassy, rainbow-colored slag, unlike any Don had ever seen. Somewhere deep underground a monster dynamo was throbbing like a giant heart. The whole place was permeated with a mounting air of high expectancy, of imminence. Don sensed that he must act quickly, if he was going to act at all. Time was turning on its axis. He crept along the canyon's brink until he found a large, loose rock. He looked at it, and at the guard's head below.

"What's the matter, buddy? Lost?" inquired a voice behind him.

Don nodded and turned around with an agreeable expression. A third guard stood behind him with a submachine gun cradled in his arm. He looked Don up and down. "You're the new radar man we sent for, aren't you?"

Don shrugged modestly. "And I'm off the beam," he confessed.

"Come with me." The third guard marched him down into the canyon, to the tunnel's mouth.

The second guard sprang up and scowled. "So you're the guy who threw that poor girl out on the road last night!"

Don hung his head.

The first guard came out of the tunnel, talking. "The Reverend says that if we should catch that sex-fiend—" He stopped at the sight of Don. "Caught him already? Good. I'll take him in." He paused and stroked his unkempt beard. "Isn't it typical of a degenerate's psychology, Doctor Blake, to return to the scene of his crime next morning?" He raised his rifle and poked Don in the ribs. "Stay well in front of me," he warned. "I want a clearly defined target."

The tunnel rose steeply into the mountain, Don discovered. At the upper end they stopped before a tall, curved, shining door of armor plate. It was not attached to the rock, but was separated from the rock by a bottomless black chasm that had to be stepped across. Don had a fleeting, fantastic impression that the tall curved door was only a tiny segment of some huge inner structure delicately suspended within the mountain. From somewhere far below came the sounds of heavy pumps working hard, like labored breathing.

The guard rang a bell. After a long time the door slowly opened with a hiss. It seemed to be self-sealing and immensely heavy. Martin Madison stood inside, operating hydraulic controls.

Don felt the old missionary's piercing gray eyes upon him. "Are you sure this is the man?" Martin Madison inquired. "He doesn't look the part."

"He says he did it," said the guard.

"I did not," said Don. "Doctor Madison, I've just come from your publisher—"

"Come right in!" said Martin Madison hospitably. "I've wanted to have a talk with you for years. You got here just in time." He added to the guard, "You needn't worry. He's all right. Just wait outside. We have private business to discuss."

Don stepped across the black crevice, from rock to metal. He felt a delicate trembling of the new floor beneath his feet. Martin conducted him along a passage.

"Now about your January royalty statement," he began. "I've just made my last will and testament—"

Don looked about in wonder and in growing fear. He had a nightmarish feeling that he had been here before— in books. The corridor's walls and ceilings were lined with an intricate tapestry of colored wires and numbered tubes. Every inch of space was utilized. And the atmosphere— Don breathed deeply. The air was more than fresh. It was alive. And the fragrance— It was like a hothouse full of exotic flowers and rare fruit grown out of season.

"You're not listening to me," said Martin Madison. "But I dare say the circumstances are a bit unnerving, even for a publisher. How did you persuade Leigh to give you a pass? The press was not supposed to come till evening."

"I'm just lucky, I guess," Don mumbled. His breath failed him. They were emerging from the mystifying corridor into the most unusual and beautiful living-room that he had ever seen. The vaulted ceiling shone softly with a metallic luster. The furniture was all built in. Deep armchairs were upholstered in foam rubber a foot thick. The carpets were as soft as mattresses. And flowers grew everywhere, climbing up the walls; fruit and flowers and bearing vines, spreading a never-ending feast and freshening the air.

Martha Madison was seated on a divan with Holly. She turned to her husband with her lips compressed. Holly kept her eyes downcast. Martha said quietly, "This girl is exaggerating, Martin. She's had a fright. Nothing more. Look up, girl. Tell me, is this the man?"

Holly nodded without looking up.

"Then you're not from my publisher," said Martin Madison indignantly. "Or did you combine business with pleasure, on this trip?"

"I'll marry the girl if you want me to," said Don, looking eagerly at everything but Holly. At both ends of the arched living-room were massive bulkheads, dials, and indicators. The whole room was on a slant, but the deep foam-rubber armchairs and the ankle-deep carpets kept them from slipping.

"I don't consider marriage necessary, under the circumstances," Martha said dryly. "Besides, that kind of marriage never lasts."

Martin had started to say something emphatic to Don when an orange light winked on an intricate control panel at the upper end of the tilted living-room. Martin waded up the soft-carpeted slope, picked up a mouthpiece, flicked a switch. He spoke in tones too low to be audible. A blue light began to flicker. A red needle crept forward on a luminous dial.

"You've fooled us," Martha was saying tartly. "We thought this was something serious."

"It is serious," said Holly, and raised her eyes to Don.

Martin climbed down the soft floor of the listing living-room. The whole great shell seemed to quiver around them.

"You'll both have to leave immediately," he said. His manner was urgent but calm. "They probably won't let you out of the canyon until after midnight." He shook Don's hand, and with the pressure steered him toward the door.

Don twisted his fingers out of the firm, large hand, and stopped. "Just a minute, please," he said, dropping all pretense. "Let's not go any further with this masquerade. We weren't parked on any road last night, or any night. This is strictly business. My name is Don Brook. I am a private investigator, hired to trace your disappearance. This girl is working with me. We're here to find out how you are and what you're doing."

The Madisons exchanged thoughtful looks. "I knew it," said Martha to her husband. "I've told you both a hundred times you couldn't keep this secret. It's too *big*. You should have let the whole world in, as witnesses." She was curiously undisturbed.

"We didn't dare," said Martin. "Pritchard would have

been stopped." He turned to Don. "Was it our lecture manager who hired you? He's been trying to find us for another tour."

Don said, "I am not at liberty to disclose my client's identity."

"Nor am I at liberty to disclose what we are doing—*yet*," said Martin. "As for how we are, we're fine, as you can see."

"How nice to know that someone cares that much about us," said Martha. "I thought the world had forgotten."

Don took out the telegram. "I stole this from your mailbox," he said. "I don't know what it says." He handed it to Martin, who tore it open, read, and smiled; handed it along to Martha, who also read, and also smiled. "We have only a few minutes left," said Martin. "But we're going to show you around quickly. You'll have to listen fast, and figure it all out later." His voice picked up speed. "The plants. We've collected them from all over the world. Grown by hydroponics under sun lamps, they provide food and oxygen. After years of experimenting, we have succeeded in creating a miniature replica of a natural environment—a terrarium for humans."

"We lived all last year in here," said Martha, "hermetically sealed up, except for radio. Like a pair of guppies in a balanced aquarium. Don't ask why. Hurry, Martin. You're so long-winded. Use short words."

"I'm hurrying, dear," he said quickly. "Look sharp, young fellow. These cabinets. Ten thousand books on microfilm. Ten thousand musical and dramatic recordings on microwire. The world's great art on ten thousand color film slides. Dictating machines with mini-cylinders enough to last two lifetimes. Sufficient reserve provisions and supplies to stock an ocean liner on a world cruise." He was climbing toward the upper end, beckoning impatiently.

Don had difficulty in keeping up with him. Signal lights on the control panel were winking frantically. "In there," the old missionary panted, his deep eyes burning with a determined light, "in there are our instruments. Tele scopes. Cameras. Tons of motion-picture film. A complete astrophysical laboratory!"

"Please let me look," Don begged.

"Only for a minute. You must not go in." The thick bulkhead swung back, and a sun lamp came on. There was even more to see than Don expected. But in the middle of all that advanced design, like a jarring note, stood the oldest and most decrepit typewriter he had ever seen.

"That's my lucky typewriter," said Martin defensively. "Wouldn't part with it for the world." He firmly shut the door. "You'll have to get out of here now. Time won't wait." They clambered softly down the sloping carpets. Don looked about again with growing wonder. This inspired interior could have been designed only by a woman who had dreamed all her life of having a model home, and had lived instead in tents. Each square foot combined space-saving conveniences with every comfort of a millionaire's private yacht. So restful was the atmosphere, so sweet the perfumed air, that Don had to fight off an almost irresistible impulse to drop down in the deep soft upholstery and sleep till Judgment Day.

They were approaching the lower end, where Martha was showing Holly her stainless steel electric kitchen. It was the quintessence of a dozen dream homes. "Eggs wouldn't break on my rubber floors," she was explaining.

As they came up, Don turned to Martin and said huskily, "But you've both had so many adventures—"

"So many," said Martin, "that for us there is only one sublime adventure left."

His wife silenced him with a warning look and turned back to answer Holly's question. "But of course it must be beautiful, my child. We're going to enjoy a well-earned rest in here." Her eyes twinkled at her husband. "This is one trip where we're going to revel in sinful sloth and luxury!" She turned Holly toward the door. "We studied the failures of the past. The engineers all laughed at me, but I contended that their whole approach had been too bleak, impersonal. Too *scientific*, in the tiresome sense.

51

I said that it didn't have to look like a submarine on the inside, too. No wonder the others couldn't stand it out there. They had too much time on their hands. Look at the colors in this room." Her fingers played along a keyboard resembling an electric organ. A hundred hidden sun lamps simulated dawn, high noon, a glorious sunset; then darkness, and a silver crescent moon, that waned and waxed.

"Essential to the biologic cycle," Martin explained. When the lights came up he had his arms around his wife. "I've stood her this long," he chuckled. "I can stand her a while longer." They smiled at each other with a strange and tender radiance of anticipation—and yet they were so *old*. Only their dauntless spirit of discovery, shining bravely from their dimming eyes, was unquenched by the rising tide of time, that all-devouring myth which in the last analysis is man's only enemy.

Don and Holly looked at one another in pain and grief; but Martin Madison was proudly showing them a broad double desk stocked with writing materials enough for a small college. "We've always longed to write and illustrate a ten-volume set of books. 'Our Lives,' by Martin and Martha Madison. Now we can."

Martha said, "We won't get started on it if we stand here bragging. Good-by, children. God bless you." They put their young guests out into the corridor.

Don took out the three violet papers and showed them to Martin Madison. "You wrote these on that old typewriter of yours, didn't you?"

The old missionary glanced at them and nodded. "Notes for an old sermon. Never used them. Tore them up. Too highfalutin. Leigh must have picked them out of my wastebasket. He saves every word I write, poor fellow. Thinks he's going to make a fortune because I'll be a collector's item. Bunk." As he spoke, he was urging Don toward the exit, walking with his heavy limp.

Don said, hanging back, "I'd like to read the rest of that sermon, Reverend Madison."

"If I can find it, I'll give it to you—in a little while. Step lively now. Go ashore."

Martha was handing Holly over the gaping threshold, with its awful crack. Leaving the enchantment of the past few minutes, suddenly aware of what awaited them outside, Don blurted, "Did that telegram say that we were to be silenced, after what we've seen?"

"Here, you decide." Martin thrust the telegram into Don's coat pocket. "Good-by, son. We'll be seeing you—I hope."

Martha Madison was in no mood to speed the parting guest. "I'm so glad that everything's right between you and your young man," she told Holly. "How glorious it must feel to be as young as you two are!" For a moment they looked deeply into one another's eyes, the young woman and the old, in wordless understanding.

Holly said impulsively, "I am Burgess Wood's grand-niece, Holly Summers."

Martha gave her a little hug. "I'm glad. Now I begin to understand Leigh's wire. Good-by."

Don broke in stubbornly. "But why in God's name at your age—" he burst out.

"Wait and see," said Martin Madison. "All my life that astigmatic astronomer, Burgess Wood, has been calling me a crazy sky pilot. Now I'll show him who's crazy! Now I'll show him who is *really a sky pilot!*" He threw back his shaggy gray head and roared with the hearty enjoyment of a man who has the last laugh on an ancient rival.

Martha said mildly, "Burgess was a fine young man. There have been times in our lives together, my dear, when I—remembered him." The massive door cut off her words with the cold and final silence of the tomb.

Don and Holly found themselves in the empty, echoing tunnel. They moved close together. "They were so *happy*," Holly said in a trembling voice. "They were so *sure*—of something. Oh, Don. Can't we do something to get them out of there?"

A tall new guard with a carbine stepped out of the darkness and touched his helmet politely. "My orders are to invite you to come with me."

With a look at the carbine, Don took his hand away from his hip pocket where his pistol was. The guard conducted them through a short side passage that opened out into the air. A few steps, and they found themselves standing in the twilight on a small platform about halfway up the rocky slopes of Meteor Mountain. Far down at the bottom they could see a tiny cable car creeping upward like a beetle. Its cables led past them to the peak, towering high and forbidding above them in the cloudless sky.

"You are to get on this cable car as it comes by," said the guard. He went inside and shut the door, locking them outside on the little platform in the wind. In the west, a blood-red sun was sinking toward a range of rugged mountains.

"Do you mind if I sort of cling to you?" said Holly. "High places make me dizzy."

Don took her in his arms and held her tight. "You gathered what that was, where the Madisons have been living?" The cable car crept slowly toward them.

She nodded. "The biggest ever built." She looked along the mountain. "That must be where it will come out." She pointed to where workmen were removing camouflage netting from a great opening as round as the barrel of a giant cannon.

She put her face against Don's shoulder. "It was so pitiful to hear them talk of the future." He could feel her long slim body trembling from withheld sobs. "All those books they think they're going to write. And all that scientific work they've planned— Oh, how frightening it is when old people refuse to give up the ghost. The Madisons will both die of old age before they even get *started!*"

Don watched the cable car ascending. There was someone on it. Someone who looked very much like someone who could not possibly be on it. Holly's face was still hidden in his arms. "Well, at least they'll get to die together," he told her. "That's the way they'd want to go, I know.

With their boots on. But such a fantastic, futile death! So much worse in their cases, than in all the other volunteers', because the Madisons have so little time left, anyway. Professor Leigh must be criminally insane."

"It's such a pity they never had any children," said Holly. "That makes death so damned final—"

The cable car creaked closer. Holly raised her eyes and gasped at whom she saw. Then she whispered quickly to Don, "Promise me you won't tell *him* you've found her here. The shock would kill him!"

The cable car swayed up to the platform and stopped. In it, looking ruffled and indignant, sat Dr. Burgess Wood. "Well!" he snapped. "At least *this* much of what that science-charlatan says is true. That I'd find you two here together." He looked resentfully at Don. "So this is how you hunt Martha Madison. By forgetting all about your business and running off with my niece." He looked sternly at Holly. "Where did you spend last night, young lady?"

"In a crowded airplane, uncle," she said demurely. "In separate, adjoining seats. Excuse me, but we were ordered to get in this cable car with you, and go somewhere."

He waved them back with his cane. "You can see there isn't any room," he said. "Incidentally, I am so close to being in a state of kidnap that any distinction is purely academic."

"There's room enough," said Don. He and Holly stepped in. The cable car began to crawl again. The horizon expanded, league on league. The sun sank lower. The searching wind grew chill. From deep in the bowels of the mountain below came a symphony of ordered sounds. Whistles, winches, sounds of loading, as if a great ship was preparing to set out to sea.

The car stopped with a bump at a platform near the mountain peak. The hemispheric dome of an astronomical observatory loomed up from the solid rock like a great pale mushroom pushing through dark soil. The old astronomer looked reluctantly impressed. "I don't believe it," he grumbled. "There can't be anything inside. I'd have known about it." He clambered out of the swaying cable car and entered the observatory through a door that stood invitingly open.

Don and Holly paused outside. "Pinch me, please," she said. "We'll wake up back in Burbank, waiting for a plane."

"I was going to ask you to pinch me," said Don. "I'm afraid I'll wake up back in my office, as I so often do."

"Careful! Don't let's wake up too far back. Or we won't have met."

He nodded. "Then let's keep on dreaming. I want to see how this dream ends." He took a long last look around the desolate mountain, surrounded by empty desert. The indigo shadows of the night were deepening their dye. No light of human habitation showed anywhere on the horizon. But in the secluded canyon far below there was a bustle of activity and the clatter of a donkey engine.

From inside the observatory came words of erudite profanity. Don and Holly hurried in. Doctor Wood waved his arm angrily at the huge charts and graphs laid out beneath the telescopes. "These are enlarged copies of my quadratures!" he sputtered. "My corrected measurements have all been entered." He glared at tiers of unfamiliar equipment. "What are all these dial settings? This place looks like a television station had eloped with a planetarium." He noticed Don and Holly standing arm in arm. "Have you really eloped with her? This human anaconda?"

"What makes you think so?" Don inquired.

"Why, your obliging secretary said you had, when I phoned your office this morning for a progress report. Otherwise I wouldn't have let Leigh bring me to this Godforsaken place!"

Don gave Holly a sidelong glance. "What did you say in that telegram you sent Miss Mosely?"

"What you wanted said, boss. Naturally, I signed my name, as traveling secretary."

"Telegram," said Don, and slapped his coat pocket as if a live coal were in it. He whipped out the wire which Martin Madison had handed him, and scanned it swiftly. Pritchard Leigh had wired to the Madisons from Pasadena, the night before.

TRY TO CAPTURE TALL THIN COUPLE WHOM WOOD IS SENDING TO SPY ON US. THEY WILL MAKE CREDIBLE WITNESSES AS THEY HAVE THE PROPER BACKGROUND. LET THEM IN UNHARMED AND SHOW INTERIOR. AM BRINGING WOOD MYSELF BY FORCE IF NECESSARY AS YOU INSISTED. QUADRATURES COMPLETE. AM NOTIFYING SCIENCE REPORTERS AND NEWSREELS TO COME AT SEVEN.

Don handed it to Holly. She read it, and gave him a wry glance. "What a brilliant team of bold detectives we turned out to be," she said. "Excuse me while I take care of Gramps. He's sputtering." She took him off to one side and spoke soothingly to him, explaining something earnestly. Feature by feature, his dour expression softened and he began to nod. Holly left him studying the charts again, and went out on the terrace.

An impersonal voice gritted faintly through a loudspeaker. "Please keep your places. There will be a slight delay. A minor accident. No cause for alarm. Doctor Geeble, please. Doctor Geeble—"

Don crossed the observatory and squatted down on the immense plotting-board where the starry charts were spread. Wood was checking the co-ordinates of a majestic curve with a look of grudging approval.

"Excuse me," said Don. "Did you ever see these before?" He held out the three violet slips of paper.

Wood looked up and snorted. "Seen them too many times. Leigh calls them his litmus-paper test of people's minds. Claims where cosmology is concerned, there are only two basic types. He tried them on me, surreptitiously. Left them lying around mysteriously. Seems I'm acid." He leaned across the chart, did a little higher mathematics on his cuff, and nodded reluctantly. "Right on the button," he said to himself. Then he noticed Don again, holding out the violet slips with a look of silent accusation. "Now don't start looking at me like a detective," he said defensively. "I found Leigh's litmus paper so irritating I thought I'd better try you and Holly. Test your mettle. See if I had traitors in my camp. Trouble is, Leigh can't find how the damn thing ends. Now go away and stop bothering me, young fellow. I'm looking for Pi in the sky, like Martin Madison."

Don went out onto the wind-swept mountaintop and looked for Holly. The sun had set. The moon had not yet risen. It was the hour when there is nothing in the sky but stars.

"It was nice of you to offer to make an honest woman of me," Holly said. "But it was just part of the act, of course —wasn't it?"

"Not necessarily," said Don. "You're tall enough for me to dance with, without feeling like a cradle snatcher. I don't have to dislocate my sacroiliac to whisper in your ear. We could take it from there, and sort of see what happens."

"That's much too offhand a proposal to consider, Don. Sssh! Something more important is happening, down there."

Far off in the direction of Highway 70, the headlights of many automobiles were bobbing slowly through the sand dunes. They were at least two miles away.

"Why is it," said Don, "that every time you shush me, you're doing the talking?"

"Sssh!"

From the first car an inquiring yellow signal flare arched into the air, a curve with a dot on the end, a burning question mark. From the mouth of the canyon below them, two red rockets soared up in warning answer. The motorcade stopped. Like a row of dominoes falling over, the headlights went out, all along the line.

She slipped her arm through his. "I'm sorry," she said. "I'll stop shushing. It comes from having brought up a houseful of wise old men."

Far behind the jagged mountains in the east, the full moon rose, pouring moonstain down the slopes, bleaching out the stars, and turning the desert below into a silvered wonderland. Mile on rippled mile of snow-white gypsum crystals in the torrid desert seemed an Arctic wilderness of freezing cold, its dunes heaped up like sparkling snow drifts. Somewhere far away, a coyote howled.

Don bent and kissed the tall, cool girl beside him. While their lips met, asking and answering an eager question, the whole mountain began to shake and rumble beneath their feet. Startled, they sprang apart. Doctor Wood ran outside in alarm. "Earthquake!" he cried. Don pointed silently to the huge pit in the mountainside not far below them.

From the tunnel mouth emerged, with a majestic slowness, a shimmering pointed shaft. It had the exquisite symmetry of strength. Searchlights played upon its shining surface from a dozen angles, so that the far-off spectators could see the stupendous sight.

From their closer vantage point, the three watchers on the observatory terrace could see the vessel's name: "?." Beside the sign of Man's unanswered question was emblazoned boldly, in the celestial heraldry of the astronomers, the symbol of the ship's home port, $\oplus$, Terra, gem of the ocean, home of a brave, free-minded race. The Madisons' new houseboat, *The Question Mark II,* was spanking new from stem to stern. Quivering with nascent beauty, like a gigantic butterfly emerging from the long preparatory dream of the cocoon, the sleek cruiser slid up the launching-ways with her prow lifted to the stars.

The rumbling grew louder. Meteor Mountain shook so violently that tons of loosened boulders went crashing down the mountain's quaking flanks. Scarlet flames began to spurt out of the launching-pit as the slim silvery shape slowly gathered speed. With the sound of a million blowtorches the scarlet flames quickened to bright orange and began to climb the spectrum, hue by fiery hue. Orange was consumed by searing yellow fire. Yellow soared to brilliant green, to burning blue, up the last blinding step into fading violet, and then out into the unimaginable colors that lie beyond the range of the merely human eye.

An incandescent cloud of rainbow flames boiled up miles high into the sky, and with a final roar like all the bass chords of a funeral march struck simultaneously upon a celestial pipe organ, a pillar of fire ascended into Heaven.

In a few seconds the giant rocket had vanished straight as an arrow into the western sky. Its twinkling point of light was soon swallowed up in the immensity of icy ink-black space. Then all grew still. The searchlights snapped off, one after another. Soon the only illumination left, other than the pale moonlight, was an infernal crimson glow from the rivers of molten rock that drooled slowly down the smoking face of Meteor Mountain and dripped off into the desert in a man-made lava flow.

Doctor Wood was the first to recover his voice. "That lunatic Leigh!" he gasped. "Trying it again, after it's forbidden. I hope he was in that one."

"I wish I were," said Pritchard Leigh, behind them. Don whirled. The professor's shirt was torn, his face was blackened by smoke, and his eyes flashed jubilantly.

Wood turned on him furiously. "I'm going to have you arrested for murder, kidnaping, and fraud."

"Very well," said Leigh pleasantly. "I'll give myself up in an hour. If you still want me to, then." He ushered them back into the observatory and hospitably offered chairs.

Wood angrily remained standing. "To what pagan diety did you sacrifice your victims this time?" he demanded.

Leigh pointed to a symbol on the chart. His three involuntary guests stepped close and looked.

The sign was ♄ .

Wood whirled and cried, "That's eighty million miles away, you maniac!"

"He's killed them," said Holly, and began to sway. Don caught her and helped her to a bench. His own knees were shaking. He reached for her hand. It was as cold as his own.

Leigh went calmly to the washstand and unwrapped a cake of soap. "Colloquialisms like 'millions of miles' are meaningless out there," he said, lathering his hands. "Distance means nothing where there *is* nothing. Only time counts. The time it takes to get out there and back." He washed his hands thoughtfully. "Places you think are very far away may thus be brought very close, in terms of *time*." He dried his hands on a ragged old Army towel that was none too clean. "Space is a string of empty zeros," he went on. "Our concept of the cosmos should not be spatial, but temporal. Time, not space, was the only barrier left between man and the stars he's always wanted."

Wood pounded with his cane. "Time is what I'm speaking of, you fool! The round trip to Saturn will take fifty, sixty, maybe eighty years! Whom did you send, Methuselah?"

Leigh bent double to wash his blackened face. When Wood saw him with the soot off, he went to him grumbling, "You've burned yourself, you bungling ape. Playing Prometheus. Here, let me put something on it." He took ointment from the medicine cabinet above the washstand and applied it gently to Leigh's reddened face. "Think you're pretty smart, don't you?" he growled. "Doing all this on the sly."

"Like other scientists who have stumbled upon a really basic discovery," Leigh explained, turning the other cheek, "I was forced to work in secret, like a medieval alchemist—" He was trying to be very nonchalant, but Don noticed that he glanced anxiously whenever possible at a huge chronometer overhead. It had three pairs of different-colored hands.

Wood daubed salve scornfully. "What basic discovery did you ever make?"

"Superphotic speed," said Leigh.

"There's no such word," Wood scoffed.

"There will be, after tonight."

Wood flung down the ointment tube in disgust. "Nothing can exceed the speed of light. It says so right in Ein-

61

stein." Then he cocked a quizzical wise eye at his old rival. "How'd you do it, Pritchard? There isn't enough energy in atomic fuel to boost a rocket into an escape-velocity anywhere near the speed of light."

Leigh shrugged modestly. "I didn't do it. The Master Scientist did it. He put the facts there for us to find. We finally got tuned in on His beam, the cosmic rays. That ship sails before them, like the Mayflower rode the wind."

Wood put his hands in his long white hair and clenched both fists full. "This is scientific heresy!" he groaned.

Leigh was looking into the mirror. "Science and its mirror-image religion both have risen from the primeval cave on a ladder of the rankest heresies," he said, combing back the two faint wisps of hair above his ears. "I want to look presentable for the news photographers," he said hopefully, and stole a furtive glance at the big clock.

"Why do you keep looking at that Rube Goldberg clock?" Wood demanded. "You act as if you had planted a time bomb in there. Have you? Anyone who thinks something can travel faster than light is capable of anything. Why, that would punch holes in the Einstein Theory!"

"Einstein's theory punched holes in someone else's theory," said Leigh. "I can't remember whose." He looked long and hard at the colorful clock, reading it like a chain of signal flags. Don noticed that each of the six hands was painted a pure prismatic color. Each hue was gradually finding its right place in the spectrum, the faster colors passing the slower ones.

"We haven't time for a game of chess," Leigh announced. "We might smoke half a short cigar." He went to his desk, took two small panatelas from an onyx humidor, and gave Wood a light, carefully letting the sulphur burn off the match before the flame touched the tobacco. The two old enemies sat down together and puffed companionably. Out in the night, a giant searchlight began to sweep restlessly back and forth, questioning the sky.

"How much do you pay for these cigars?" Wood asked, wrinkling his nose.

"I buy them across the border, in old Mexico," Leigh said apologetically. "Five centavos. I've had to economize, these last few years. You want to know what happened to the others we sent out from here? They were caught and crushed in the frozen seas of time. This last job is an ice breaker. She'll crash through the barrier of superphotic speed and sail in the clear, just as in the old days daring pilots crashed through the barrier of sound to supersonic speeds, after the experts said that it was heresy to try."

"By the way," said Wood, "where do you get your pilots, Pritchard? On parole from insane asylums?"

Leigh did not answer. He was watching the big clock fixedly, and counting on his fingers. Its six hands were arranging themselves into a rainbow.

"What type of victims did you blow to glory this time?" Wood persisted. "Another crew of Air Force volunteers? Brave men, those."

Don and Holly sat wringing each other's hands.

"No, not this trip," said Leigh carefully. "Tonight we were faced with an entirely new personnel problem. We weren't afraid of mechanical breakdowns. The thing flies herself, with a little trimming here and there on the approaches. What concerned us was the human breakdowns. Our machines can now stand anything. Unfortunately there seems to be a limit to what our human minds can stand." He blew a wreath of smoke. "We learned to our sorrow that a man alone, even the strong silent type, didn't last long enough to get anywhere. There is a kind of solitude out there, face to face with all Eternity, that no mortal can long endure in loneliness of soul. He must have companionship, or he starts sending garbled messages. One poor chap's last radio message to us read, 'It is not well for man to be alone.' " He flicked off an ash.

"We further found, to our regret, that crews of trained, disciplined air officers eventually reached a point where they—no longer answered signals. Perhaps they didn't get along well together, in close quarters."

He puffed reflectively. "However, by keeping at it, we

discovered that when mature males and females are brought together under ideal circumstances, given proper guidance, and then make the attempt together, some extremely interesting new reactions are obtained."

Wood gave a ribald guffaw. "You call *that* a discovery? You spent millions finding *that* out?"

"I refer to courage," said the professor loftily. "The only lasting solution to the human equation is love. Not the selfish, shoddy grasping that too often passes for love nowadays, but the genuine, abiding love that inspires great poetry and music, and lasting marriages, which are even harder to create." He nodded happily to himself. "Yes, Burgess, our tests proved that a harmoniously married couple, in perfect agreement as to the historic importance of our work, could sustain each other's morale long after other volunteers had, to use the vulgar expression, cracked up." He sighed. "That left us with only one logical alternative."

Wood examined the fraying tip of his cigar. "Those must have been some tests."

"They were indeed," said Leigh. "In fact, I'm working on a theory that people in love inhabit their own time dimension. Time passes in a different way, for them."

"I've noticed that," said Wood. "There are times when time just seems to stop."

"Why, Gramps," murmured Holly, but she could not smile.

The old astronomer did not hear her. "So you sent a young married couple, did you, Pritchard?" He turned and winked at Don and Holly. "There sit a pair of likely candidates for the next excursion. I have always contended, ex officio, that suspended animation is the only solution to the time problem in space travel. These two haven't breathed for the past ten minutes. What's the matter with you, Holly? Have you seen a ghost? Don't tell me love has reared its tousled head among the cathode tubes!"

Don and Holly sat speechless with grief, unable to meet the old man's twinkling eyes. Wood turned back to Leigh and persisted with rough jocularity.

"Well, who were the poor devils, Pritchard? As Devil's Advocate, I'll send flowers to their next of kin. Pale, waxen immortelles should prove appropriate, in the language of the flowers. Corpses keep, at absolute zero."

Leigh glanced inquiringly toward Don and Holly. "You haven't told him?"

Neither of them could find the strength to speak. They gripped each other's cold hands tightly.

Leigh turned his big bald head and looked straight at Wood. "The volunteers you just saw take off," he said quietly, "were Martin and Martha Madison."

For a minute Wood sat as if he had not heard. Then his ruddy face drained gray. He struggled to stand up, brandishing his cane at Leigh. He slumped back in his chair. The half-smoked cigar fell from his fingers, and rolled across the smooth stone floor.

Holly sprang up and ran to him. "Now you've killed him, too!" she cried furiously at Leigh.

"He has not killed me," said her uncle hoarsely. "He's not man enough. But I'll kill him, as soon as I catch my breath." Wood shook his fist at the professor. "For this I'm going to put you in a cell, padded or penitentiary, if it takes me the rest of my natural life!" He breathed heavily. "Before, our differences have been professional. Now they're personal!" He lurched up to his feet and lunged at Leigh.

Holly threw her arms around her uncle and restrained him. Don pulled Leigh back to a safe distance behind a spectroscope of unorthodox design.

Leigh called plaintively to Wood, across the echoing observatory. "Please try to understand, my friend! The Madisons were the only qualified scientists who were *old* enough to go!"

Wood shouted back in fury, his voice ringing hollowly around the vaulted dome. "Old enough to start on a voyage that will last at least fifty years! Why, the Madisons will be dead of old age before they pass Mars!" Wood shook his fists. "Tie him up, Don! He's a murderer!"

Don expertly pinioned Leigh's arms. They were thick and hard.

Ignoring Don, the professor pleaded, "The speed of the Madisons' ship is so great that they are literally ahead of time. That's why we had to send *old* people, with lóng lifetimes *behind* them, not ahead of them. The Madisons are traveling *backward* in time, not forward."

"My poor Martha!" Wood groaned. "What a ghastly way to die!"

"She isn't dead!" cried Leigh. "She is alive! And I can prove it! Let me go!"

Holly said sharply, "For a man who has failed every time, you seem rather sure of yourself tonight!"

"I am sure," said Leigh. "In fact, I'm positive."

"Of what?" Wood snapped.

"That the Madisons have *already returned from Saturn.*"

There was a sinking silence. At the icy bottom of it, Leigh added, "Relatively speaking. And one must always speak relatively, mustn't one?"

Don Brook and Burgess Wood exchanged significant glances. In a wordless flash of understanding they agreed that the safest course would be to humor this dangerous madman until they were all out of his reach.

At a nod from Wood, Don freed Leigh's arms with an apology and faced him with a smile he did not feel. "Very interesting, professor. Would you mind telling us where the Madisons are at present?"

"Look in the telescope," said Leigh.

A trick to get me to turn my back, Don thought. He did not move. Doctor Wood was weeping on Holly's shoulder. Somewhere outside an electric gong began to hammer shrilly.

"Your telescope is aimed to the east," Don politely pointed out, keeping a heavy chair between himself and Leigh. "Our friends the Madisons went west."

"The Madisons will land from the east within seventeen minutes," said the professor, consulting the complex color clock. "Naturally, they would have been here long ago, if it had not been necessary for them to slow down considerably toward the end."

"Natch," said Don soothingly, edging sideways toward the telescope. "The velocity of light being a mere one hundred and eighty-six thousand miles per second, it would take some time to de-accelerate to a safe landing-speed." His hand crept toward his hip pocket. Feeling that he had to keep Leigh entertained at any cost, he went on brightly, "For, as every schoolboy knows, a really hot ship like yours, landing out of control, would punch holes in more than the Einstein Theory. It also would punch a large hole straight through the earth, thus altering the political situation on both sides at once."

Leigh nodded vigorously, with approval. "I'm glad to see I did not underestimate your qualifications as an expert witness for tonight's unusual events, Mr. Brook. May I call you Don? You have the face of an open-minded thinker. You also enjoy the immense advantage of being an ignorant layman, free to admit the existence of a new datum when it thumbs its nose at you. Whereas my learned colleague over there"—he looked sadly at Doctor Wood— "is so rigidly disciplined by scientific dogma that he righteously excludes every observation that does not fit in with his preconceived prejudices. What he's going to learn tonight will hurt him more than pulling teeth."

Don smiled agreeably. "Thank you so much. And what new datum will you demonstrate?"

"That for a superphotic rocket, the slowing down takes longer than the trip," said Leigh. "As we measure time, the trip took no time at all. The trip took time-minus."

Holly raised her head from taking care of Doctor Wood. "Minus how much time?" she asked ominously.

"I wish I knew exactly," Leigh replied. "It should take at least minus-fifty years." He went to an intricate control panel. "Maybe minus more than fifty years." He tapped a sending key of curious design. "It all depends upon the accuracy of Doctor Wood's measurements, here on our charts." He threw a switch and waited for an answer. "I don't get any signal from the Madisons," he complained. "Of course, they may be busy at the moment. Two isn't much of a crew."

Wood said savagely to Don, "Don't diddle with that gun, Don. Draw it. Put him under arrest."

Reluctantly, Don pulled out his small, flat automatic, feeling it a futile toy against the forces around them on the mountain.

Leigh looked at the pistol and sighed. "I thought our world was rid of men who shoved guns in scientists' faces rather than face the facts of scientific progress. I dare you to look in that telescope, Burgess! If you don't like what you see, shoot me. But look first, please!" The earnestness about him began to prevail upon them.

"Keep him covered, Don," said Doctor Wood. He crossed the laboratory and squinted into the eyepiece of the telescope.

The old astronomer stared skyward for a full minute, slowly stiffening all over.

Outside, in the desert night, three green rockets flared and fell.

At last Doctor Wood straightened up and rubbed his eyes, smiling dazedly. He walked across the laboratory, tottering a little. His face was chastened. He said to Leigh in a shaken voice, "I can't believe it, but it's true. Of course, you're lying about the Madisons. They couldn't have warped that ship around into so tight a turn about the earth, at *their* speed. And yet there's really something out there." He looked up with new eyes at the open sky. "It must be one of your early, lost ships finding its way home at last, from God knows where. That, in itself, is big, good news for everyone on earth. Big enough to put your bullethead in the hall of fame." Then he remembered, and his face grew stern again. "But though they wreathe your brow with laurel, I cannot forgive what you have done to Martha Madison! For that I shall destroy you, if I can. As you have destroyed her."

"I set her course by your quadratures," said Leigh mildly.

"You used my work to kill her," said Wood in deepening anguish. "You tricked me into killing her myself!"

"If your calculations were correct, Burgess, she will return unharmed," said Leigh reassuringly. "Perhaps *unharmed* may prove to be an understatement. If you had not worked so hard to prove my life's work wrong, I could not have been right tonight. If I am."

Above them, the six-armed clock drew its colored hands together like a closing fan. Outside, far below them, landing-lights blazed on across the desert, as far as the eye could reach.

Don put his gun away and went to the telescope. The eyepiece felt cold. The wrinkled face of the moon came crisply into focus. Silhouetted against the silver disc was a tiny, pencil-shaped splinter. It grew swiftly larger.

As he watched, he also tried to listen to the two scientists arguing behind him, not hearing all they said, not seeing all he looked at. The pointed thing was falling toward the earth at meteoric speed.

"If the Madisons die," Leigh was saying, "it will not be of *old* age."

"How did you get them to go?" Wood raged, paying no attention to Leigh's words. "The Madisons—I mean Martha—had too much sense for a suicidal stunt like this! You must have used torture, hypnosis, and drugs to make them do this."

"The fact is," Leigh replied, "it was Martin Madison who sought *me* out, urgently, ten years ago . . ." Don stopped listening, and watched the approaching rocket. Fire was spurting from it, as its braking jets blazed into action. Streams of violet flame shot out a mile ahead, fighting to retard its swift fall toward earth. Like fiery hands, the bow-jets pushed against the first faint traces of the upper air. A faulty jet cut out. The ship began to spin like a flaming pin-wheel, hundreds of miles above the earth.

Don shut his eyes until the observatory stopped spinning. He could not bear to watch that fiery dance of death. Leigh's voice swam up at him again. ". . . Martin said he'd given up his search for some way to renew man's lease on life. All he'd found was deceit, and self-deception. Radio-active fountains, yoga, yogurt, serum, cereals, and weird baths of one thing or another were all wicked pagan rot, he told me. The most that any of them did was to prolong an obscene caricature of life's outer husk while the jaded spirit died inside, and sank into corruption. And yet, there it was, repeated forty-three times, in the Book he loved and lived by. That man shall find eternal life, if he be worthy. Being a scientist, I tried to explain to him that Scriptural promise is purely spiritual. Being a medical missionary, he had a practical turn of mind. He wanted to *apply* what he devoutly believed was true. . . ."

Don forced himself to look back into the telescope. The rocket had stopped spinning and was falling like a stone. As he watched it in horror, his hearing of Leigh's voice dwindled to a thin and tiny piping, millions of miles away. " . . . and on his seventieth birthday he declared his firm conviction that the truest promise ever made could come true only when man perfected himself enough to turn time backward in its flight, as happens every night in dreams. That, Martin said, would automatically mete out each individual reward and punishment with a poetic justice truly divine. For by having to live his old life over again before he could get a new one, each man would get precisely what he had coming to him, according to the ticket he had written for himself, each passing year. What could be more fair? And as I happened to be working on the same problem of turning the raveled sleeve of time inside out, we joined forces, pooled our resources. Fortunately we could extract the rare minerals we needed right here inside this mountain." He tapped with the toe of his moccasin against the natural rock floor.

Don grew conscious of Holly standing beside him at the

telescope. "Let me look," she begged.

"Better not," said Don. "This rocket is going to crash. It could wipe out a whole city—"

She pushed him gently away from the eyepiece and looked. "Not with that hot pilot at the helm," she said presently. "He's nosed her up into a stall, and lost momentum. Want to see for yourself?"

"Sssh," said Don. "I'm listening—"

"But where did Martha stand on all this rot?" Wood was roaring. "She had a fine mind of her own. Wrote that preacher's books for him, I'll bet. She was too smart to believe this nonsense."

Leigh stroked his chin and smiled reminiscently. "Martha didn't say much one way or the other. She just pitched in and helped. She and Martin made a perfect team. Their strength was in their dependence upon one another. There are times when one and one add up to more than two, as you will see tonight. Martha had a genius for humoring men with grand obsessions. She held my staff together, with her tact. I don't know yet whether she believed in this experiment or not, but she made both of us believe in ourselves. She tortured, drugged, and hypnotized us with her faith—*in us*." He sighed wistfully. "Martin Madison was the luckiest man on earth—"

A siren screamed. Leigh started violently and looked at the big clock. Its hands had converged to form a perfect rainbow. He sprang up shamefaced. "We're late," he said sheepishly. "With all these super-gadgets rigged up to remind me of the time, I sit dreaming of a dear little old lady's courage! Please come with me. And hurry! I need all of you as eyewitnesses."

They hesitated. Leigh seized Wood's arm and hustled him out to the cable car, protesting. Don and Holly followed, and crowded into the swaying, creaking car just as Leigh kicked off the brake.

"I loathe being dragged around," Wood told him coldly, hanging onto his hat and cane as they rocked down the sickening descent. "Even upon occasions of undoubted historic importance, such as this."

"Let me apologize for telling you that your detective had turned criminal and was holding Holly in a desert shack," said Leigh smiling. "I had to get you here somehow, Burgess, to keep you from denouncing me in front-page interviews tomorrow morning as a science faker. And a pious fraud."

"I didn't believe it," said Wood, "and I don't believe this other story of yours, either. The Madisons aren't in this ship any more than Holly was in that shack. Any mere man who tried to hold Holly anywhere against her will would have his hands full. And as for one-hour flights to Saturn—hooey!"

Don gave Leigh a reproachful look.

"Well, you *are* holding me," Holly murmured in his ear. "But not against my will." Don held her tighter and admired Leigh's bald head shining in the moonlight.

Despite the growing chill of the desert night, Leigh's scalp was beaded with perspiration. The man was bearing up under terrific strain. "Yours will be the first opinion skeptical editors will ask for," he reminded Wood.

"I withhold comment," said Doctor Wood, "until we have opened that rocket and have seen what, if anything, is left inside. Something I hope never occurred to Einstein has just occurred to me, unfortunately."

At the bottom of a slope a large, old-fashioned touring car was waiting. Its wheels were fitted with out-sized airplane tires. "Sand buggy," said Leigh. "Unfortunately our landing-technique may prove a bit primitive. We've never landed a big one before, in one piece."

Leigh took the wheel himself and drove along a sandy road among the dunes, followed by a dozen jeeps carrying his assistants, reporters, and photographers. Don also saw an ambulance, bringing up the rear. Guided by the living star above them, the caravan wound through the desert.

For an anxious minute it appeared that the rocket would fall south of the Rio Grande in Old Mexico. Then, righting itself in a fountain of flame, it swooped to the west, over Arizona. A touch of the main jets brought its nose up into a stall, and with most of its momentum lost, it dropped off in a glide toward the three hundred square miles of sparkling white gypsum sands that are one of Earth's most conspicuous landmarks, by day or night.

The professor pushed the old car to reckless speed. He zoomed over dunes and dipped into gullies like a roller coaster on a spree.

Leaving a cometlike trail of fiery gasses, the rocket crossed high in front of them, about a mile away, glinting dully like a tarnished metal pencil in the bright moonlight. Its appearance had somehow changed in the short while since they had seen it leave. Now it was roaring past, less than a thousand feet above them, settling tail first toward the sand. Parts of it grew incandescent from the friction of the air. A huge tail-vane melted and broke loose and slashed down.

The accident caused the rocket to veer erratically, like a wounded bird. It yawed to the east, toward the city of Alamogordo.

The professor swung the car around in pursuit. The engine screamed up to sixty miles an hour in second gear. Leaving all semblance of a trail, they careened through a labyrinth of dunes, fighting blindly in the direction the rocket had taken. The following convoy was scattered and confused.

All at once a white wall of sand loomed up. Leigh had run into a dead end, and was going too fast to stop. The car reared up like a bronco, blew both front tires, and buried its radiator deep in the sand. The rocket was lost to sight.

The professor climbed over the windshield and scrambled up the slope. Don followed him. Holly stayed behind to assist her uncle. "Don't help me," he sputtered. "Help him." He pointed to where Don had slipped to his knees in the shifting sand.

They climbed a crescent dune, floundered to the crest

together, and sank down out of breath. From their high point they had a view for a mile or more ahead. The level sands were empty, a lonely sea of silver in the moonlight. "Lost it," said Professor Leigh. "Now we'll have to search by plane. They might need assistance quickly."

With a rushing sound the rocket re-appeared less than half a mile away, headed directly toward them, skimming low above the sand. Don flung his arms around Wood and Holly, and threw them to the sand, shielding them with his body.

There was a sound of thunder and a shower of red-hot sand. The dune shook like flour in a sifter. It seemed hours until the burning dust had settled. Then they crept cautiously to the crest of the dune, and looked fearfully down the other side.

Scorched and scarred and spilled on its side, a battered old rocket lay smoking like a husk of burned-out fireworks. No light was visible from its smashed portholes. No sound was audible except the crackling of cooling metal.

Professor Leigh leaped up and ran toward it through the sinking sand. He made little headway. He lifted his feet and put them down with the leaden-footed horror of a nightmare chase. He stopped and sank to his knees.

One by one the others came up abreast of him and looked silently upon this derelict that the tides of time had cast upon our island shore, from out of the deeps of space.

In the general outlines of its radical advanced design, it resembled *The Question Mark*. In details, it could not be, unless the times were out of joint. *The Question Mark* had been new. This thing was old, a relic from the ancient past. Even in the flattering moonlight they could see that insatiable Time, the all-devourer, had eaten into her like acid. Her beauty was burned up in the long, lost race with Time. To blast and sear her shining armor so hideously must have taken eternities of torment in the super-hells of heaven.

Reason said this could not be *The Question Mark*.

Reason erred, against the New. There was her name, ?, still faintly legible across her dented prow. And below it, not yet quite erased, showed the brave insigne of this argonaut's home port, ⊕, tight little isle of a proud, seafaring breed who would not give up reaching for the stars. She was Earth's ship, and she had come home to Earth, full circle, back around the breaking-wheel of time.

All about them in the dunes, Don could hear the other cars approaching. Subdued, excited voices called back and forth across the sands. A flash bulb popped.

Holly said softly, "At least they got to die together."

Don shook off his numbness. "Let's open this thing and get the bodies out," he said dully, and waded grimly forward through the sand.

A dozen of Leigh's assistants and a score of newsmen were closing in on the smoldering, silent rocket, shielding their faces from the radiated heat. It was still too hot to touch. They stopped and waited.

A slow pounding, as of a hand-wielded hammer, began to ring inside the hull. A square plate on the downward curve of the tilted hull began to grit loose, crookedly. With a shower of rust, the hatch fell open and hung down like a broken jaw.

From the dark interior, a bent figure appeared, crawling up the slanting passage on slow hands and knees. Reaching the air, it stood up straight, a shadowy outline. It seemed to be a man. He looked around silently for a long time, breathing deeply. The tense watchers could hear his long, deep respirations. All he seemed to want to do was breathe and look at the surrounding mountains.

Professor Leigh pushed forward. "Ahoy, there!" he called. His nonchalance was gone. His voice was frankly shaking.

"Ahoy yourself," said the man doubtfully. His voice had an unfamiliar ring. Don's heart sank. This was not the voice of Martin Madison as he had spoken two hours before.

The shadowy figure lowered a swinging ladder. Its bottom rung dangled high above the moonlit sand. The man hesitated, peering down. "Are you—Professor—Pritchard Leigh?" he asked, speaking with difficulty, in a dazed and distant way, as though awakening with reluctance from a deep, sweet dream.

"I am," Leigh cried.

"Glory be," exclaimed the stranger. "So you are." He came part way down the ladder, turned, and looked again. "You must have found the fountain of eternal youth," he said. "You don't look a day older than when I saw you last." He stared about incredulously at Leigh's assistants. "None of you do. I can't believe it!"

More cars were arriving. Their headlights found the ladder, spotlighting a sun-tanned, clean-shaven young man, with curly blond hair. His bare legs were muscular and straight. At the end of the ladder he halted, and for the first time seemed conscious of himself. "Excuse my appearance," he said. "We haven't bothered dressing much. It's been like the Garden of Eden." Newsreel cameras began to grind.

The young Greek god on the swinging ladder made an effort to get his bearings, and failed. Some strange doubt crossed his handsome face. He asked in a low, bewildered voice, "Is this still the United States of America?"

Don was one of the few who stood close enough to hear. "You bet your sweet life it is," he said proudly.

The golden youth looked relieved. "I'm glad," he said, and dropped lithely to the sand. "I began to worry on the last lap, coming in. When I put on the brakes, my old memories of the past got mixed up with my new memories of the future." He passed his hand across his face in a gesture of confusion. "I remembered disunity, sabotage, commies—"

A young reporter whispered in Don's ear, "What's he talking about?"

Behind his hand, Don told him quickly, "You're too young to remember. It was long ago. Mentally, this man must be living in the past, to use such archaic words."

The young man's hearing was acute. He heard Don's muffled whisper twenty feet away. "I guess you're right," he said, coming closer. "We have re-*lived* the past, not merely remembered it." He slapped his right leg heartily. "Just got this pin back a year ago." He groped for words, smiling at them in a strange new way; with the vigor of youth and the wisdom of great age. "You see, it all comes back to you out there, just the way you lived it. Wisely or foolishly, with every pain and pleasure in its place—" His lost eyes came to rest on Don.

"I don't recall your name," he said slowly, "but your face reminds me that I promised you something, many years ago." He reached in the pocket of his shorts and handed Don an ancient, wrinkled, almost illegible torn scrap of violet paper with a few words typewritten on it. "Finally found it," he said. "Had plenty of time to look." Then he turned, tipped back his head, cupped his hands, and called to the open hatchway.

"Aren't you *ever* coming?"

A second shadowy figure appeared in the dark opening. "I have to put on something," said a voice. "I couldn't come as I am."

Don felt his head spinning. It was the voice that he had heard on the sound film the afternoon before. The gay, young voice of Martha Madison, as she had been in her twenties on her honeymoon.

She stepped part way out into the light and paused. Blinded by the spotlights, she could not see the crowd. A sudden silence fell upon the crowd of jostling men. Unaware of watching eyes, she stood looking about, breathing deeply, and smiling to herself, as if she were glad to be alive, and back on terra firma. Then she started nimbly to climb down the swinging ladder. The increasing glare of headlights spotlighted her. Red-gold hair gleamed richly, long glossy hair, tumbling unbound down her back.

Part way down the ladder, she heard the whirring of cameras. She turned around on the ladder and waved cheerily. "Oh, hel-*lo* there, everybody!" she called. "This *is* a surprise!"

An agitated photographer elbowed in beside Don, to take a closer shot. *There goes that same scene again,* Don thought dizzily, *the second time around the reel.*

She dropped lightly to the sand, and stood beside her husband. Leigh's bearded, armed assistants formed a protective ring around them, holding back the growing crowd. On the sand flats beyond, planes were flying in and landing in close order. Army planes, Navy planes, the FBI.

Burgess Wood plucked at Leigh's sleeve. "Let me speak to her," he pleaded. His thin white hair blew wanly in the desert wind. "Martha—" he called. She could not hear him in the growing uproar.

Wood looked up at Don with tears in his eyes. "You *did* find Martha Madison for me!"

The press was firing questions at the travelers.

"What did you find out there?" a science writer demanded loudly.

Martin Madison said softly to himself, his eyes shining, "We found the love that is literally the life eternal. Love and the laughter of the stars—"

"We said, what did you find on Saturn?" a reporter shouted impatiently.

"Nothing there," he said. "Nothing anywhere."

"Show us the stuff you brought back!" a photographer yelled. "Hold it up to the light!"

Martin put his arm around his bride. "She is all I brought back. She is all I wanted."

"Talk louder!" bellowed a radio engineer, moving a microphone closer.

Young Martin Madison good-naturedly raised his voice. "We brought back a few home movies, to prove where we have been." He waved a hand at the block-long hull. "We exposed one million feet of three-dimensional, one-millimeter color film. With sound effects and telephoto close-ups of every blessed ball of fire we passed." He chuckled at Leigh. "That should keep you scientists out of mischief for the next ten years."

"Nothing else?" cried a columnist. "You found no new elements or unknown creatures?"

"One new element, called Time. One unknown creature. I saw him every morning in the mirror, when I shaved. I see him all around me now."

There was a murmur of disappointment. A leather-lunged radio commentator bayed hopefully, "Then at least you'd definitely state we're not in any danger from weird enemies out there on other planets?"

"Definitely not. Our enemy is here. On this planet. Unregenerate Old Adam." Seeing their falling faces, he relaxed his stern mien, and grinned boyishly. "Of course, we'd all rather face a seven-legged monster than ourselves, wouldn't we? It's so much more fun. But all there is out there in space is the projection of our minds. The cosmic joke is on Homo Sap." He pointed to the blackened rocket. "Get in there and go back to your boyhood. If you dare—"

There was uneasy muttering among the newsmen. "You're not co-operating with the press, young man," said a middle-aged editor. "We can't print sermons." Then he noticed young Martha Madison, standing modestly aside to give her husband the spotlight. He turned eagerly to her. "Ah, you, my dear! How about it? Was it really as bad as all that?"

She smiled enigmatically. "Wouldn't that depend upon what kind of life you'd led? We learned everything in life anew, out there, and yet we had forgotten nothing—"

"The hell with that," called an impatient voice from the shadowy rear. "We've got deadlines to meet. Give us the *story*, please."

She colored a little with surprise. Then she remembered where she was, and smiled with tolerant amusement. "All right, I'll try. We had to work hard, every day. That made time pass quickly. We had our ten volumes of memoirs to write. And I do mean memoirs. Observations, gardening, and keeping everything shipshape gave us plenty to do.

One of us had to stay on duty all the time, to spin the wheel, in case we ran afoul of sunken hulks of old wrecked stars, the asteroids. We slept and worked in six hour shifts. Sometimes I fudged an hour on the captain. Set my clock back. My rank and title? Why, first mate, of course!"

"Stick to what you *saw* with your own eyes," a wire-service reporter pleaded.

She closed her eyes, as if remembering, and then she said slowly, "With our own eyes we saw the rings of Saturn whirling like merry-go-rounds. We saw Jupiter juggling his eleven moons. We saw endless meadows sparkling with stardust like fields of wild flowers in the spring. We saw bright comets switch their fiery tails like cats. We saw the past lie down beside the future in the cradle of the Now. We sometimes saw little unborn worlds, smiling in their sleep."

She broke off, moved out of the light, stepped close to Holly, and whispered, "Lend me your cape—"

They withdrew from the crowd.

A gray-haired newsman said accusingly to Leigh, "You've dragged us out here in the desert for nothing, again. First your rockets didn't come back at all. Now they come back with nothing. What about our vital interests? What profitable purpose do these flights serve?"

Leigh faced his accusers with a defiant gesture. "You're still talking like eighteenth-century buccaneers, looking for new lands to plunder. Suppose there's nothing out there but immortality? Just like it says in the Book? Can't you see they have brought back the most precious cargo of all? Look at them. They're young again."

Uniformed men from the planes were pushing in among the civilians. "What's going on here?" an officer demanded. "Who are these people?"

"A couple of kids we never saw before," the Albuquerque Tribune man complained. "Nobody knows who they are. This rocket shoot was a misfire. The thing fell right back on the earth. We saw it all!"

Burgess Wood raised his quavering voice. "I know who

these people are. They are Martha and Martin Madison, the famous missionaries and explorers!"

Sounds of derision arose from the crowd. "The old coot is off his nut," a brash youngster said. "Why, those old fogies died years ago." The crowd began to mill around Martin.

Don and Holly helped Martha Madison slip away to one side, unobserved, disguised in the long cape. Holly gave her an understanding smile. Martha Madison nodded happily. "This was the only joy in life we'd missed. Now we shall be completely happy, knowing what we know, of life and of each other."

Burgess Wood tottered after them, holding out his shaking hands in a piteous appeal. "Martha," he implored. "Don't you remember me?"

The beautiful young bride looked closely at him. Studying her from a step away, Don saw that she was radiant with youth; and yet there was now a richer, subtle difference in her smile and eyes. Suddenly he understood. *If old age* could; *If youth knew* how. *She had them both. To have forgotten nothing,* Don thought, *and to have a second chance at everything— That would be a heavenly reward beyond man's fondest hopes of paradise.*

Young Martha bent and kissed the old man's withered cheek. "You could do what we did, Burgess," she said softly. "More rockets can be built, now that they know how."

The old astronomer shrank back in horror. "What, live my life over again, backward in relative time? Aching with the heartbreak of those years without you, Martha? Knowing the disappointments that are coming, every morning I wake up? Foreseeing my bad dreams each night?" He gave a short, harsh laugh. "I'd sooner cut my throat than go through all that again." He held her at arm's length in the moonlight. "Let's leave Father Time alone. He knows what he's doing. Now stand just so, my dear. Let me see the moonlight in your hair. All I want is a last good look at you." He nodded happily, and let her go.

"Yes, that's just the way you looked when I first fell in love with you. Divine. This is the way I shall now remember you forever." With a courtly, old-fashioned gesture, he bowed and kissed her warm young hand, then turned his back on her and slowly walked away, leaning on his cane.

Martin Madison detached himself from the noisy crowd and intercepted the slow old man in a few long strides. He stooped and peered curiously into the wrinkled face. "You must be Burgess Wood."

"And you must be feeling mighty cocky," said the old man with a wistful twinkle in his smile. "You found your fountain of youth, after all. Right in my own back yard. The stars. Well, enjoy your encore, sonny. It's too strong a drink for me, your time-elixir."

The muscular young man said sympathetically, "I'm sorry—"

"Don't be. You're the one who's going to be sorry, Martin. I'll have the last laugh yet. You see, the trouble with men's lives is not that they're too short, but that men live too long. Outlive their usefulness— No, I'll take the proper kind of life eternal, thank you. It's been good enough for mortals up to now. It's good enough for me. Good-by." He turned his back again and plodded off. The moonlight flung his shadow far ahead of him, a black forerunner undulating on the snowy sands.

Looking for his bride, Martin Madison pushed on through the dissatisfied, gesturing crowd. When he found her he said nothing. Only smiled, and took her hand.

Don spoke up. "Aren't you bitter about their not believing you?"

The Madisons looked at each other and burst out laughing. "We're used to that," Martin said. "Nobody believed what we tried to tell them, the time before."

Martha corrected him sweetly. "A *few* did, dear. The few who deserved to believe. Well, let's go back and reason with the cannibals. Remember that night in the Congo? It seems only yesterday."

"It *was* only yesterday," he reminded her, and they both

laughed again. Don and Holly watched them push back into the gesticulating crowd, shoulder to shoulder, tall, young, strong and unafraid of scorn and skepticism.

Holly gripped Don's arm. "What about us? Will we have been so happy that we will dare to go around a second time, when we reach the age they were a few hours ago?"

Don kissed her long slim fingers, one by one. "Ask me that again in about fifty years, my love. They may have excursion rates by then. But how many takers? Say, we've got to keep an eye on Gramps. He may get lost in the desert."

They found his dragging footprints in the sands and followed them. From the top of the high dune they saw him trudging far below, waving his cane at his shadow, like a little boy with a stick.

"When he walks like that," said Holly, "it means he wants to be alone." They turned and looked the other way, down at the spotlights and the churning crowd.

The Madisons were trying to climb back into their space ship, but now their listeners would not let them go. A few were beginning to believe. Martin hung on the swinging ladder, speaking to the upturned faces.

"Can you hear what the sky pilot is saying, Holly?"

"Not a word. Let's see that slip he handed you."

"Slip," said Don blankly. "Oh, that." He took the violet scrap of paper out and held it in the moonlight helplessly. "I can't read this without my glasses," he said. "You put yours on first. We've deceived each other long enough."

Holly took out a handsome pair of tortoise-shell rimmed glasses, studded with tiny rhinestones, and read aloud:

"—you forget that the Kingdom of Heaven is not on this Earth. In reaching for the stars, man can find nothing but his own soul."

Gravely, Don added it to the three other slips in his wallet. They slowly walked along, scuffing thoughtfully at the soft warm sand, sending it splashing in little sprays.

"I like you in your glasses," Don remarked. "Men have to make passes at girls who wear glasses like yours. They sparkle in the moonlight like tiny, unborn stars, or something." He put his arm around her. "I'm satisfied with everything except my solution to this case."

"What does it take to satisfy you? The pearly gates ripped off their hinges?"

"Well, no. But there are at least three known planets out beyond Saturn."

"You mean it isn't settled yet?" she cried in dismay.

"Not for me," he said solemnly. "Uranus, Neptune, Pluto—"

"Oh, shush your mouth," she said. The moon went behind a cloud. The stars looked out.

He regarded her face in the starlight. "I wonder if it's safe to kiss you again without bringing on another earthquake?"

"The scientific approach would be to try and see."

After a long time he raised his head and softly asked, "Did you hear what I heard? A far-off, musical sound."

She nodded, her eyes sparkling. "I really did hear *some*-thing," she admitted.

Don suggested, "Let's try again. Maybe we've made a discovery of the first magnitude."

They experimented. After an interval he announced, a little breathlessly, "That was definitely out of this world."

"What *is* it, dearest? Celestial wedding bells?"

Don stroked his chin and looked quizzically at the starry sky. "What we hear," he said gravely, "must be the laughter of the stars. Yes. Look up, and you can see them twinkling with laughter."

MORNING STAR

WE KNOW NOW, you and I and all of us within sight of a headline or earshot of a radio this morning, that Brian Dale was right, after all. Last year, you recall, there was talk of stopping him. No one could, because there was no law against it. No man before had ever tried what he has done. He was the first.

(First, but not last. My radio announces a wild rush of volunteers.)

And, as you know, before anyone could write a new law to restrain Brian Dale, he was gone where none could follow, and given up as worse than dead.

This morning he returned. Listen to Lewis Fremont on the air, calling him "Galileo, Columbus, and Lindbergh rolled into one."

Rather a large order for the modest, quiet young man I knew so well, back in New Mexico before this happened. Remembering those starlit desert nights when he secretly prepared himself for his supreme adventure, I can't help wondering what it felt like to be Brian Dale then, when he was the only man on earth who knew what every news-boy knows this morning. He confided in me, the night before he vanished, because he more than half expected to die, and wanted to get off his chest the crushing weight of a beautiful and terrifying truth.

If I told you what really happened the night this all began, I'm afraid it would sound like an adventure story, full of spies and guns and detectives in the dark. For they were there in force. Yet that would be merely the physical shell enclosing a bigger story, far more exciting, in the lasting sense. The adventure of the open mind, when Brian Dale met the Impossible and mastered it—or her, I should say. The mental courage, not the gunplay.

That is what I am pleading for against the tumult and the shouting. We miss the point of this historic morning if we cheer Brian Dale's amazing achievement as a mere feat of physical strength and daring. He has these, of course, in abundance, along with his rare good looks and all the other stock qualities of the hero. Listen to our friend Ariel Hotspur, voice shaking with emotion, calling Brian Dale, "Superman in the flesh!" I can imagine what Brian would say to that. One short word.

I know what Brian went through that first awful night, because he told me all he thought and felt; and I beg you to believe that it took more courage and will power for him to keep his mind open, in the blinding face of a vast new truth, than it did to rock the universe. For this is what makes a man divine. Not his animal nature, but the spiritual bravery to believe in a miracle when he sees one. The sheep, that night in Bethlehem, merely bleated at the Star. It took three wise men to follow it, to hope, to find.

And so the real story of Brian Dale would be, not this parade down Broadway now going on, but the eerie events of that night he stood beside the crater of an extinct volcano in America's Tibet and knew, but dared not tell.

I suppose I had better write this in the quickest, clearest form known to man, the straight adventure story, although it's so much more than that. I tried a philosophic version, full of depths and terror, and threw it in the wastebasket. The real terror of that first night, when a man's soul burst its bonds and soared into infinity, cannot be described. I shall give you the facts of what occurred, and let you imagine how you would have felt, had you been Brian Dale.

His story would begin like this, breathlessly: "Brian Dale hung up the receiver of his field telephone, sat down on a chunk of lava, and lit a cigarette with a steady hand;

but he could still hear the chief's deep voice warning him from far-off Washington—"

One moment, please. A false report about Brian Dale is on my radio—and on yours, too, for nothing else is on the air today. A flustered newscaster, caught at the mike with his script down, is ad-libbing, "Brian Dale was one of the brilliant young scientists in the atomic-bomb laboratory at Los Alamos, New Mexico."

How Brian would laugh at that, his deep, masculine, ribald laughter. You see, I happen to know that Brian Dale was a policeman. A Federal law enforcement officer in plain clothes. Before that, a Marine combat pilot. He was brilliant, yes, at guarding his country's scientific secrets. But not at creating them. His science was counterespionage, the nuclear physics of power politics. His salary was $4500 per annum. He was worth at least $45,000,000 to our country's safety, that gossamer web in which our lives hang like fragile spiders. He was no visionary dreamer. He had an FBI man's mind, factual, deductive, tough. Your kind of guy. To me, that makes his fantastic exploit all the more remarkable. Because Brian Dale laughed heartily at the merest mention of just the sort of thing that then happened to him. But when he had his facts, he believed, though sanity itself must have strained on its hinges. For Brian Dale, like you and me, comes from a good family, Homo sapiens—Man the Reasoner. Not unjustly, it seems this morning, called The Lord of the Universe.

Now let's start again, and this time I promise to keep going.

Brian Dale hung up—and so on—could hear the chief's deep voice saying, "I just got a tip from a certain embassy that extreme efforts may be made to learn what's going on out there in New Mexico tonight. Brian, you've got the most responsible job on earth!"

Brian took a deep drag on his cigarette and tried to be

thrilled at having the most responsible job on earth, but all he could feel was the New Mexico sunset hot across his face, and in his heart the cold knowledge that he must not fail.

A peak of the Jemez Mountains bit a black wedge out of the sun's orange rim. It would soon be dark. And darkness favors the attacker.

I don't see how there can be any slip-up, Brian thought, tense but unworried. *This is an airtight job.* He raised his binoculars and made a last inspection of the two-mile circle around him. Electrically charged fences. Searchlights. Armed guards outside. Inside, barren desert, up to the foot of the hill where Brian stood. Under the hill, the volcanic crater where the Thing stood, shimmering faintly under its acres of camouflage netting.

Brian skipped it. He did not like to look at Project Nine. He considered it a waste of his fellow taxpayers' money. He thought it goofy, and guarded it with his life, because those were his orders from the chief.

He swung around and closed his circle at its only entrance, a mile away. Barred gates across the one narrow road. A sentry post, with motorcycles and machine guns. A naked bayonet flashed blood red in the sinking sun, as though it had already been used. And it would be, instantly, on any prowler.

Brian shook his head impatiently at the sound of a plane. Couldn't be. Not for forty minutes. No one would dare. All aircraft had been ordered to keep out of New Mexico's skies till morning. "Testing a new rocket," the chief explained to irked airline lobbyists in Washington. It was not exactly true, but it was kinder to the brain than the real reason.

The sound persisted. Brian raised his glasses and swept the sky. It really was a plane. Small, fast liaison type, coming in low at reckless speed. One wing tip whipped a plume of snow from a mountain peak as the pilot dived in over the rocky wall to the hidden valley of the crater and the Thing.

Brian picked up his field telephone and spoke quietly to the radio truck at the landing-strip, down in the distance. "Get that plane's number. Tell pilot to alter course or be shot down." Brian had the laconic manner cultivated as a professional virtue by those of his dangerous calling, Democracy's Praetorian Guard. It went well with the casual look that masked the hair-trigger alertness of his clean-cut face, the vigilant efficiency of the steel-trap mind inside.

Ortiz, the radio operator, was back on the phone. "It's the general."

"What's he say?"

"For you to go to hell, Mr. Dale."

"Tell the general to do the same. Then let him land."

"But he's not on schedule. You said shoot all—"

"I know, Ortiz. The general is snafu. We'll shoot the next one."

Brian replaced the receiver with the deadly gentleness that was his only outward sign of anger. The exact timing of tonight's secret meeting was a security safeguard. And if there was anything that Brian Dale hated more than enemies of the United States of America, it was people who violated security safeguards in these crucial days, when a moment's carelessness could cost our country the upper hand it now, so briefly, held.

Brian swung into a jeep, bounded downhill, and jockeyed alongside the taxiing plane, his sandy hair blowing in the prop wash. The general jammed on the brakes and jumped down into the jeep beside Brian. He had learned to fly at fifty-nine and, like most fierce and wonderful old men, was a distinctly hot pilot. The general looked like an apoplectic moose, redder today than Brian had ever seen him.

Brian turned on two wheels and gave his passenger the roughest possible ride up the rocky hillside. After four years' flying with the Marine Air Force, mere Army generals cut no ice with Brian. Especially when he outranked them, as he did tonight, as civilian chief of security on mighty Project Nine.

The general grunted between boulders, "All right, I'm ahead of your schedule. Death penalty, apparently—Ouch! But if you think I'm breaking your rules, my lad, wait till you hear what your wonder boys have just done. That's why I flew in early. To warn you there'll be hell to pay tonight."

Brian slowed the jeep to a considerate canter and listened.

The general said, "Today noon your starry-eyed intellectuals invited a refugee scientist to sit in on our super-hush-hush huddle tonight. A complete stranger who is legally a prisoner of war!"

Brian's square jaw hardened. "What's the name?"

"Doctor Morgenstern."

"Never heard of him."

"It's not a him. A her. Miss Eva Morgenstern."

"My aching back," said Brian. "In which plane?"

"Worse yet. She's coming in by car. Under guard of two MP captains. They flew her up to Santa Fe this afternoon from Dayton. She's one of our menagerie of captured German scientists working at Wright Field. Supposed to be the world's greatest authority on some damned nonsense I can't even pronounce."

Brian shifted thoughtfully into compound low. "Means she was a real Nazi. Big shots had to be."

The general's face darkened to purple. "She's not. I haven't told you the worst yet. The woman is not a German. She is a Soviet Russian scientist."

Brian parked the jeep carefully on the hillside, and gently said, "Here, general. You drive. I'm going over the hill. To the bughouse."

The general nodded sympathetically. "Yes, I considered doing that myself. Or committing hara-kiri on the White House steps with my old cavalry saber. Then I got so hopping mad I hopped on out to see what happens tonight. You can't arrest her. They cleared her through channels. She has a signed pass. That ends it for us of the lower echelons. Start the jeep, soldier."

Brian drove grimly to the hilltop and parked by the phone. He said, "Something fishy about this. I just talked to the chief. He didn't say a word to me about any Doctor Eva Morgenstern having permission to attend. He did say certain parties might risk anything to break in tonight. I'm going to call Washington just to double-check your story, general." He picked up the receiver.

Ortiz presently reported. "It's ten p.m. in Washington, you know. Chief just left the office. Quit early. Secretary is trying to find him for you. Call you back."

The general was staring down into the crater. When Brian came up beside him, he grumbled, "All I asked for was a simple little rocket that would rub out any city on earth. Look what I get!" He shook his head incredulously at the exquisite, impossible, inevitable Thing, standing steeply on its half-mile ramp. Far down in the crater, tiny figures in white coveralls hammered faintly and trotted in and out the fortress doors of the vast underground laboratories. Modern science had put men back where they started from—in the cave.

The general muttered, "Haven't we got trouble enough here on earth without goofing off looking for more?"

Brian shot him a sharp sidelong smile. "Don't tell me you're beginning to fall for this Buck Rogers stuff."

"I didn't fall. It knocked me down. There she stands, ready to go. My fault, too. I'm the one who insisted that all our laboratories drop everything else and concentrate on cooking up an atomic rocket fuel, so that we'd be rid of this nonsense of lifting four tons of alcohol and liquid oxygen for every ton of warhead. How did I know our scientists were going to hit the jack pot again? Why, that dream-boat down in the hole will fly practically anywhere and back on a barrel of the new juice. It makes me dizzy, thinking what happens next."

Brian said, in pity, "If you're dizzy, general, better come in out of this hot sunset."

The general turned away reluctantly from his vision

of the future. "All right. Show me your layout for tonight so I won't be breaking any more of your ground rules. Not that it matters, with Tovarisch Eva Morgenstern of Moscow attending our meeting!"

"Maybe she won't get here," Brian hinted. As they passed the phone, he paused. "What about my call to Washington?"

Ortiz said, "Chief is at the White House. Can't call him to the phone there."

"Leave a message with the White House switchboard for him to call me as soon as he's free. Say it's urgent."

Brian conducted the general on a quick tour. "My layouts are always simple. Beef up the perimeter defenses, strip down the center. As you can see, there's not even a bush for a dog to hide behind for a mile around. Beyond that, not even a puppy could get in or out through those electric fences. But only two men here at the house, besides my driver and me. One on the front porch. Trent." A small thin man in a gray raincoat stood at the top of the steps, looking the general over with impersonal cold eyes.

"The house has only one door," said Brian, opening it. "And two rooms. In the first room, here, one man. Parker."

Planted solidly against an inner door stood a large square man. Not until Brian nodded in a certain way did he move aside to let them through into the room where the history-making conference of the world's four greatest scientists would, in a few minutes, begin—if all went well.

From the ceiling hung one shaded bulb. It threw a circle of light on a plain table and six chairs.

"Now you'll need another chair," the general said. "You can't leave our lady colleague standing."

Brian said, "She can have my chair—if she gets in. I'll stand—where I can snap the cuffs on her, but quick."

The general banged admiringly on the barred and blacked-out windows. "Not taking any chances, are you?"

"I never take chances. Especially tonight. For a few hours all our prize eggs are going to be in this one little basket. Over my dead body will one get busted. I don't count those who are already a little cracked, from working too hard on Project Nine." Brian circled the room, making a last inspection. "Do you realize this is the first time we've risked having Berkley, Jameson, Capri, and Zweistein in the same place at the same time?"

The general nodded uneasily. "I've been thinking about that all day. If a meteor or something should hit this house, with the real Big Four in session—" He broke off nervously.

In mutual reflex, they glanced at their watches. "Yes, they're due in ten minutes," Brian said.

The general yawned. "Your turn to worry. I'm going to sleep. I'm still on Eastern daylight saving time." He lay down at attention on the conference table. "I shall enjoy a brief preliminary nightmare, before our physicists arrive with a real one."

Brian turned off the light, hiding his smile in the sudden dark. He felt sorry for the old cavalryman, wrestling with the maddening concepts of push-button warfare.

Brian strode past Parker, past Trent, outdoors. The sun had set. Night fell swift as rain through the thin mountain air. Brian read the recognition signals winking back and forth between the radio truck and a plane approaching high from the west. He was reaching for the telephone when it whirred. Ortiz chanted, "Says Pasadena, in proper code. Is on schedule for Pasadena plane."

"Land him. Warn all incoming pilots to stay in the ready room and not wander around. How's about my call to Washington?"

"Bad luck. Chief left the White House by the side door a few minutes ago and didn't get your message. Wherever he went, he's not there yet."

"Try headquarters again. Code this: 'Request authority prevent Russian alien Eva Morgenstern from entering experimental area. After all, Ed, what the hell?' "

"Code that last, too, Mr. Dale?"

"Code all I said. I mean it." From the corner of his eye he was watching the first plane land safely. He sent his driver, Munn, down in the jeep. In a few minutes Munn was back with Professor Hector Berkley, the world's greatest nuclear physicist. He was a bubbling, bald little man, brisk and candid, but naïve as only a learned scientist can be in worldly matters. Brian and his staff of guardians sweated blood for Berkley. The physicist was carrying Nooky, the much-photographed black-and-white terrier that accompanied him everywhere. Nooky was short for "nucleus," according to one version.

"Inside," said Brian.

"Oh, not until I've seen my baby!" Berkley said gaily. He ran to the edge of the crater and peered under the camouflage netting. "Please turn on the lights."

"I will not," said Brian. "This whole area is blacked out tonight, absolutely. This is supposed to be a secret meeting—remember?"

"Oh, my, it's so hard for me to keep remembering all these silly rules you make. Don't you policemen realize that any industrial nation equipped to build a modern submarine can build a successful space ship? Our only secret is our new fuel."

"If they can, then let them," said Brian. "Don't deprive them of the fun of figuring it out for themselves, the way you had to do! My orders say 'secret,' and she stays secret. You'd better come inside now, professor. The general is waiting for you." He guided the physicist through the dark.

Overhead a streak of fire flared and faded. Then another, and another; faster, closer. Brian stopped and eyed them suspiciously. "Shooting stars, I suppose?"

Berkley chuckled with condescension. "Meteoric shower. This is August eleventh, you know. The Perseids are due. Tonight should be a beautiful display. Simple folk will tremble. Can't we hold our meeting outdoors to enjoy it?" Brian shepherded his costly charge silently into the house.

The general was snoring. Berkley said, "I wish he'd stay that way all evening. He understands less of what we're talking about than Nooky here."

The general said thickly, "I heard that." He swung his legs off the table and sat down. "Berkley, your dog would know better than to bring a communist scientist into this room tonight."

Berkley put the little animal on the table. "What an intellect! Her monograph on astronautics—"

"Don't monograph me," said the general. "How can she be anything but a spy? She's after the formula of our atomic-rocket fuel—a secret more vital than the bomb itself!"

Berkley made a hoop of his arms. The terrier jumped through. "Spy for whom, general? Doctor Morgenstern is a woman without a country. She fled from Russia one jump ahead of the firing squad. She was in a Nazi death camp awaiting execution when we liberated her."

Brian asked, "What's her description?"

Berkley said, petting his dog, "I've never met her— Oh, don't look so cross, general. Scientists and authors become intimately acquainted through their work, without ever meeting in the flesh. Ah, those charming formulae of hers—"

Brian persisted. "Don't any of you know her when you see her?"

Berkley said, "Zweistein might. He met her in Leningrad at a scientists' congress back in the old Intourist days, about 1934. Zweistein vouches for her."

Brian relaxed. At the mention of the name Zweistein, he felt better all over. He had the deepest respect for the judgment and the loyalty of the grand old man of modern physics.

Brian went out and watched for Zweistein's plane. He hoped the old man would not be tired from his long flight. The sleek private plane came in from the east. It was too dark now for Brian to see the airstrip. He heard the jeep laboring up the hill, guided by the faint blue glow of its blackout lights. Brian ran over to help Professor Zweistein from the jeep. The great scientist's halo of white hair shone in the darkness.

His voice was gently guttural with the ghost of a German accent. "Ach, what a romantic place for a scientific meeting! Why is so secret a little trip next door? Every American newsstand is covered with magazines giffing exact details of interplanetary travel—most of them so nearly right I read them for my own delight!"

Brian guided him inside and seated him between the general and Berkley. The dog barked happily at Zweistein. Children and animals loved the old professor on sight, as if they sensed, with their purer instincts, the profound goodness in him, the compassionate vision of an Old Testament prophet.

He looked about and asked, "Und where is my friend Capri? I thought he lived here."

"He lives down in the hole," Brian said. "He wanted to tinker till the last minute. I'll send for him. Jameson's due, too."

He went out and phoned the underground laboratory at the bottom of the pit, and a little later saw corpulent Doctor Capri start waddling up the long stairway that climbed the charred cliffs, soon to be burned again by the fury of a man-made volcano from the rocket's huge jets. The crater made a natural launching-pit.

While Brian waited, the last plane appeared, precisely on schedule from Chicago. It brought Sir Jules Jameson, the astronomer. He stumbled out of the jeep into Brian's arms and mumbled an embarrassed apology. Protecting the eminent Englishman was a sore trial to Brian. Sir Jules, who knew his way around the universe as familiarly as his own London garden, could get hopelessly lost returning from a washroom in the Pentagon Building. He seemed always to be more than half asleep, never recognized anyone, not even Lady Jameson; but on the rare occasions when he spoke, in his almost unintelligible British accent, planets turned over in their orbits, and stars changed their names.

Brian led the astronomer to the chair at the foot of the table. Sir Jules opened a huge brief case full of charts.

Brian bent down beside Professor Zweistein's bushy head. "Could you identify Eva Morgenstern if you saw her?"

The picturesque old man pursed his lips doubtfully. "Ach, it has been so long. One meets so many women scientists in Russia, and they all look alike. And no woman's face could be the same after what she has been through." He added hopefully, "However, she should recognize me. I have looked like this—so funny—for thirty years."

Brian hurried out at the sound of a loud voice. It was Capri, on the front steps. The fiery Italian scientist was remonstrating with the guard. "I live here! I work here! I design most of this, and you keep me out of my own conference!"

Trent stood motionless before him until Brian nodded and took Capri in himself. He had glittering black eyes and a waxed mustache, and believed passionately that there was intelligent life on other planets—a view for which he had been widely ridiculed.

The room was already resonant with talk. Only the chair at the head of the table stood vacant. Brian suggested, "The sooner you start, gentlemen, the quicker you can leave."

Berkley said, "Oh, but we can't start without Doctor Morgenstern. Go see what's keeping her, won't you?"

Brian bit back a sharp answer. He knew that Professor Berkley meant no offense, speaking to him as if he were a bellhop, and yet it always irritated him. He went out and snatched the telephone receiver off the hook.

Ortiz said, "Just going to ring you. Here's Washington."

Brian drew a deep breath and prepared to talk fast and rough, but when he heard the voice and what it said, he let his breath out in a low whistle of chagrin.

It was merely the chief's secretary. She said primly, "All I can tell you, Mr. Dale, is that he received your request ten minutes ago."

The guarded manner, the brush-off answer, cut even

Brian's thick skin. The chief was not one to speak through secretaries. Was he powerless to act in the Morgenstern case and loath to admit his humiliation to his agent in the field?

Brian stood in the darkness, feeling his cheeks burn. Far to the south, a pair of automobile headlights swung into view, bobbing up and down as a car raced over the rough desert road. *Here she comes,* he thought. *Your Trojan horse. Bet she looks like one, too.* Brian felt an inexplicable uneasiness come over him. In his business there were no such things as nerves. There couldn't be. And yet Brian was a keenly sensitive man, as they must be who live by having sharper wits than their antagonists. He thought he heard a faint rushing sound high overhead. He fought off an impulse to turn on the floodlights.

Irritated by the loss of his habitual calm, he dialed the sentry post at the gate and told them, "Send out a motorcycle patrol and tell that driver to turn his lights out. Take your time about examining that woman's papers. If you find a flyspeck on them, let her cool her heels. My phone won't answer."

He hung up without waiting for a reply. He turned his back on the distant headlights. He did not want to watch the car enter or be on hand to greet the woman. If she called him "comrade," he'd blow his top, he knew.

A freakish gust of wind swirled up from the desert below, showering him with sand and dust. Shielding his eyes with his hands, Brian groped back toward the porch. Off to the left, the garage door blew open a crack, banged shut. Brian had a glimpse of Munn servicing the two jeeps.

He sensed Trent's presence, rather than saw him. Brian said, "If a woman arrives, send her in."

Trent's voice replied, startlingly close in the gloom. "Okay."

Brian gave the same order to Parker, who was standing under one dim light, and went through into the conference room.

Professor Zweistein was saying sadly, "No, our refugee committee could not help her. They would not let me see her at Wright Field. Her application for American citizenship has been refused. Tomorrow she must leave the country. We are fortunate to have her consultation for this one meeting. Sir Jules, these magnificent planetary charts you've made will help us get from her the data we need, in concrete form." Professor Zweistein paused, and his voice grew stern. "And even though Doctor Morgenstern is a homeless, harmless refugee, I must caution all of you not to make the slightest reference even to the existence of our atomic jet-propulsion fuel, let alone its formula!"

"We're not children!" protested Berkley. "I have the formula here in my pocket, where it's perfectly safe!"

Brian mopped his forehead. He wished the priceless paper were somewhere else. He drew back into the shadows, outside the pool of light, and stood where he could watch everything that happened in the room. His heart was sick. For the first time in his hard-hitting, successful life he felt discouraged. He looked at the floor. He decided to resign from his government job in the morning. If the woman got in. The scientists' voices droned learnedly of perturbations and interorbital curves, solar acceleration and the velocity of escape. At some point in their discussion the door must have opened silently, for when they looked up, the woman was there alone. Brian could never be sure, later, how long she had been standing in the shadows, watching and listening. The general saw her first, as he was not listening to Capri's wild plan for packing samples of earth's culture—books, pictures, figurines—into the robot missile.

The general cleared his throat. "Er—here's Doctor Morgenstern."

Seeing that she was observed, she took one lithe step out of the shadow into the light. The five men arose to their feet as if pulled by invisible wires. There was an electric silence. Then Berkley and Capri collided in their haste to hold her chair for her. She clasped her long white hands over the back of it and remained standing, tall and slender, looking slowly about the room, as if trying to get her bearings in unfamiliar surroundings. Trapped in the circle of light at the table, she could not see Brian in the shadows beyond, but Brian could see her with the merciless clarity of a prisoner under the sweat light at a police station. And the first thing he noticed, with the impact of a mule's kick in the pit of his stomach, was that she did not recognize Professor Zweistein, one of the dozen most unforgettable faces on earth.

Zweistein was the first to recover from the magnetic spell her entry had cast upon them. With an Old World aplomb, he made the introductions. "Doctor Morgenstern, these are my colleagues: Doctor Capri, Doctor Berkley, Sir Jules Jameson. You know their work, of course. I shall now disclose to you the highly confidential subject of tonight's meeting, with the strict and solemn understanding that you will never—" The great man faltered.

She was smiling down at him, a curved, strange smile of pale coral lips and jade-green eyes, a fond smile of such tenderness as a mother might give a precocious child. And yet she was a young woman—magnificently young, Brian saw. But there was more to her than that—much more—qualities that defied description.

Zweistein said weakly, "So you already know the subject of our conference?"

She nodded with amusement. Swiftly her eyes explored the faces and the forms of the men around the table, and Brian thought he detected a look of disappointment in the unearthly beauty of that heart-shaped, opalescent face. *Prison pallor,* he thought. *But what skin.* Every inch of her beautiful figure was tense with an excitement that seemed akin to curiosity. Carefully, Brian moved closer, observing with wrathful admiration how cleverly she masked the eagerness with which she inspected each of the men, in turn, and somehow subtly dismissed them.

Trying to explain to himself her curiously eager air,

Brian classified her as one of those hot-blooded super-women with the tastes of a medieval tsarina. A superb female who had been too long deprived of the company of men of her own considerable caliber. A feminine woman with a superior intellect, perhaps, but a still more superior body, to whom tonight's meeting with free men meant more emotionally than it did intellectually. Brian thought, *After all, she's been locked up for years. This is her first time out. I know how I'd feel.* Then he was furious with himself for so digressing, when the woman needed watching, not sympathy.

Her searching eyes lighted on Berkley's little terrier. He began to wag his tail and whine in a most peculiar manner. The woman's face brightened as if she had made a discovery. She held out her hands to the dog, and, for the first time, spoke, forming her words slowly, as if English was very hard for her. She asked, pointing to the dog, "May I touch it?" Her voice was like no other voice Brian had ever heard. It made the short hair bristle on the nape of his neck. It had a bell-like quality of song that made mere words sound like interruptions. And her accent was like nothing on earth.

The men exchanged puzzled glances. Berkley smiled and said, "Why, of course, Doctor Morgenstern. He's just a common terrier."

She nodded. "Of course." She repeated the words, as if learning them. "A ter-rier."

Professor Zweistein's deep eyes filled with tears. He leaned toward the general and murmured, "Poor woman, they haff kept her locked up so long she has forgotten what a dog looks like."

The general nodded without taking his eyes from her glowing face. His red skin had gone white.

The dog crept toward her, quivering. He threw back his head and softly howled, not the yelp of fright, but the eldritch keening of a dog to the moon. Then he fawned before her and began hungrily to lick her hand, as though it were coated with some delicious substance. A look of inexpressible delight overspread the woman's sculptured features, and she hesitantly stroked the terrier's short fur.

Embarrassed, Berkley pulled the dog away, but he darted to the woman's feet, lay down between them, and growled when his owner tried to remove him.

Again Zweistein came to the rescue. "Gentlemen—and Doctor Morgenstern—we must begin. Our time is limited. Please be seated."

Her grace, as she seated herself, was fluid, like a swimmer's. The movement brought her head down where the light fell upon it, and Brian saw that she was wearing a close-fitting turban, suggestive of a helmet. It completely concealed her hair. Her dress was a plain dark traveling suit of some odd, lustrous cloth that Brian could not identify. She wore no jewelry, no rings on those delicate long fingers. Her hands themselves were jewels.

None of the men paid much attention to Berkley, acting as chairman, as he quickly summed up progress to date. Fuel tested. Rocket complete, ready to aim, and set for flight. Whether it would find its target or be forever lost in space depended upon the accuracy of tonight's calculations.

But the woman paid attention, Brian noticed. She absorbed the summary with the intense concentration of a gifted linguist memorizing a lecture in a foreign language that supplies many new and needed words.

Watching her, Brian decided she was the cleverest woman he had ever seen, as well as the most beautiful, in her other-worldly way. She would have been formidable but for a puzzling quality of innocence that prevented her from hiding her emotions. Her intellect was keen, but it could not control the delicate play of light and shadow across her ivory features. Brian saw hope in her face, and fear that she would fail, and a deep and nameless longing.

It was her unworldly air of naïveté, her lack of guile, that first soothed Brian's cold fury of enmity and suspicion. Spies weren't like that. She must be something else. Maybe she was really what the others thought she was—an honest refugee scientist, more feminine than scientific, her emotions overwrought by the importance of the occasion, and trying hard to make a good impression that might enable her to remain in America as an assistant on Project Nine.

Brian leaned down in the dark behind Professor Zweistein and whispered, "Is this the woman you met in Leningrad?"

Zweistein shrugged the philosophic shrug of his ancient race, a sad and shrewd salute of the shoulders to the essentially enigmatic nature of life. "Who else could she be?" he whispered. "Your military police would not bring Madame Molotov."

"But that accent of hers—it's neither German nor Russian!"

"*Ja,* it is *outré.* Russians are eccentric linguists. There are as many different kinds of Russian accents as there are Russians. Remember she has lived long abroad."

Brian said, "All the same, I have a hunch I'd better go out and speak to her guards. I'd like to see her identification papers with my own eyes. There just aren't any women like this."

Professor Zweistein reached out and caught Brian's departing hand. "Please don't go away," he whispered. "I have the queerest feeling. As if I needed someone like you near me tonight. Someone—how do you say?—hardheaded."

Brian let himself be drawn back. He squeezed the old man's hand with an almost filial affection. What difference did it make, inspecting her papers now? She was in, and had the Big Four eating out of her hand. Brian couldn't blame them. She was as bewitching as a beam of moonlight turned to more than human form.

Berkley was finishing. "And so, gentlemen, and lady"— he gazed at her like a smitten schoolboy—"tonight we must make our final calculations and compute the exact time at which our rocket ship must leave this earth."

She said calmly, "Four a.m., September first." It sounded

to Brian as if she had rehearsed it, and he wondered—but he was wondering about so many things that he did not know which to wonder about first. Wondering about the delicacy of those pale coral lips, the unimaginable color of the hair she hid beneath her helmet.

Sir Jules blinked and mumbled, "I say, that would be a most unfavorable time to launch a rocket to Mars. The distance then will be nearly three times the minimum, when Mars is in opposition to the sun."

She threw back her sleek helmeted head and softly laughed. The music of it was low and vibrant, and brought Brian's heart bobbing up into his throat.

"Not Mars," she said. "Venus."

The silence of an impasse congealed upon the room. Sir Jules came fully awake. "Doctor Morgenstern, with all due respect to your outstanding knowledge of this field, I must remind you that the sole purpose of this meeting is to chart a rocket flight to Mars."

She shook her head at him sweetly, as if he were a naughty, but rather nice little boy. "Oh, no. Please. Venus is better for men—and so much warmth. On Venus you could leave your rocket without special suits. Surface conditions"—she groped for a word she had apparently learned for the occasion—"resemble tropical jungle."

Berkley and Zweistein exchanged startled glances. Capri's mustache quivered. Sir Jules screwed in his monocle and said, "My dear girl, how can you possibly know what you have just said? Venus is always veiled in clouds. No astronomer on earth has ever seen her surface."

She said gently, "Even so, it is as I say. Hot rain and rich vegetation. Men could live there. Strong young men able to stand—the jungle."

Professor Zweistein had been studying the woman closely, with a quizzical look. He said, "Here in the United States we had no idea Soviet astrophysicists had made such astounding progress. What instruments did you use? Why didn't they publish your observations?"

She smiled at him, sensing that he was on her side,

rather than comprehending what he had said. Before she needed to reply, Berkley had leaped into the role of her defender, and answered for her. "When a Soviet scientist makes a discovery with as much potential future military value as hers has, you don't think they'd publish it, do you? Neither would we!"

She flashed him a grateful smile that melted him in blushes. There was another on her side. And yet Brian detected again that subtle air of disappointment, as if she wished Capri and Berkley were younger and more virile. She turned her extraordinary green eyes on the general. "And you?"

He swallowed hard and said huskily, "Let's see how a shot at Venus works out on your sky maps, Sir Jules. If it's really a better calculated risk, sound military doctrine demands we take it."

Sir Jules thumped his bulging brief case indignantly. "We selected Mars because its cloudless air will let us see the signal flash of the atomic bomb our unmanned rocket will carry in its nose and explode on landing."

Her face clouded over with swift dread. "Bomb? Unmanned? Oh, no. Neither. Think how you would feel!"

"But, my dear lady, we just can't go shooting hundred-million-dollar rockets off into space without some proof that we're getting where we want to go!"

Zweistein held up a trembling hand. "One question. Doctor Morgenstern, what you have said about Venus agrees with my own hypotheses—theories I've never dared publish. Tell me, from your—er—unique observations, do you think that the flash of an atomic bomb could be seen through the clouds of Venus?"

Her breathing grew rapid. In a low voice she answered, "And what if those you have exploded here on earth—were seen there?"

Sir Jules stood up and said icily, "Unless this wild talk is stopped, I shall withdraw from the committee!"

There came a dangerous pause. She seemed alarmed. Brian narrowed his eyes at her. He recognized, even under her ivory immobility, a trace of that trapped look the cleverest women get when they have overplayed their hands with men. That inner panic of loss they try to hide beneath their most alluring smile, as if by blind biology they may win back what their incautious words have lost them.

"I apologize," she said haltingly. "I am unfamiliar with English and I use wrong words."

Capri cut in defensively. "What she means to say, Sir Jules, is that these are her hypotheses. Every scientist has a right to express a theory, the same as you. Sit down."

The Englishman grumbled, "They didn't sound like hypotheses to me." He reluctantly resumed his seat.

Berkley said, "I vote we consider her proposal for setting the rocket at Venus. Let's see how it works out on the charts."

The general spoke, his brassy voice softened. "Do I understand, Miss—Doctor—that you are advising us to send a manned rocket on this first test flight?"

"Yes," she said, "manned."

The general insisted, "But wouldn't it mean almost certain death?"

She said, "No. The opposite. Plot your curves correctly —I am here to help do that—set your instruments accordingly, and you will reach Venus safely. Out in space"—she tossed her helmeted head in a casual nod—"there are no winds to blow your ship off course, no fog to blind you. Space is safer than your sea or air, but automatic instruments cannot anticipate unknown situations. Only men, pilots, can make original decisions. Send men, but no bomb, I beg you. Send life to life, not death."

Sir Jules raised one eyebrow. "Come now. Surely you don't expect to find life like ours on other planets?"

She pressed her pale, exotic lips in a firm line, whether to suppress impatience or to keep from laughing in the astronomer's face, Brian could not be sure. She said, "You have a Book here. I read it, preparing myself for—tonight. It says, 'In my Father's house are many mansions.' If you knew what those words mean—" She broke off quickly, as if afraid that she had said too much, but the men were drinking in her voice, her face, rather than her reasoning. She went on, "Life like yours, no. Different conditions create different forms. But life, yes! Everywhere the sun touches. Light is life. Life is light. That is in your Book, too—if you would read it!"

Brian noticed that each of the men at whom she had looked directly and smiled upon was not afterward quite the same. Only Sir Jules remained unwon. He said gloomily, "If these hypothetical Venusians of yours know anything about the black history of mankind on Earth, they'd fight off our rocket landings as you'd defend your home from lunatic cannibals! We're a bad lot."

She nodded with a manner that to Brian seemed forgiving, and said, "There is much truth in what you say. Yet have not the women of Earth"—her voice broke and she continued with an effort—"have they not loved their mankind these many centuries, despite cruelty and war, simply because they were men?" She pronounced the word with cryptic emphasis, caught Sir Jules's elusive eye, held it, and slowly smiled upon him. The great astronomer thawed and began to beam, and Brian got a glimpse of what he might have been like forty years ago, a pink-cheeked, eager lad on the playing fields of Eton. She said earnestly, "Mankind may soon need a safe refuge to flee to from his own radioactivity." Her listeners stirred uncomfortably. Brian noted how swiftly she sensed that they were not pleased, how adroitly she changed the subject, and her manner with it, with the grace of a tactful hostess. Now she was laughing, bantering with them, subtly coaxing. "Imagine what amusing biological specimens you might find out there. Here on earth men and women are so nearly alike one can pose as the other by exchanging clothing. Yet the biologic odds were that two quite different creatures would evolve—as happens among so many lower forms of life." Her eyes began to glow with a singular intensity. "As scientists, we may easily visualize some hypothetical planet where the female of some biped mammal compares favorably in structure with the human female of Earth, but where there are no corresponding males —a tragic race whose other half failed to evolve beyond mere pollen—a mindless germ—a mocking dust on the winds of eternal loneliness!"

She sank back trembling, exhausted with her effort, struggling for breath.

Capri pounded on the table, his black eyes snapping with excitement. "She confirms what I have been ridiculed for saying, that there is life out there, waiting for us to find it. Under the clouds of Venus, the Cytherean veil, there is surely an atmosphere dense enough to support a safe rocket landing, and perhaps even to return from. I must insist that our ship be zeroed in on Venus!"

Berkley, the general, and Zweistein all nodded their assent helplessly, as if hypnotized. Sir Jules spread out his charts before her and offered her his fountain pen.

When her alien hand touched the confidential papers, Brian felt a shock go through him. He clenched his fists and shook with rage. He took one quick step forward to declare the meeting over, and to hell with consequences, but Professor Zweistein caught his coat sleeve, shook his head, and laid his finger to his lips. With a quick nod he returned Brian's attention to the woman's face.

She was smiling at Sir Jules's precious charts. Smiling fondly, as Sir Jules himself might have smiled at a caveman's animal pictures, amused by their crudity, and yet touched by the dear knowledge that this other mind, so remote in time and space, had drawn his animals about as well as Sir Jules could, for in them both burned the same sacred spark of Reason, and made them kin.

Berkley bustled to bring out his papers, too. Among the documents he handed her was a red sheet stamped TOP SECRET. "Here is the formula for our atomic-rocket fuel," he said.

The general struck his forehead with his palm and moaned, "My God!"

Before Brian could draw his gun, the woman tossed the red page aside without a glance and sat examining Sir Jules's fountain pen as if it were an archaeological treasure. Suddenly, conscious of Brian's astonished eyes upon her, she put the fountain pen down and tried to hold it casually. She held it wrong, he noticed.

She said brightly, smiling at them all, "Shall we compute our curve into the orbit of Venus?"

It seemed to Brian that they all said in unison, "Please do, Doctor Morgenstern!" Their heads bent over the table. She asked a few short questions: "The rocket's weight?" They told her. "Its speed at leaving the stratosphere?" They told her.

They told her everything she wanted to know, but not one of her questions concerned military secrets. The lovely stranger who had walked in out of the night was no more interested in the construction of the earth's first space ship than Brian was in the specifications of Hiawatha's birch-bark canoe. She was concerned only that it reach Venus with its crew alive and well.

As the world's four greatest intellects watched, fascinated, she traced a parabolic arc, writing in beside it, as she drew, a series of complex equations. Brian was very close to her now, giddily aware of her disturbing beauty; aware, too, that she printed her figures in an oddly unreal hand, as an American might paint Chinese ideographs, faithfully learned, but lacking the Chinese look.

Professor Zweistein's face grew troubled. "Excuse me, please, but I assume you have memorized these equations?"

She shook her head and continued computing swiftly.

Zweistein passed his hand over his face in a gesture of stupefaction. "You mean that you are solving these problems in your mind?"

She laughed, looking from face to staring face. "Yes, of course. How else?"

Capri murmured something in Italian that was either a prayer or an oath. Sir Jules blinked rapidly. Berkley's bald head broke out with bright drops of sweat.

Zweistein pointed to the complex equations with an unsteady hand, and said, "I am called the world's greatest mathematician, but for calculus and mechanical quadratures, I need paper and pencils and many hours alone. What you are doing, Doctor Morgenstern, is beyond human powers!"

She saw that she had made another mistake. Brian could guess now what she was going to say. Oh, she was clever, this bold creature with the jade-green eyes and coral lips, but not quite cunning enough to conceal her amazing performance of imposture, slips, and recoveries from eyes as trained as Brian's. He began to edge toward the door behind her silently, so as not to attract her attention. For some reason that he could not explain, he felt very glad she had not noticed him yet.

She assumed an expression of innocent confusion and said with a humble smile, "Excuse me, please." Brian noticed how quick she was to use a phrase once she had heard it. "Again I make mistake in English."

Brian thought, *That omitted article was overloading it just a bit, my dear Eva.*

She went on apologetically. "The truth is I have many times worked these equations, and so remember them. Forgive me, please. Let us sit closer together." Five chairs scraped eagerly toward her, and under cover of their noise, Brian opened the door and slipped out.

Parker was standing motionless. Brian asked him, "Where are those two MP captains who brought the woman in?"

The big man hesitated. "They must have stayed on the porch. She came through here alone. Your orders were to let her in."

"H'mm. What do you make of her, Parker?"

Parker smacked his lips. "Out of this world!"

Brian emerged upon the pitch-black porch. "Trent?"

"Right here beside you."

"Where are the woman's guards?"

"Uh—I guess they're out there with Munn. I see a cigarette."

"Didn't they bring her up to the porch?"

"No, she just came walking up the steps out of the dark, right after you came by. I thought she was with you. I flashed my light on her; she smiled and nodded to me, and I let her pass—like you said to do."

"Okay, Trent."

Brian felt his way down the steps and out toward the red spark of a cigarette. By the time he reached it, his eyes had dilated enough for him to see that it was Munn, sitting in the jeep alone. Brian stood beside his driver for a full minute before he said anything. Munn silently handed him a cigarette and lit it. Brian needed it. He inhaled deeply. Finally he inquired, as casually as he could, "Seen anybody?"

"Not even a jack rabbit."

"What happened to the car that started up here?"

"That's what I've been wondering," said Munn. "I saw two motorcycles stop them right after you phoned the road block."

"Munn, be exact. How soon is right after?"

"About one minute."

"You must be mistaken. Our motorcycles aren't jet propelled—yet."

"These first motorcycles came from the other direction, from Los Alamos. Ours came up later. Dark out there ever since." He stepped on the starter. "Maybe I better—"

Brian said, "Yes, and hurry. If I'm inside when you come back, have Parker call me out of the meeting. Got your flare pistol? Good."

After the jeep had crawled off slowly down the dark slope, Brian stood alone in the moonless night, his head thrown back to the starry sky, breathing deeply of the cool, rarefied breeze, trying to clear his orderly mind of the fantastic feeling of ecstasy and adventure the woman had given him, a mad impulse to break all bonds and precedents and have her at whatever cost. It crossed his mind that if she married an American citizen, her deportation could be stopped; and it bothered Brian that he should think things like this.

And as he stood with face uplifted to the depths of heaven, another meteor fell. A big, rose-colored one, majestically slow, mysteriously silent.

Behind him in the dark, Trent spoke. Normally a laconic man, his voice was edged with excitement. "That was a beauty, but you should have seen the one that sailed over an hour ago! Just before the last time you came out. Green! And hummed! I'll swear it landed somewhere near!"

Brian jumped. Then he forced himself to relax. To say, as he passed Trent, "It was probably fifty miles away. Stop stargazing. Keep your mind on your job!"

Like I'm doing, he thought. *Which isn't much.*

At the door to the inner room, he paused. From within came happy laughter. Half-forgotten words bobbed up in Brian's mind. *"Except ye become as little children—"* He couldn't remember the rest of it.

He went in. They were admiring her work. Her words came more easily as she gained confidence in speech. "How many men will your space ship carry?"

"That's the rub," said Capri ruefully. "With food, water, supplies, and oxygen enough for any emergency, only one man can go with safety. It's too late to change the ship's design. We'll make the next one bigger."

"But you will send one man? Not one of you, of course. You are too—valuable as scientists."

"Yes, if we can find such a man, and he is willing," Capri said. "The right man would be one thoroughly experienced in high altitude military aviation. We could teach him the rest of what he needs to know while we are installing the instruments between now and September. The main thing he'd need would be nerve. The rocket is designed for automatic flight."

Her attention was fixed on Capri with such hopeful intentness that she did not sense Brian coming closer to her in the shadows at her side, his eyes drinking in every detail of her loveliness as a photographic film absorbs its image, helplessly, totally, forever. Tiptoeing, so that she would not turn those fatal eyes on him, he moved over where he could see her profile, delicate and darkling fair. She breathed, he saw, with difficulty. Each inhalation seemed to pain her. And, although the airless room was hot and stuffy, she shivered.

Professor Zweistein noticed it, too. "Doctor Morgenstern, you are suffering. Are you ill?"

She shook her head and smiled, trying to conceal her distress. "You may call me Eva," she said.

"*Ach,* but you are choking, my dear Eva. Mr. Dale, can't you open a window?"

"Oh, no, please do not open a window!" she begged.

Capri cut in before Brian could move. "It's the altitude here. Coming up from Ohio in a few hours, she feels it. Isn't that right, Doctor Morgenstern—Eva?"

"Yes," she said. "Of course. Altitude."

Brian passed close beside her, letting his gaze linger on the exquisite curve of her throat. From her arose a flowery fragrance, as of a living blossom. His heart leaped and hammered. He wondered what the penalty was for kidnaping a prisoner of war. He understood suddenly what made the men of olden times fight bloody battles to capture fair women. With a lump in his throat and a stinging in his eyes, he knew now that he was indeed this night going to resign from his exacting duties, not in protest, but to capture and keep this woman, this original Eve, and not to let her get away. The hell with who she was, or had been. That did not matter now. Getting her, crushing her in his arms, was all that he could think about—for several minutes.

Then he righted his mind, as he would pull a fast plane out of a spin, went behind the general's chair and whispered in his ear, "Something's wrong. Step outside with me a moment. Those MP's have turned this woman loose and scrammed."

Without moving his rapt eyes, the general murmured,

"Good. I mean shut up. Nothing's wrong. Everything's right around here, since she came in. Man alive, this scramble for bases on other planets is just beginning, and we've got to be thar fustest with the mostest men."

The woman looked up swiftly and tried to pierce the shadows beyond her pool of light. "Who is this other man who stands always where I cannot see him, and whispers and watches me?"

Berkley said, comic in his jealousy, "He's no one of importance—not a scientist. Just a sort of strong-arm man."

She said eagerly, "Let me see this—strong-arm man."

Brian thrust himself into the light. He saw the pupils of her green eyes dilate and her lips part slowly. They stared at each other as if an eternity had been compressed into seconds. Unwaveringly, he met her amazing eyes, forced her to drop her gaze. *I know,* he said in his mind to her. *You can hypnotize these old men, but you can't fool me.*

She raised her eyes shyly, and a coral flush came over her ivory face. She gave him back a yielding look of pleading, and of promise. She said softly, "Better one man than none."

Brian withdrew from the light, and unsteadily left the room. He found himself wandering in the dark some distance from the house. As soon as he was able to think connectedly, he thought, *Damn it, I wonder what's keeping Munn?* He stared in the direction of the road. As he watched, a red signal flare soared and fell like a silent scream for help. It took Brian twenty minutes to reach the spot in the reserve jeep. When he saw shadowy shapes ahead in the road, he switched on his headlights.

A large military car stood crossways in the narrow road, its front and rear wheels bogged down hopelessly in the sand. In the car Brian saw the grayish splotches of four faces—a driver and three passengers. Around the car stood six motorcycles. Three were his. Three were from the special anticommando forces at Los Alamos.

Nine men, three of them MP's, were arguing with Munn and with one another. Munn held a flare pistol.

"Our orders were to stop her before she got here, and bring her back to Santa Fe," said a Los Alamos guard. "Orders from Washington!"

One of Brian's men retorted, "And our orders were to meet her and bring her in through the gate. Which is it, Mr. Dale?"

Brian said, "I'll tell you in a minute." He opened the rear door of the sedan and flashed his light inside.

Hunched down between two large and exceedingly peeved captains of the military police sat a wrinkled little old woman with a wise, kind face and tortured eyes. When Brian spoke to her, she answered in an accent that was like sauerkraut laced with borsch. Years of refugee horror had reduced her to a point where she saw nothing worthy of remark in the senseless confusions of this mad and futile night. She had no idea why she was brought here. She cried only a little when Brian told them to take her back to Dayton.

Brian stepped around to the driver, a surly sergeant gnawing a cigar stub. "How did your car get into this position, sergeant?"

"Beats the shucks outa me, mister. Some kinda wind just turned us around, gentle-like, before the cops got here. What goes on here, anyway?"

Brian said, "You wouldn't believe me if I told you. Nobody would."

It took all nine men to turn the MP's car around and start it back toward Santa Fe.

Brian got in with Munn, leaving his motorcycle men to bring his jeep back. He was in a hurry to get back to the house on the hill, and he felt too shaky to drive.

"Step on it," he told Munn.

On the way he watched several meteors flame across the sky. They reminded him of the fiery trail left by the high-altitude jet plane he had test-piloted in the last week of the war. Zip, and gone. The way he must have looked to lonely ranchers on the Mojave Desert. He began to wonder, more amused than anxious, how many of those streaks in the sky were bona fide meteorites, and how many might be—something else.

That wild ride through the dark desert from the road where the real Doctor Morgenstern had wept, to the house on the hill where the lovely woman smiled, was in its weird way the happiest twenty minutes of Brian Dale's twenty-nine years. Happiest because most exciting mentally. His fearless deductive mind now had a totally new case to work on, the toughest case of his career. He was even a little grateful to this other Eva—he decided to call her Eva from now on—grateful to her for flinging him a challenge that took all his manhood to answer.

As the dark wind whipped his face, Brian swiftly added up the clues he had gathered. Put them together as he had once watched a young physicist assemble an atomic bomb. Cool, efficient, unafraid of the blinding outcome.

First, Brian knew now that Eva had come straight down inside the guarded area. She had not jumped in a parachute. Even our meager radar defenses would have picked up an outside aircraft by the time it reached Central New Mexico.

Second, Brian had noticed something that the four scientists, in their enthrallment, had failed to detect. When Professor Zweistein protested that no earthly mind was capable of the exhibition of mental mathematics that she was giving, Eva had quickly belittled herself. Yet before she began to write in that quaint, unformed, childlike hand, she had not known the rocket's weight or speed. Hence, reasoned Brian, gingerly placing another part in his spiritual atomic bomb, she could not have memorized her equations in advance, since two basic factors were unknown to her until a moment before she began.

Third, as he passed beside her on his way out of the room, he had seen a lock of her hair. Had one tantalizing glimpse of it before she flicked it out of sight again beneath her helmet. And that bright instant had done more to prepare Brian's mind for the impact of the only possible solution to his case than had all his other deductions combined. For, while a cunning enemy might just possibly have found such a woman somewhere and trained her for this daring feat, he would not have let her come with hair like Eva's. No wonder she kept it hidden. What Brian had seen was incredible. And yet a man must believe his own eyes or declare himself insane.

Brian decided he was not insane. He had never felt saner in all his rocksteady life. Coolly he added the final ounce to his atomic bomb of logic: Eva could not escape. By whatever means she had arrived, out somewhere on the ink-black miles of empty desert, one click of a searchlight's switch and it would stand revealed, with a hundred armed men converging. By coming here tonight, Eva had trapped herself as hopelessly as the real Doctor Morgenstern's car had been trapped in the sand. What good was her reckless gamble when it placed her completely at his mercy? His, personally. For only Brian Dale, as chief of security, was in a position to piece together what had actually occurred tonight, to appreciate her masterpiece of timing and imposture. No one else knew or could ever know the whole story—unless he told it. It was almost as if Eva knew him intimately, and was depending upon him to let her go, when she had completed her bizarre mission. She had not yet played her trump card—and that card was Brian Dale.

There it stood, complete, the reasoned bomb. Brian closed his eyes and waited for it to go off. It fissioned in his mind, pleasantly, a light growing brighter until everything was clear as in the noonday sun, in one blinding flash of revelation the old Brian Dale, earth-bound scoffer and exclusionist, crisped to ash, and from it rose, phoenix-like, the complete man of the open mind, his horizon the universe. If she had told him who she was, an hour before, he would have laughed at her and reached for his handcuffs; but now that he had reasoned it out for himself, he had to believe it, because it was true.

Brian said to Munn, "Can't you drive faster?"

Munn said, "Yes, if you'll let me turn on my lights."

"Not yet," said Brian. "But in a minute I'm going to turn on all the lights." *Or am I?* he wondered. For all at once he had begun to feel very good all over at being Eva's trump card, the man she needed to make possible her escape.

Munn speeded up. A sudden crash threw Brian from his open seat to the sand. As usual, he had neglected to fasten his safety belt in the jeep. He picked himself up, hoping very much that he was uninjured. He was.

Munn said, "Chalk up one jeep, chief. Radiator's busted. Hit a boulder. Can't I turn on my headlights, just once?"

"Blackout," said Brian, "means no lights. Go back to the gate and get the other jeep. I'll walk up."

Brian ran as fast as he could, but it was slow going, and some time had elapsed before he reached the hilltop. A high-pitched humming, as of some unimaginably rapid vibration, pulsed in the air. Brian sprinted for the house. He brushed past Trent and Parker, although both tried to speak to him. The only thing he could see in the conference room was her empty chair. He fought to keep the scientists from seeing his confusion. Not hard, because they were happily discussing the beautiful curves she had drawn on their charts, the long columns of equations and esoteric data.

He asked as nonchalantly as he could, "Did she step out for a minute or something?"

Berkley said waspishly, "As if you didn't know. Fortunately, she'd finished her work for us—or I wouldn't have let her go. She told us you said for her to meet you outside."

Brian whirled and raced out into the night, ran to the edge of the hill. Below in the empty desert, he heard a dog bark. Berkley's little terrier. He plunged down the slope toward the sound.

He called, "Eva, wait!"

Her lips brushed his cheek in the darkness. He groped and caught her in his arms. She was supple as a mermaid. "Bri-an," she whispered.

120

He asked her, trying hard to keep his mind on who he was, not who she might be, "If I kept you here by force—"

"I would die." She gasped for breath. "Another five minutes and this thin, cold air will kill me." She shivered pitifully. Brian held her closer. Her shivering stopped. "You are so warm, man," she murmured.

Brian heard his own voice saying, to the astonishment of his mind, "I could be shot for this—but I'm going to let you go—the way you came. I don't want you to die. Take me with you, Eva."

"I want to! But I do not dare. You would die, the way we travel. That is why I came, to help you to come to us— to me. Come in your great clumsy boat and you will be safe. Oh, we have waited so long for you to learn!"

"How did you plan this tonight, timed so perfectly?" he asked.

She answered, "As you would—if you had, as we do, a way to listen. Most of what we hear from earth saddens us —poor frightened children plotting to set fire to their own nursery! And as we watched you starting that fire with your atomic-bomb explosions, we knew what any woman knows when she is in danger—that we must come to you."

She laid her head on his broad shoulder timidly, like a young girl, excited and a little frightened by a new and wonderful experience. "I heard your voice, Brian Dale, planning this meeting long ago. I loved you then. I volunteered to try. I studied hard. What I did tonight was our only chance. As I listened to your voice, man, you sounded —brave enough—in your mind and in your body. Only a very brave earth-man could dare to believe what you have guessed about me, and guessed correctly. That is what makes you so—so much a man. And I listened to your orders again tonight, as I came in, riding with the meteors. I hope the old woman was not hurt."

"She wasn't. Have you come and gone before?"

"Only a few times, long ago. Before we learned to disguise ourselves as earthlings, and came as we really are, men knelt and called us angels. It was safer for us in earth's childhood when men believed their eyes. But it did no good, and we stopped coming. Now your earth is dangerous with troubled adolescence, and a trip here is so awful that when my sisters quarrel, one tells another 'You go to Earth!' I came here once before for a load of books, to learn your language, and was shot at and almost caught! You are such a ferocious species!" She stroked his sandy hair wistfully, as if it were infinitely precious. "But quite the sweetest species in our dull little solar system. No, do not let me go, man. I would rather die here on this strange cold planet in your warm arms than go back to our eternal loneliness of futile hoping."

Brian felt the rapid beating of her heart, come so far to be so close to his. A heart like his. He shook her. "Eva, go while you can. I'll come to you."

She nodded, too out of breath to speak. Through the pitch-darkness he helped her across the flat sands in the direction she wanted to go. Then a last streak of Brian's stubborn common sense asserted itself, as a man transfigured by conversion might struggle once with the old Adam in him before surrendering to a state of grace.

He said harshly, "How can I be sure I'm not dreaming? Things like this don't happen!"

She laughed softly. "You have a saying here on earth, 'There has to be a first time for everything.' Tonight is the first time this has happened, and this is my first kiss. Show me how."

He showed her with a rush of tenderness and adoration he had not known was in him. Her lips were like fresh tropic fruit. Suddenly he understood the meaning of his austere, lonely life, his discipline, his training. It led like footsteps straight to—tonight.

She took his hand and guided it under the edge of her helmet. Her hair was crisp and cool, like a bed of maidenhair ferns. "Men have dreamed this dream for a thousand years," she said. "Yours is the first to come true. Here is your proof, man—and my promise." She left a wisp of her hair in his hand and, with a last lingering shy caress, twisted free and vanished in the blackness toward the humming sound.

He stumbled in the direction he thought she had taken. Tugging at his flashlight, caught in its belt holster, he ran headlong into the steel framework of one of the huge Army searchlights that ringed the hill. Stunned, he sank to his knees. Seconds or minutes later, he had a vague impression of a rising shape, some distance off, that left a brief streak of green flame and vanished. A violent wave of compressed air threw him off his feet.

Sand was still falling when he picked himself up, dazed. He staggered around the searchlight, fumbled for the controls, and switched it on. The desert blazed. Far out on the edge of the night, a mile away, groups of guards shielded their eyes with one hand and held their guns at ready with the other. Nothing moved on the barren land but a desert owl, fluttering blindly in the sudden glare. An owl and some eddies of dancing dust, such as the freakish little whirlwinds of the desert so frequently arouse.

Finally he remembered the wisp of hair in his clenched fist. He held it into the searchlight's white dazzle. It was a delicate soft green, the green of jungle ferns. Its flower-like fragrance came from within, not from added perfume. Very thoughtfully he put it in his wallet, in a little pocket that had always been reserved for a lock of hair, and never used before.

Leaving the searchlight blazing he walked slowly back toward the house. The field telephone was whirring as he approached.

"Hello, Brian," the chief said briskly. "Sorry to keep you waiting, but I've been busy since noon chopping my way up to the President to spike this Morgenstern business. Your message expressed my sentiments exactly. Then I had to burn up the wires to Los Alamos to send out a flying patrol and nail her before she got to you. Every second counted. There wasn't time to return your call. Where is she now?"

Brian said, "Doctor Eva Morgenstern is on her way

back to Dayton."

"Good. We'll deport her in the morning. Are our great brains safe and sound?"

"They've never been better, chief."

"Hold on, here's something special coming in on the Teletype." Brian could hear the ticker beside the telephone. "No, it's nothing. Just the usual dither about shooting stars crossing the sky. Here's a statement from the Naval Observatory: 'Captain Marshall Decries Hysteria over Harmless Meteoric Shower.' Say, are you all right, Brian? You don't sound like yourself."

"I'm not, chief. That blood vessel I popped flying high altitude is giving me some trouble. I'd like to resign."

"Blood vessel, hell. I saw your last physical. Perfect specimen, the medics said. What is it, a girl at last?"

"I guess so. I've got to—make a little trip and meet her family."

Behind him, as he hung up the receiver on his past, Brian could hear the scientists talking excitedly as they came out of the house. He joined them with a feeling that he was one of them now, committed to a cosmic venture. The reflections from the searchlight's glare cast a false moonlight around them.

Berkley turned to Brian and complained, "I've lost my dog. Find him for me."

"Your dog is gone," said Brian. "And I mean really gone away."

Capri said, "Yes, Hector, you gave her your dog, remember?"

"Did I? I'm not surprised. She earned several dogs tonight. Her last suggestion was a brilliantly simple solution to the safe return trip. But I'm glad she's gone. She was too disturbing to have around the project."

"Yes, wasn't she?" Capri agreed.

They walked to the top of the stairway that led down into the crater, Sir Jules with his brief case full of charts.

Capri said, "Let's wait for daylight before we go down to start work. It won't be long." They sat down on chunks of lava, lit cigars, and spoke of the advantages of semi-automatic over automatic flight. Brian listened carefully.

A faint flush of light, pearl-gray and rose, spread in the east. The meteors faded. Into the dawn a huge bright star rose dramatically from behind the Sangre de Cristo Mountains, the Mountains of the Blood of Christ. It drew their eyes.

Brian asked, "Sir Jules, what is the name of the morning star this time of year?"

Before the slow-moving Englishman could reply, Berkley had turned with a condescending smile. "The so-called morning star is never a star at all. Stars are suns. The morning star is always one of our close neighbor planets. But since when have you become interested in astronomy, officer?"

Brian returned his smile without rancor. He was going to have to get along with Berkley—for a little while. Berkley knew about orbits and bow jets and such. "Since tonight, Professor Berkley, thanks to you. I've just resigned from the force. I'm an unemployed civilian."

Sir Jules awakened with a start. "By Jove, come to think of it, that's Venus!"

Berkley said, "Amusing coincidence, isn't it?"

Capri laughed. "Astrologers would claim there was some connection between our decision tonight and Venus being the morning star."

Zweistein said, "Her name, *Morgen,* morning. *Stern,* star—" His voice trailed off.

"Superstitious rot!" Sir Jules declared.

"Yet my horoscope foretold—" the general began, thought better of it, and changed the subject. "Where on earth are we going to find a man in his right mind willing to pilot a rocket to Venus?"

"Right here!"

Five heads turned and stared at Brian. The general nodded. Berkley smiled, almost friendly. "The world's first space pilot would require the highest scientific degrees. What are yours?"

Brian came forward, and for the first time in his life, drunk with the wine of her lips still on his own, made a speech. "My qualifications are what you need for the job. Five years of big-ship flying. Test pilot on pressurized jobs and high-altitude equipment. Know radio and radar. Taught instruments and celestial navigation at Quantico. Single and no dependents. And I love—the tropics."

Capri began to gesture with excitement. "Military aviation is the best possible preparation for space flight. The rest we can teach you as we install the instruments together."

Berkley said, with a friendly grin, "I guess the only way to get free of your vigilant guardianship, Mr. Dale, is to shoot you off the earth into space. I've tried every other way, and failed."

Sir Jules said, "Yes, this young man is the type of steady chap we need for the flight. No nerves. I've watched him as closely as he's watched us, for the last few years, and I must say that anyone who would take care of four old fools like us the way he has, and not lose his mind, or us, deserves a go at something good. I'm for him, as you Yanks say."

"Thank you, gentlemen," said Brian, and stepped forward to sit down among them; but old Professor Zweistein cocked a shrewd eye and beckoned him aside, out of earshot. From the glowing vision in those deep, far-seeing eyes, Brian knew that Zweistein was the only one among the technically minded scientists to grasp what had really happened tonight.

Brian held up a warning hand. "Let's not either of us say anything," he pleaded.

The moist eyes twinkled. "I was not going to. Some things are better left unsaid. All my life I have prayed this night would come in time—and now it has."

Brian opened his wallet and by the first pale light of morning showed him the wisp of her hair. "What would you say this is?"

Professor Zweistein examined the green fluff for a long time with the strong pocket magnifier he used for reading fine print. Finally he said, *"Lieber Gott!* I must show this to a plant biologist. It seems to be human hair, but instead of the usual animal pigments, it contains chlorophyll, the green of leaves. Look, here is a faint streak of xanthophyll!"

"What the hell is xanthophyll?" asked Brian.

"The orange-yellow dye that frost brings out in leaves."

"You mean that hair like this, as it grew old, instead of turning gray, would change to brighter colors?"

The scientist nodded gravely. "Like a maple tree in autumn. Except that this sample cannot be hair—see, it has tiny branches, finer than silk. It must be some rare desert air plant. May I have it to take back to my laboratory for analysis?"

Brian shook his head and put the wisp of tender green carefully away. "No, I need this. But I'll get you some more—if you'll teach me how to fly that crazy crate down in the hole."

The old professor gave him a knowing smile. "I'm going to give you every minute of my time—until September first."

"At four a.m.," said Brian softly. They raised their eyes together, the young man who dreamed dreams and the old man who saw visions, and beheld the tender glory of the morning star.

By now, you know the rest, if you've kept your radio on. How, at dawn today, Brian Dale came gliding back from another shore of our sea of space in a scorched and battered rocket packed with proofs and specimens of a world that is to ours as ours would seem to cavemen.

Newscasters are choking as they try to describe the value to earth's ills of the wondrous gifts this Marco Polo of the spaceways has brought to us as tokens of peace and friendship.

Hold it! Here is Brian Dale himself. Tom Lowell, mike in hand, has cornered Brian as he leaves the White House. I can predict his first question. "What's it like on Venus,

Mr. Dale?"

Hear the chuckle in Brian's voice as he answers cautiously, "Are we on the air? Well, in that case I'd better not go into detail, except to say it's rather warm, and that the nights are very long on Venus. Er, I mean by that the planet rotates so much more slowly than our earth that every night seems like a week. Uh, that is, Venusian nights are literally a week long—I guess. Well, anyhow, it shouldn't be long now until we have what you might call a half interest in the place. It was hard to get away, and I'm in a hurry to get back with our first hundred colonists."

Hear him pause, assume a serious tone, say straight-faced, "However, because of the exhausting nature of space travel, and the really indescribable hardships imposed by surface conditions on Venus, I have urged the President, and he has agreed, to limit our colonists exclusively to men —picked men." Beneath his solemn official manner he is closer to laughter now than he was a moment ago, when he was openly chuckling.

In fact, if Brian Dale threw back his head and let out the ribald laughter that is in him at this instant, I suspect your radio and mine would emit the oldest and the newest sound on earth, the battle cry of history, the lusty laughter of a male creator's own fertile image, insatiable migrator from land to land and star to star; Man, pledged by the sacrament of his birth from Woman to sow his seed beyond all seas and skies; Homo sapiens, of the roving eye, father of the rainbow races, tireless weaver of all loves into one bright tapestry of life triumphant, conqueror of time and death and space by the divine right of his eternal and sublime desire.

THOSE MEN FROM MARS

THERE ARE THREE YOUNG MEN in Washington who see as much of our President as do his Secret Service bodyguards. We sometimes glimpse their faces in the newsreel backgrounds, out of focus. They are background men. One or more of them is always near the Chief Executive, yet few of us outside official circles could guess all three names correctly on a quiz program, no matter how fabulous the prize.

These three hard-working, unobtrusive gentlemen are the special White House correspondents of the major news services. One or more of them is always at or very near the White House, standing by to cover possible emergencies. They watch and wait, upon the theory that when and if the Story of the Century should break, there won't be time to notify the hundred-odd Washington correspondents eligible to attend a general press conference at the Executive Mansion.

My frank young friend, Ted Bonifield, was one of these three special White House correspondents until last night. It doesn't matter which he was. All three are ace newspapermen, and in a pinch they pool the news, the way our free press did throughout the war.

A national emergency more grave than any war has come, and gone, as everybody knows today. The theory of the wire-service watchers at the White House proved correct. Ted Bonifield was on duty when the Story of the Millennium broke, like an egg, on the White House lawn at sunrise, Easter Sunday. Not the most convenient moment, you'll agree, for rounding up the working press in nothing flat.

And so, if it hadn't been for Ted and his two competitors, our still-trembling world might not have read an impartial eyewitness account of what actually occurred during those first few crucial minutes on this fantastic Easter from which all Earthly history will now, of course, be dated. In a way it was funny, but it was also rather terrible. One square mile in the center of Washington was, as you recall, evacuated.

I had the rare good luck to be with Ted the morning that it happened. I wish my luck at pinochle the night before had been equally good; but it was not. I lost more dimes than a biochemist can afford. The Senator was too worried over world affairs to sleep. He kept us at his suite till four a.m. That is why Ted Bonifield and I happened to be walking southeast on Pennsylvania Avenue just before daylight on Easter Sunday and thereby came to be among the first few men on Earth to see the strange egg-shaped contraption dropping out of Heaven straight upon the White House—

Pardon me. In my haste, I've skipped a very important part. It's this: Before the pinochle, Ted had a dinner date with Bette. He met her at her office. He hadn't far to go. Bette works in the White House as private secretary to my boss, who is not a politician, but a physicist.

We edged in past armed guards, who always eye my beard suspiciously. It was past six, Easter Eve, with enchantment in the air. Everybody else had gone home, but poor little Bette was still transcribing some long-winded man's dictation. Ted and I were furious. We also knew better than to breathe before she'd finished.

I tiptoed to my desk. Again it was piled high with telegrams from good Americans who did not want a war. No one where I work wants war, either; but anyway, we'd sweated out the worst week ever. At noon on Good Friday, the Air Force was alerted, globally. Saturday night, Alaskan cities were blacked out. Downstairs, the President was still at his desk, with coffee and apples for his dinner, watching the Intelligence ticker tap out history's closing quotations on the falling stocks of peace. Calmly he issued the precautionary orders that kept our country on its toes. His wife and kids were at the farm for the week-end. He had no house guests, and was quite alone. It must have been the loneliest job in the world that night, looking at those push buttons on his desk, knowing if he pushed a certain one what would happen to some hundred million simple folk who personally meant us no harm, but were misled. For this time, we were ready. On mountain peak and desert island, the launching-pits were loaded with the deadly fruit of science.

Knowing what we knew, Ted and I were glummish; but Bette, who pretends she knows nothing and is smarter than us both, soon cheered us up. She whipped the last page from her electric typewriter and swung around in her posture chair with a sparkling smile, and flashing glasses.

Bette wears these newfangled glamour-glasses that dazzle the male animal, as the spinner hooks the largemouthed black bass. Maybe Bette invented the fancy frames so popular nowadays. I wouldn't put it past her. Fine art is her hobby, and subtle are her ways. She has converted the liability of being nearsighted into a sensational asset. Her super-spectacles have streamlined golden frames inlaid with ivory arabesques, and are studded with tiny rhinestones. Her odd-shaped lenses are tilted slyly, like a wood nymph's sidelong glance. My superior officer must be the original absent-minded professor to concentrate on his formulae with a jeweled hummingbird flitting around his office.

Ted tipped back her swivel chair and captured her. This is my cue for a tactful turning of the back. What happened then is restricted information. While no authoritative statement was available at press time, it is believed probable (by usually well-informed sources) that an accredited White House correspondent was carefully and completely kissed.

Replacing her super-specs, Bette resumed her pint-sized dignity as the official private secretary, who vouchsafes nothing to no man. She handed me the page she'd typed.

"Initial this, please, Doctor," she suggested shyly, and I hastened to obey.

I read her perfect typing with respect. It turned out to be her transcript of a ssh-ssh report I'd made that morning on climatological bacteriology. I saw to my surprise that Bette had recorded every dismal scientific term correctly. The little girl could not have known what some of those nine-legged words meant. I'm none too sure myself, and I invented them. I looked at her pretty little face and shook my shaggy head in wonderment.

"How do you do it, Miss Pringle?" I marveled.

"Oh, I just keep my mind a blank," she laughed. "I let dictation whiz through me as if I were a radio."

"A small portable," said Ted, picking her up.

"Don't put me down," she said. "Honestly, Doctor Waggonner, I don't know what I'm writing half the time." She tweaked Ted's nose, being in a rather handy position. "Do you, big shot with the cute nose?"

"Not over half the time," Ted confessed, standing her up on a desk like a doll. "If things don't start making sense pretty soon, I'm going to buy us a country weekly, and write English."

"I wish you would!" she said, looking domestic. She hopped down like a bird and put away her water colors. "I'll leave my paints and stuff here," she said. "I'm coming in tomorrow."

Bette paints her water colors early in the morning, and on Sundays. They are said to be collector's items. Lately she hasn't had much time for hobbies. She'd been coming to the office on Sundays to type top-secret papers for the President's Monday meetings with the Supreme Scientific Council. She has a special pass to come and go.

They ran off happily together. I fondly sighed, and ambled over to the Senator's for dinner. To the man from

Mars (as the saying goes), we would have been a grotesque sight: two sad old fat men, both with beards, choking down choice terrapin and sherry while the lights went out around the world.

Ted dropped in at midnight to hear the European news broadcasts on the Senator's short-wave set. That was the recent Saturday, as we all remember, when our crooners and comedians were rudely interrupted in mid-gag three times by calm-voiced appeals from the governors of each state, saying, "Keep your heads, folks. Don't repeat rumors. Obey your air-raid warden, and above all, fellow citizens, *stay off the highways.*"

Yes, we were on the ragged edge for a few days there, up till Easter Sunday. Now, of course, the world situation is entirely different, thank Heaven. And I literally mean Heaven. After all, where are the planets?

Now we have played pinochle all night, my dimes are gone, and Ted and I are back where we were a minute ago, strolling down Pennsylvania Avenue toward the White House at the crack of dawn on Easter Sunday.

Ted saw it first. He had thrown his head back, and was drawing a deep breath of fresh dawn air to flush that senatorial cigar smoke from his healthy lungs. His eyes swung casually across the grayish sky, snapped back to a speck, and narrowed keenly. After a while he relaxed and yawned and said, "It's only a weather balloon. For a minute I thought I was seeing things."

We strolled along. An early sparrow chirped in the dim stillness. I looked where Ted pointed, very high and straight ahead of us. The sky was clear and cloudless. The sun began to rise. I yawned, too, and said, "The darn thing seems to be falling."

Unconsciously we'd both begun to walk a little faster. Ted said, in a wide-awake voice, "Balloons don't fall straight down unless they're busted. This one isn't. See, it's oval."

We were taking long, fast steps now. I said, "It must be a barrage balloon, being pulled down on a cable."

Ted took longer steps, and faster. "Couldn't be. A cable that long would weigh more than a balloon that size could lift so high."

We jogged into a trot, not taking our eyes off the sky. "Then what the hell is it?" I wheezed.

Ted said, his words joggling out as he passed me, "Whatever it is, it's falling on the White House, and that's my beat." He broke into a run.

Ted had been talking to the guard in the booth at the White House gate for a minute before I lumbered up. They were both on telephones, talking fast. As we hurried in, Allen darted out buckling on an extra gun belt.

Allen is the chief of the White House detail of the Secret Service. His duty is to guard with his life the life of the President of the United States. Allen is a craggy, crusty man, because he has to be. He grazed us with a fast hard look and raised binoculars. Ted came up beside him and asked quietly, "What is it?"

"Don't know. Don't like it. Radar should have picked it up long ago. We'll soon see what it is." He stepped back into his office. Through the lighted window we could see him at three telephones, wasting no words.

By the watch upon my shaking wrist, I timed what happened next.

One minute. Swarms of extra guards came boiling out of somewhere and surrounded the White House. They wore steel helmets, carried Tommy guns and gas masks.

Two minutes. Police radio cars were stopping all civilian traffic into the White House area.

Three minutes, and a squadron of our fastest fighter planes were roaring up into the sunrise sky. In the cold upper air their hot jets left fiery trails like comets.

As you have read in Ted's dispatches, no one tried to run away. Scientist and non-scientist alike intuitively knew, if this was war, there would be nowhere for men or mice to hide from it in all our lost and lovely world. Not in heroism but in numb despair we stood with backs against the wall and watched the show and let the cold sweat trickle. At least we'd know what hit us. Millions wouldn't. For in a minute now, if the President pushed a little button, our trans-hemispheric guided missiles would be on their way around the world, each carrying an atomic bomb.

Our jet fighters reached the thing in thirty seconds. At their approach it stopped in mid-air and hung motionless. Now we knew it was no stray balloon. The thing was consciously controlled. It could perceive.

The squadron leader looped in alone and looked it over. Banked in tight spiral turns, he examined the object closely from all sides.

In the Smithsonian Institution today you can hear those priceless wire-tape recordings of the historic words that baffled major was reporting by radio to his colonel on the ground. (Many taxpayers have commented favorably upon the fact that this time we had an automatic record of who said what to whom, and when.) With Air Force informality, unaware that he spoke for posterity, the laconic phrases filtered down with a Texas drawl. Let's listen in.

"Mac, this baby sure don't look like anything of ours— It's red, a metal shell about thirty feet in diameter, tapered at one end, like an egg— It's got a funny mark painted on the side like identification. A circle with an arrow pointing off at two o'clock. Does that mean anything? It does not answer signals— Can't see how this damn thing stays in the air. It's got no jets, no prop, no control surfaces, no nothing. Something's screwy up here. We'd better get rid of it, Colonel. It is not ours. Repeat: *It is not ours.*"

His commanding officer must have remembered Pearl Harbor, another peaceful Sunday morning when Americans trustfully slept. He decided that this time things were going to be different. The order to attack was given six minutes after the object was first sighted.

One by one our sleek fighting planes peeled off and dived at the intruder. The rivet-hammer racket of machine guns split the hushed Easter sky above the Capital, bringing frightened faces to hotel windows. A soldier handed me a helmet and a gas mask. I stood holding them foolishly in my arms.

Allen said, "I'm putting the President in the bomb shelter. I'll be back in a minute." He sprinted into the White House and bounded up the stairs.

Our fighter planes threw everything they had at the invader—but nothing happened. Somehow, impossibly, our best combat pilots missed a stationary target bigger than several barn doors. Nothing was wrong with their ammunition. They were loaded for bear. Live shells were cutting into roof tops all over Washington, and starting fires.

Something was spoiling our pilots' aim. Something uncanny. They couldn't all have missed. By rights the red thing should be falling now, shot down in flames. But it was not. It just floated there serenely in the blushing sky, not offering resistance, not doing anything.

I think we all understand by now how that last pilot felt. He was end man on the squadron line, and he had seen it all, the valiant dives, the futile misses, the target still unhit. There is probably a boy or two on your street—in your house, perhaps—who would have made the same decision.

Put yourself in his cockpit and feel how natural it must have seemed. You are up there alone in the sky facing a mysterious enemy poised like a bomb above your country's heart. Your orders are to shoot it down. You obey orders. You have watched your buddies do their best, but the enemy is still untouched. You're mad because it somehow made your buddies miss. You're mad because the enemy deliberately chose Easter Sunday, when there are lilies on the altars. You're also mad about a lot of other things that have been happening, and this red Easter egg from out of the stratosphere is the last straw.

Now it's your turn to peel off. You kick your hot new ship wing-down into her last grand screaming dive, knowing that you, at least, are not going to miss, because there is always one last way to keep from missing, once. Above the cold upcrawl of grav's in the stomach you feel a little glad it's going to be this way instead of later, in some accidental, less important way. At the final instant, perhaps you close your eyes and say good-by to someone—

The President appeared in the wide-open window of his bedroom. He leaned out and looked up. He was in rumpled blue pajamas and his hair was tousled. Allen appeared behind him, trying to pull him back out of danger. An aerial cannon shell exploded in the White House driveway. The Chief waved Allen back and watched the battle in the sky intently, with no trace of fear.

We all saw it happen, though many tried to look away. The last pilot dived to crash his target. He came in straight and steady, firing everything he had without effect, but when he was almost there, his plane was flung off to the right by an unseen force. His left wing broke off against thin air.

A second later, the ejector under the pilot's seat threw him clear of his spinning plane. Another second, and his parachute ripped open, fluttered out, caught the rushing air, clung, and blossomed, round and white as a carnation.

The wingless plane crashed into the Potomac River with a splash explosion that threw a column of smoky water as high as the Washington Monument. The rest of the squadron, traveling at four miles a minute, were by now far out over Arlington, regrouping. Two more squadrons were ordered aloft from different fields, north and south of Washington.

The parachuting pilot sailed slowly over the White House, directly underneath the big red thing. We saw him turning in his harness to get a closer look at it.

The President called down to an aide who had arrived in haste. "Have them bring that pilot here to me, if he's not hurt." Then Allen firmly drew the President inside, out of danger. Fire engine bells were clanging closer.

Left alone in the smoke-streaked sky, the big red egg started to come down again, more slowly. It dropped toward us in a vertical controlled descent, hesitating now and then as if anxious not to alarm us any more than we were already. Which was plenty. If I had not been scared stiff I would have noticed, as Ted did, that the weird craft was coming in cautiously for a landing in much the same manner as you or I might hopefully approach an unknown shore.

But it was too late now for such fanciful notions. Our hair-trigger machinery of defense had swung into action, according to law. Someone threw the master switch on the air-raid siren system. For miles around a dreadful wailing rose, like brainless banshees keening at the scent of death.

A motorized antiaircraft battery arrived at fifty miles an hour, skidded to a halt, swung into position, and began to pump ten-pound projectiles into the sky at the rate of one per second.

The red egg halted its descent and hung unharmed in the stream of high-explosive shells. Now it was less than five hundred feet above our heads. My boy could have hit it with a BB gun. But artillery could not.

Ted was telephoning the news for all papers in short, quick "takes." It had happened too quickly for censorship to clamp its clammy hand upon the mouth of factual reporting. How well we all remember those first terse news bulletins. Families stopped on their way to church and started digging foxholes. Later, of course, when the nature of this unprecedented phenomenon became known in Moscow, certain precautions had to be observed.

"What's that identification mark painted on the thing?" Ted asked at a pause in the firing.

"Hammer and sickle," said the battery commander.

"It looks to me more like a circle with a short arrow on the upper right-hand quarter," Ted said. "What country uses that wing marking?"

"We don't," said the battery commander. "Fire!"

I could see the symbol plainly now. It was ♂. It seemed to me that I had seen it somewhere years ago in a book about astrology, but I could not remember what it meant. When they asked me, I shook my head. It was no time for guessing games. Hell was popping.

A second antiaircraft battery opened fire from the roof of the Treasury Building. How they got up there so quickly, I don't know. Maybe they had been up there all along, under camouflage. In crises, personal or national, surprises have a way of coming out of the woodwork.

The second battery was firing shells equipped with proximity fuses. These sensitized projectiles burst all around their target, as close as ten feet, but could not seem to touch it. The fragmentation was terrific. Shell splinters showered down like smoking hail. I put my helmet on. Somewhere I heard windows breaking. Ted ran past me with a camera. His face was cut.

The same idea occurred to both baffled battery commanders at the same minute, as often happens with well-trained officers. Both ordered tracer shells. And then, for the first time, we understood why the big red thing could not be hit.

The invader was surrounded by an invisible envelope of some totally new kind of force. It shed shellfire like raindrops. The tracers flew at their target leaving white ribbons of phosphorous smoke to mark their trajectories, but at the last split second, about ten feet from their goal, they snapped into a smart outcurve, like something thrown by a pitcher.

Through a broken window behind me I heard Ted's steady voice at a telephone, reporting.

"The tracer shells are curving around the unidentified object and caroming off into the sky. Nothing has yet penetrated the mysterious ring of—" I heard him pause for a word—"let's call it *air armor,* which surrounds the mystery aircraft."

Seeing how there's so much in the papers today about the secret of air armor, both here and in Soviet Russia, it's interesting to know when and how the fateful phrase was born, in the heat of battle.

A star-flagged staff car screamed into the driveway. The General emerged surrounded by his aides. He was red in the face, as well he might be. Allen met him, bluntly asked, "How did that get past your radar?"

"It doesn't show on radar," the General growled. "We're beaming it from every side, but get no image on the screen!"

"Why can't you hit it?" Allen asked.

"Because it isn't there!" roared the General. The anti-aircraft batteries stopped abruptly to reload. In the sudden pause, the General's next roar carried farther than he knew.

"Anything that doesn't show on radar and can't be hit at point-blank range by massed artillery, just *isn't there*, I tell you!"

"Then what is it that we see, General?" the President inquired, and his voice was honestly puzzled.

We whirled. He was coming out of his house in his bedroom slippers pulling on a pair of coveralls over his pajamas. Allen rushed at him anxiously, but the Chief shook his head. "I don't like that bomb shelter," he said. "Never been in it before. Churchill must have left this air-raid suit." He zipped it up. "May I borrow your binoculars, please, Allen?"

Allen reluctantly handed him the powerful field glasses, and put his own helmet on the tousled head.

The Chief calmly studied the red egg in the sky. The ack-ack whanged. The jet fighters whooshed by at house-top level in another gallant, ineffectual attack. Ten truck-loads of Marines rolled up in battle dress, piled out, fixed bayonets, and deployed into a cordon, taking over from the Washington police, who by this time were urgently needed elsewhere.

An Intelligence officer rushed up and tried to whisper something into the President's ear, but it was impossible to hear above the mounting shriek of air-raid sirens. The President cupped his hands and shouted to the General, "Please shut those off!"

The sirens stopped almost at once, no thanks to the General. Their three-minute warning had been given and they shut off automatically. The General looked relieved.

"Well, what is it?" the President repeated, now that we could hear ourselves think.

"It's mass hysteria," the General snapped, not looking at the evidence. "It's an optical illusion. Some kind of freak reflection in the sky."

The egg dodged sideways to avoid taking the wing off another suicide pilot. The President followed it with the field glasses. "What do you think, Bonifield? Allen says you saw this first, and gave the alarm. Incidentally, thanks."

"I have no idea what it is, Mr. President," Ted replied. "But from watching it, I'd say the pilot knows where he is, wants to land here, and will then identify himself."

"That's the way it looks to me," said the Chief, his eyes at the binoculars.

The big egg dropped another hundred feet.

"Flame throwers!" the General ordered. His chain of command began to relay the order down through the stars, eagles, leaves, and bars to the stripes who have to go in and do it.

With a worried frown, the President lowered the binoculars. The morning sunlight accidentally flashed upon the polished lenses.

An answering flash of light came from the object overhead. Then another, and another flash, blinking out some incomprehensible code.

"He wants to talk to us," said the President. He scratched his stubbly morning chin. "General, I think we'd better stop all this shooting. It isn't doing any good, and I'm afraid we're hurting lots of our own people." At a crash in the distance the President raised the binoculars again. "Yes, there went the Indian off the Capitol dome," he said. "I order cease fire. Let's use our heads instead. Bring Doctor Zweistein here. He's over at the Mayflower. We were going to have breakfast together this morning."

The General barked at his aides. They scattered. The President stepped out on the lawn in plain view.

The big red egg dropped lower and swung toward him.

Allen ran out and tried to bring him back. The President said patiently to all of us, "Steady, everybody. We've been firing on this thing for twenty minutes. It has not returned our fire. What else must it do to prove it's friendly? Sing songs?"

Instantly the egg began to sing. From inside its shell came soft, sweet sounds, rising and falling in unearthly harmonies that sent shivers down my spine.

"Well, I'll be God damned," said the President of the United States reverently, and if you had heard his tone of voice, you would agree with all of us that it was not profanity.

The singing egg came down another hundred feet. Now it was near the treetops. A branch brushed it. A huge spark leaped out and crackled.

"Take cover!" the General bellowed. "This thing is set to go off when it touches the ground!"

"I doubt that," said the Chief. "Someone is inside it."

"No, it's being operated by remote control," the General insisted. "That humming you hear is from radio tubes."

"Will somebody please hand me a mirror?" the President asked.

So simple a request threw his staff into confusion—until Ted Bonifield quickly unclamped the outside rear-vision mirror from the General's staff car, three steps away.

"Thanks," said the Chief. He flashed the mirror and received intelligent signal flashes in return. What he sent it repeated. He showed the queer craft where to land. It settled swiftly toward the White House lawn, casting a huge black shadow ahead of it like a solar eclipse. As it passed over me, I shuddered.

The General said darkly, "I predicted war would start with the President's assassination. This is suicide!"

The President waved cheerfully to the thing. The thing bobbed politely in reply. The eerie humming had grown louder.

At last the cease fire order began slowly and imperfectly

to take effect. It is so much easier to start a war than stop one. Mean-looking assault bombers were winging up against the rising sun for a final all-out attack with heavy rockets that would have mowed down half of Washington, when their radioed cease fire orders reached them. They turned back to base, wheeling in formation like a flock of birds. It was beautiful to see them come, when they were needed, but it was even more beautiful to see them fly away.

Gradually the air grew still and clear again. The day began to feel a little bit like Easter, in an ether dream.

The big egg, following the President's directions, came in near a corner of the White House on an open stretch of lawn between two flower beds.

With growing faintness I observed that even in the bright morning sunshine, the answering ray from overhead burned brilliantly blue white. It flashed across the lawn beside my feet. I looked down and saw a swath of green spring grass turn autumn brown, go crisp, begin to smolder, smoke— Then the shaft of light curved back, looked at the killed grass, and softened itself to a rosy glow, as if sorry for what it had done.

I rubbed my eyes. Curved light? Professor Zweistein must be inside this Easter egg!

The President called to us. "Did anybody see what I saw?"

"Yes, sir," said the General promptly. "We could use that curved light in night fighting."

"I mean someone not subject to mass hysteria and optical illusions. Preferably a scientist. Hasn't Zweistein come yet? Then where's the old boy with the beard, the bio-something?"

"Here, sir. Yes, I saw it, too. It really curved."

"How does he do it?" the General demanded.

"Well, Doctor Zweistein says all light rays curve eventually, in space time, so this may be a compression of that inherent curve—" Ted nudged me. I shut up. Things were happening.

The big red egg was hovering ten feet off the ground at a point about one hundred feet away from us. It was having difficulty in getting down to Earth. An unseen cushion or buffer kept bouncing it back up into the air. The melodious humming grew shrill. Behind me I heard Ted's level voice phoning.

"The unidentified object is now landing on the White House lawn, under the President's bedroom windows. The air armor which protected it from shellfire seems to keep it off the ground. The humming sound it makes is not a voice, at least not any human voice. It sounds more like the drone of precision machinery operating at extremely high speeds. . . . The President steps toward the thing. . . . I just caught a whiff of ozone in the air. That means some powerful electromagnetic forces are operating near us. . . . The humming stops. There is a click. The thing falls suddenly to the ground. Did you hear that thud? I felt it shake the White House. . . . The thing must be incredibly heavy, to create such a tremendous impact from a ten-foot drop. . . . Now it's lying on its side. No noise, no movement. Maybe it's dead. It's so heavy that it's sinking into the solid ground making a deep, cup-shaped depression."

As I write these words today, I can look out of my window and see that historic hole. It is fenced off now and guarded from souvenir hunters. You can see it for nothing if you want to stand in line all day. People who are still skeptical as to whether all this really happened last Sunday are coming into Washington from points as distant as Missouri to look with their own eyes upon the only depression this administration has produced.

A second car sped up the drive behind us. "I hope that's Zweistein," said the President. "This thing must be made of something heavier than uranium."

It was not Zweistein, but the fighter pilot. A flustered secretary had called the FBI. They picked him out of the air as he neared ground in DuPont Circle, and brought him in without red tape.

Still in his flying suit, with gadgets dangling, he swaggered up the walk, a cocky little redheaded lieutenant, not a bit displeased at being rushed to the White House to report to the Commander in Chief. Somehow he missed seeing the General. Otherwise I'm sure he would have saluted. He shook hands with the Chief, who gave him a cigarette, lit it for him, then lit one himself. They both took deep drags and stood looking at the big egg on the lawn.

It didn't look quite so red any more. The ruddy color had been cast on it by the rising sun, or by our fears. Lying on the green grass, it was delicately pink, the color of an Easter egg.

This simile did not occur to the fighter pilot. He was thinking of something else. He said ruefully, "There's one meat ball I couldn't hit."

"You nicked him with your wing tip, didn't you?"

"Not by ten feet, Mr. President."

"Then what took your wing off, Lieutenant?"

The pilot lowered his voice. "If the General hears this, he'll say I'm bucking for a psychoneurotic discharge." They moved off a few steps. "The truth is that this king-size meat ball is surrounded by some kind of funny business, like a magnet in reverse. It bounced me off to one side. But nobody will ever believe that, and the thing's dead now, I guess."

"I believe you," said the President. "Stick around. I like the way your mind works. You're not afraid to admit that something new can happen. I have a hard time finding men like you—"

He stopped. We all stiffened. The thing had begun to tick, not like a clock but in a curious syncopated rhythm, as if all kinds of complicated processes were going on inside at different rates of speed.

"Look out, it's going to explode!" the General shouted. He tried to throw himself between the object and the President.

The Chief steadied him and turned him around. "Take it easy, General," he suggested. "Watch what's happening!"

The big egg revived, rolled over, and put down three square metal legs. They sank deep into the soil, like roots. They must have had appalling power behind them. They steadied the egg in an upright position, giving it a semi-human appearance, like Humpty Dumpty.

Where an eye should be, a pale blue porthole opened. The ticking stopped. The tension relaxed. Then something worse began. I had a creepy feeling that my mind was being read by an alien intelligence, amicable enough, but inconceivably remote from our ways of reasoning. Strange ideas flowed into my mind—pictures—

The blue porthole closed. The feeling went away. I shrugged uneasily and called it nerves.

"Maybe we can destroy it on the ground!" the General was baying.

Bang! went something. It was a minute before I could find strength to turn around.

A third official car, stopped abruptly at the gate, had backfired. There seemed to be some forgivable distraction among the White House personnel that morning.

From the back seat of the sedan emerged the famous head of fluffy white hair. Two admirals in gold braid hustled Professor Zweistein to the President.

"This thing—" the Chief began.

Zweistein nodded eagerly. "*Ja,* I haff heard already on the radio. A Russian rocket." He walked out on the grass alone and looked it over shrewdly. As he passed me I heard him chuckling. "They should live to make such a rocket," he said to himself.

The curved light ray arched out and illuminated Zweistein's hair. The scientist smiled at some abstruse private joke.

All smiles faded when an Intelligence officer raced out, white faced, and handed the President a strip of Teletype paper. When the Chief read it his face went white, too. He handed it to the General, whose red face turned almost black with wrath. In sickening silence, the news was numbly passed around. What did secrecy matter now? Over Ted's shoulder I read with sinking heart:

ALL COMMUNICATIONS CUT OFF IN AND OUT OF MOSCOW. UNABLE REACH OR RECEIVE AMERICAN EMBASSY. LAST REPORT SAID HEAVY FIRING AUDIBLE, MANY PLANES IN AIR. RED ARMY MOBILIZING. BORDERS CLOSED. GUESS THIS IS IT.

"I knew this was it," the General rumbled. "This thing is obviously a Russian guided missile. Probably filled with germs." He coughed. "Maybe there's still time to decontaminate it. Where's that biochemist? Everybody else start running. I urge an immediate declaration of war, Mr. President!"

Nobody moved. The President was reading the report a second time, weighing every word. Then, regretfully, he nodded to the General. "Very well. Take over. Looks like you were right from the beginning, General. Yes, Allen, I'm coming. But before I can ask Congress to declare war, we ought to have legal proof of where this missile came from."

"Where else could it come from?" the General glowered. "Anything that isn't ours, is theirs."

Professor Zweistein said mildly, "Excuse me, please, but do you not see the identifying symbol plainly painted on the shell?"

"We've all been looking at it," said the Chief, "but nobody knows what it means."

Suddenly it came back to me, that meaning. The book had not been about astrology, but astronomy. I drew a breath to shout the answer, and missed by one second my chance to shine. For Zweistein was replying calmly, "That is the astronomic symbol for the planet Mars."

The General said a short, bad word. The President made a wry face and said, "If this is a publicity stunt, somebody is going to a Federal prison! The planet Mars, in a pig's eye!"

The angry disbelief which greeted Dr. Zweistein's simple

statement of fact was further aggravated by the sudden arrival of the Secretary of State. He is a hardheaded man, and he will not let his country be pushed around. His face looked like a granite mountain in a thunderstorm. He announced, "Mr. President, our Ambassador at Moscow is incommunicado. That is tantamount to war. I have taken identical measures against the Soviet Ambassador here. He threatens to break relations. What are your wishes?"

"I wish everybody would keep his shirt on," said the President. "Look, our Easter egg is hatching."

I gaped. The pink shell was opening a little, near the top, disclosing a listening device shaped like a giant ear. Turning with the awful mechanical interest of an aircraft sound detector, it centered on the vibrations of our speech.

"Hello," said the President, experimentally. "Can you understand me?"

The tin ear nodded. Yes. It understood.

"Can you talk?"

The big ear swung from side to side, rather sadly, it seemed to me. No. It couldn't talk.

"This is all oriental trickery," the General growled. "While we fool around with this dummy, they're probably attacking somewhere else."

We all began to look askance at the mysterious thing. There was something sinister about the knowing way it had dropped down and squatted on the White House lawn. I felt glad there was a hundred feet of open space between it and me. The off-beat ticking started up again, tick-tockety, tockety-tick. We all backed away fearfully.

An undersecretary of State had been struggling through the crowd to the Secretary. Now, at last, he overtook him with a new message. It was from the American Ambassador at Moscow. The President and the Secretary of State scanned it together and exchanged startled looks.

"Read it out loud," said the Chief. "This is no time for pussyfooting. Every minute counts."

In a strained voice the Secretary of State read, " 'The Soviet Government demands immediate withdrawal of an alleged American guided missile, believed to contain an atomic bomb, which fell inside the Kremlin under the Premier's window early this morning despite violent defense measures. Moscow is under martial law. The Kremlin is evacuated. All U. S. citizens not diplomatically immune have been taken hostage and chained near the alleged bomb in the event it explodes. Only an immediate denial with proof can avert war. The Russians say the bomb is painted with a fascist symbol.' "

"Round up the Russians!" the General promptly ordered.

"Now hold on," said the President, coming back. "I've changed my mind, General. Don't round up anybody. You're not taking over. I'm staying right here, where I belong." He was beginning to look like he used to during his campaign, smiling dryly through clenched teeth, balanced like a boxer in the ring, trading punches in plain words with all comers. He instructed his Secretary of State, "Unfreeze the Soviet Ambassador. Fetch him here on the double, and show this thing to him. Cable the Premier that the thing under his window isn't ours. Tell him I've got one under my window, too. Marked the same as his, unless I miss my guess. Rush radiophotos of this one to Moscow to prove it. Offer to exchange information freely. General, let's hold up that declaration of war. Something tells me we may have an entirely new situation on our hands."

He went to Zweistein, who was swiftly making sketches and calculations on a pad. "Now, Professor, how do we talk to it?"

"I don't know," said Zweistein, "but I think he does. He's come prepared. He didn't land here by accident."

In our excitement, we had turned our backs upon the thing from nowhere. Now we looked again, and there was Bette Pringle. She whisked around a corner of the White House and was in front of the big red thing before she saw it. The searching ray spotlighted her face and made her glasses sparkle. She stood frozen with terror. A curved panel lifted like an eyelid. A bulging lens popped out at her, widening at what it saw, rolling from side to side. It had a gleam in it, that big glass eye. On top of the egg, a valve stood up and blew off steam with a cheerful whistle.

Ted lunged forward. I pinned him from behind by both his arms, and held him back. For a few seconds our group stood rigid with astonishment. During those seconds, a number of things happened with the swiftness of delirium. Or perhaps our sense of time grew tangled. A science that could bend light beams like taffy could probably twist time around its finger, too.

How much Bette knew or did not know of what was going on that morning is something no man will ever find out. She claimed later that she was trying to reach her office to do what she had been drilled to do in an emergency, with the secret files. "I was scared by the commotion and took a short cut around a corner of the house," she testified. "When I saw this thing in front of me, I tried to run, but couldn't lift my feet."

I know just how she felt. My feet, too, had turned to ice.

Bette's glasses flickered in the light, for she was trembling from head to foot. The big egg winked back at her playfully. A delicate long feeler like a fishing pole glided out joint by joint, and curved around her waist.

She raised her hands to push the thing away.

A mouth opened underneath the big glass eye. The long arm drew her toward it. The thirty-foot pink Easter egg was turning, feature by feature, into a monstrous inhuman face.

Ted tore himself out of my grip and ran toward her.

As the thin arm pulled her gently but insistently to the grinning mouth, the frightened girl did something pitiful to see. Trying to hold herself back, she clutched desperately at the only handhold she could find, a flowering shrub that had just burst into bloom that morning. She tore away an armload of its fragrant blossoms, as she was pulled along.

By now, stunned spectators were recovering their wits. Several men shouted and began to run toward Bette, after

Ted. On the White House roof, one of Bette's favorite guards blew his top, aimed his tommy gun, and emptied it straight at the gleaming eye.

The bullets glanced off in a graceful curve through the window of the White House press secretary's office. Bette was inside the creature's crystal bubble of impenetrable force.

Ted was more than halfway to her now, running at top speed, calling her name.

Bette was drawn up against the open mouth. It parted to receive her. She braced her feet against the final step inside, shielding her face from the horror of the great red monster by lifting the armful of flowers she was still clutching as if they were her last hold on life. Her handbag, swinging on a shoulder strap, dropped open.

The pulling stopped. Between the mouth and eye, a shiny nose poked out, curved like a parrot's beak. The nose sniffed the fresh flowers. The glass eye lighted up with pleasure. The arm let Bette go, and took the flowers instead. It lifted the bouquet to air tubes underneath the beak, and inhaled deeply. The steam valve sighed. The eyelid drooped with the languor of delight. The frightful thing from space just sat there on the grass and happily smelled the Easter flowers, like Ferdinand the bull, not mad at anybody.

Free from the mechanical embrace, Bette began to back away. Ted was some ten feet from her, running hard, when he recoiled as if he had hit a rubber wall. He bounced off to one side and fell. Rolling up onto his feet again like a football player, he charged once more, and hammered at the armored air that kept him from the girl he loved.

Bette crept backward almost to where Ted stood, outside the dome of force, smashing his fists against thin air. When she had only one more step to go to safety, a second fishpole arm cast out to her, dropped something round into her bag, and disappeared.

Bette took one last step backward, through the unseen wall, and crumpled. Ted caught her as she fell, and carried her back to where we stood.

Her eyelids fluttered. "Put me down," she whispered. "I only fainted."

"Take her up to the guest room, Bonifield," said the Chief. "Call my doctor. I'll be up."

As Ted carried her inside, something fell out of her dangling open bag. It flashed fire, and rolled. Zweistein picked it up.

"Probably radioactive," the General gritted.

"Then so are you," said Zweistein, holding it with both hands, cradling it in wonder.

We examined the object with murmurs of amazement. The creature had given Bette a flawless blue-white diamond as big as a grapefruit. Inside the huge jewel, embedded by some miraculous art, was a cluster of nine other gems, some large, some very small, spaced about a golden core. Each man saw his birthstone there. Awed voices said, "An emerald. A pearl. A ruby. A star sapphire with rings of amethyst."

Zweistein held the treasure up for everyone to see. "As of course you all can see," he said with a courteous nod to the speechless General, "this is a model of our solar system. Each jewel symbolizes a planet, and the golden core, our sun. Its purpose is to prove—"

As Zweistein spoke, the big ear listened. The curved light ray lashed out and narrowed down to pinpoint focus on the model in his hand. It pointed out the fourth jewel from the sun, the ruby, closest neighbor to the slightly larger pearl of Terra. It lighted up the blood-red jewel of Mars.

"Thank you," said Zweistein calmly. "We understand."

The tin ear wagged.

"All rot," the General declared. "No life on Mars. Subject's closed."

"In science," said Zweistein mildly, "no subject is ever closed. Only minds."

With a shrieking motorcycle escort, the Secretary of State returned in his limousine with the Soviet Ambassador, Mr. Tvordyznak. Following came four station wagons full of reporters and photographers. Television cameras began to scan the scene with silent and unwinking eyes. They looked much like the man from Mars. Flash bulbs popped before my eyes and made me see scotomata, or spots. Radio men shoved me aside to make room for microphones. The cloven hoof of a motion-picture camera's heavy tripod came down cruelly on my toe. I tried to get away, but snakelike cables coiled around my feet. Caught in the mechanized onslaught of the media, I began to feel a little bit like Bette must have felt.

I fought my way over to where reporters were firing questions at the President and Zweistein. The Soviet Ambassador, when asked to say a reassuring word, said, "*Nyet.*"

The President went on the air at once over all networks with an impromptu breakfast table talk. He spiked the Russian rocket scare. He told the country what had happened, showed them our visitor on television, and signed off with quite a nifty ad-lib about himself and Orson Welles. That was all. He did not blame the Martian on the previous administration, or on the U.S.S.R. You didn't have to believe it at all, if you didn't want to. No thought police would call. This was still a free country, even if we were knocked cockeyed with amazement.

Mr. Tvordyznak was not impressed by any of it, nor by a new radiogram which brought electrifying news:

ALL U. S. CITIZENS RELEASED WITH FULL APOLOGIES. PREMIER AND THE POLITBURO HAVE RETURNED TO THE KREMLIN. SOVIET SCIENTISTS ARE BEING HASTILY SUMMONED. WAR DANGER APPEARS TO HAVE ABATED BUT SITUATION FAR FROM CLEAR. RADIO MOSCOW REPORTS REVOLUTION IN WASHINGTON. IS THIS TRUE? ARE YOU STILL THERE?

"Whoever asked that silly question, recall him on the first plane out," the Chief said to the Secretary of State. "He's been away from home too long."

The Soviet Ambassador, when asked to comment, stated (and I quote), "*Nichevo.*" But when a courier from his own Embassy raced up with a dispatch, he jumped, and hurried off without good-bys. He did not show his news to anyone.

The U. S. press enjoyed a field day with the Martian. It was the kind of Monday story that editors expect a man to send in every week. The character inside the egg shell appeared to comprehend the function of the primitive recording instruments around him. He co-operated with photographers in the same bewildered way as any new arrival in America, who hopes to make a favorable impression upon that fickle goddess, Public Opinion. He understood most of what they yelled at him, which is more than I did; but he could not answer questions except by pantomime. To please the press, the man from Mars patiently did push-ups on his three legs, waved his two willowy arms, rolled his big glass lens, hummed, ticked like a bebop drummer, and blew off steam upon request. Best of all he loved to smell the flowers.

The President detached himself from interviewers and ducked out to where Dr. Zweistein and the General were fidgeting. Sensing their impatience, he explained, "We'll get down to brass tacks in a minute. Right now it's vitally important to let the news get out, and stop the spread of rumors. People have a right to know."

Zweistein nodded. "*Ja,* is good. Just so they do not frighten him away before we learn from him. He has much to teach us."

"You're telling me," the General grated. We could guess by his expression that he was visualizing the other Martian inside the red Kremlin walls being studied by Soviet scientists in haste and secrecy. He pointed to the milling crowd and said ominously, "Not one of them has penetrated his defenses, except that little girl. I wonder how she did it? Where is she? We're going to need her very badly, I'm afraid."

Ted Bonifield returned alone and smiling. "She's okay,"

he reported. "She bounced back like a rubber ball. Wants to come out here again. Says she has something to tell you but the doctor wants her to rest a little longer."

"Do you mind if we go up and talk to her?" I asked. "We can't learn anything out here."

"Please do," said Ted. "She's asking for you."

In the front hall we met the White House press officer, a busy man that morning. "Give the boys five minutes more," the Chief told him. "Then clear the grounds, except for stand-bys. And see that Zweistein gets the breakfast I promised him."

In the First Lady's newly redecorated guest room, Bette was sitting up, drinking coffee, and listening with delight to the thrilling radio broadcast originating outside her window, fifty feet away. Ariel Hotspur, the fervid commentator, was describing Bette's experience in a pulsing purple voice. She was a heroine, it seemed, who had struggled in the grip of a Martian monster to obtain technical secrets for her country. "They'll have me believing it in a minute," she laughed, and turned it down.

Admiral Sarver, the President's physician, finished taking her pulse, nodded to us, and stood aside.

Bette had her glasses off, and for a moment I saw how sensitive and shy her pale small face really was, behind its brave golden mask. Then on went the glasses, making her the inscrutable Miss Pringle, White House confidential secretary to scientists, afraid of nothing except maybe mice.

"How do I feel?" She echoed our chorused question. "I feel excited, happy, proud, and very *very* curious to see who's inside the Easter egg."

"Me, too," the President agreed, sitting down in a chair facing her. "Except that I have nothing to feel proud of yet, beyond the fact of having such a girl as you around the house. I aged five years in those five seconds, while that thing had you."

"He's not a thing," she said. "He's nice."

Unable to believe my ears, I reached out to turn off the

babble on her bedside radio. Just then it was interrupted with a scratchy short-wave voice from Stockholm. At a nod, I turned it up. We listened to a new angle on the case. Said one Bjor Bjenson, "For the past quarter-hour, all Soviet domestic radio stations have been attempting to convince the war-weary and embittered Russian peasants that Soviet scientists have established contact with the planet Mars. Church bells are being rung. This ridiculous falsehood, which no child would believe, is hailed as a great victory for socialism. However, absolutely reliable reports from inside the Iron Curtain captive countries denounce the hoax as a frantic attempt to divert attention from a Kremlin revolt against the Premier which broke out at dawn today with heavy casualties and an air battle. Ninety-seven Red fighter planes are known to have crashed. Fires are raging in the city, yet forced parades of singing factory workers—"

The President turned it off. Fire engines clanged by outside. From the second floor windows we could see, beyond the cordon of Marines, vast throngs of excited but orderly Washingtonians standing in the streets and looking toward the White House. The President said slowly, "I'm glad it's not a hoax. I might as well confess that I've been praying for a miracle. Maybe this is it. Nothing less than outside allies could break the deadlock of balanced power on this earth."

His deep-set eyes, dark shadowed from his long anxiety, moved from the sky to Bette Pringle's face. He asked her, "How did you get through it?"

She said, "He let me in. He turned it off like a light. Then he turned it on again, behind me. I could feel him do it."

The General's square bulk filled the open doorway solidly. He had recovered from the natural confusion of his first encounter with a new idea, and was once more the doughty military leader who had honorably won the five bright banks of ribbons on his mighty chest. He was again a man of Mars, the warrior. To him the pink Easter egg on the lawn outside was now a military engine sent by his titular deity of armed force. He worshiped it. He said, "Mr. President, I regret this interruption, but it is my duty to inform you, as my Commander in Chief, that the defensive screen which this thing possesses has been deflecting radar impulses without sending back an echo. Therefore, it is a doubly decisive weapon which we must immediately—"

"You're not interrupting, General. Do come in. I am interrogating the only member of my staff who has any information on the weapon. Now, Miss Pringle, please think carefully before you answer. When you moved away from it, and reached the point where Ted was standing, was the force turned off a second time, to let you out?"

Her eyes, within their ornamental frames, were bright and steady. "No, sir. Not going out. It feels different when you touch it from the inside. It lets you out."

Ted said, "She's right. I was pushing with all my strength to get in, when she stepped out beside me with no effort."

The General looked portentously upon us. "This means our planes, tanks, and battleships could fire at will from inside this impregnable air armor at close range. One such bomber could dominate a country. A dozen could police the world. In war, no enemy would stand a chance."

"You mean there'd be no more war," the President retorted sharply. "Whoever gets this first, gets peace on his terms for keeps."

Bette slowly arose, a new dignity about her. "If we really got that technical secret, as the man on the radio called it, would it clear up this mess that everybody's in?" she asked simply. She looked candidly at Ted with the eyes of a wife and a would-be mother. He is the type who is the first to volunteer for the paratroops and is oftenest awarded the Congressional Medal of Honor, posthumously. I think she saw herself, in black, being handed one of those to live with for the rest of her life, and to show to Junior.

The Chief said, "Yes, it would. The Russians are realists. So are we. Individuals may commit suicide rather than surrender, but nations never do. We would have to come to terms and start disarming, because our armaments would be useless."

Bette looked out the window at the crowded streets. Over half those throngs were women, watching, waiting. "I wonder," she said. "Men have always managed to find some new way of making wars, and turning wives into widows."

"With this defensive weapon, war would become a military impossibility," the General pleaded. "Remember, even the fanatic Japanese, who had sworn to die to the last man, surrendered to us quickly and honestly when faced by a decisive weapon. They're practically our best friends nowadays. So could the goodhearted Russians be, if a few changes were made at the top."

Bette began to powder her nose carefully, making an artistic job of it.

Ted spoke for the first time, quietly to Bette. "You're not going out. That thing tried to eat you."

"That's what you're always threatening to do." She laughed. "It's not a mouth. It's a cute little door. Inside I caught a glimpse of something about your size, alive, sitting at controls. And although he obviously prefers to say it with flowers, if I tried hard enough—"

"Absolutely no," said Ted.

"Why not?" said Bette.

"Because I won't let you," said Ted.

"We're not married yet," she reminded him. "He can't stop me from doing anything I want to do, can he, Mr. President?"

"I don't mix in," came the statesmanlike reply. "But speaking for myself alone, I couldn't ask any American girl to take the unimaginable risk of doing what you seem to be suggesting."

Ted said, "What if that thing took off for Mars with you inside?"

She said, "Eventually we all take off for somewhere. I

saw what that fighter pilot tried to do. He's made me feel like doing something big today, like he did. A girl can do things for her country, too, in her own peculiar way."

"No," said the President, standing up. "Not you. We'll find out what we must know in some other way." He moved toward the door, telling Ted, "Take her home. Away from here. She's had the worst shock a girl ever had. She doesn't know what she's saying."

Right then was when we got our big surprise. Bette smiled strangely at us, and said slowly, although not without a certain sweet impertinence, "I do too know what I'm saying. Better than anybody else. After all, I *saw* him, and I learned something very important that I haven't had a chance to tell you yet, with four men saying, 'No, no, no' to me all the time."

One by one we turned around and stared at her. Her cryptic smile told nothing. The expression in her eyes was veiled by her glasses.

The President inquired, "And what is it that you have to tell us, Miss Pringle?"

Trying to be casual, he came back across the guest room, picked up a bowl of fruit, and passed it around. Nobody wanted any. I couldn't swallow, and the General was turning green.

The Chief took two apples, put one in the pocket of his overalls, and began to eat the other.

"Promise you won't laugh," she said.

"I haven't laughed since Yalta," said the General. "After today, I'll never even smile, unless we get the secret of that air armor. Speak up, child."

A faraway look came over her face. "There's something fascinating about whoever is inside that Easter egg," she said. "He tried to talk to me."

"I didn't hear him saying anything," said Ted.

"Neither did I," said Bette slowly, puzzled. "He seemed to speak inside my mind, not with words, but with ideas." She closed her eyes and sighed. "With pictures, too," she whispered, reminiscent. "Pictures no artist could paint—"

With an expression that hovered between an uneasy smile and a worried frown, the President asked Bette, "What kind of ideas has the man from Mars been putting into your head, Miss Pringle?"

"Oh, I was too frightened to—to take dictation properly. It was something about a white hat, a brother, and feeling thirsty."

The General swung off with an impatient snort. "She's hysterical. We're wasting precious time. I'll go see Zweistein. He'll know what to do. He'd better." He marched out muttering something about, "Those Russian scientists, with guns at their backs—"

We all went downstairs again. The President munched his apple thoughtfully. Ted and Bette dropped behind, deep in a domestic-sounding argument full of emphatic "But dear" and "Darling, *please!*" Bette was winning. Naturally.

The crowd outside was mostly gone, except for a handful of picked men standing by to make a sound film record of everything that happened. Zweistein was sitting at a folding table ten feet from the Martian space ship. He flashed the mirror, got flashes in return, spoke into the listening ear, and made calculations on a pad. The General was quizzing him on new developments.

"I've nothing to report except this gift," said Zweistein. With a puzzled smile he showed us a fanciful device. "He sent it out to me in exchange for some white hyacinths."

The Professor's present looked like nothing on Earth. The closest I can come to helping you see it is to say it was an intricately worked platinum bowl with two long crystal fronds like ferns growing the wrong way out of the bottom —except that it wasn't a bowl, they weren't ferns, and none of us knew what to make of it.

Bette came up behind us and clapped her hands. "That's the white hat he promised me," she said, and reached for it.

"Be careful!" Ted implored her.

"I've promised you I would be. Now let's not say careful

any more." She picked up the platinum and crystal creation. It began to look a little like a hat, the way she held it. At least the millinery from Mars was no dizzier than some of the Easter bonnets being paraded that morning on Fifth Avenue. "How cute," she said.

"Take the girl away," the General said gruffly. "This is now a military matter." He ordered an aide, "Move the entire Communications Section of the War Department here, on the double-double. We've got to find a way of negotiating with this potential ally before the Russians do!"

Bette obediently drew back. The personality inside the Easter egg, however, had other ideas about Bette. Both of his wandlike arms oozed out, and with a flourish placed the helmet on Bette's curly head.

She had looked like a hummingbird before, with her fancy glasses; but now she was an elfin princess straight out of *A Midsummer Night's Dream*. The two feathery crystal plumes stood up from her small pert head like the antennae on a beautiful rare butterfly.

As though hypnotized, she sank into the vacant chair beside Zweistein. "Oh my goodness," she said presently to herself. "This beats anything I've ever felt." She reached for Zweistein's pencil and began automatically to write.

"It beats me," said the General sourly. "Mr. President, we have no time to waste on foolishness—"

"Ssh! She's writing."

Bette wrote:

Then she sat listening, entranced.

"Read it, somebody!" the President demanded. In chagrin, we all shook our expensive heads. The shorthand of our underpaid secretaries was more mysterious to us than the hieroglyphics of the ancient Egyptians.

"You, Bonifield? Your quotes of what I say are always right. You must know shorthand."

Ted swallowed hard. "I can read hers," he said. His worried eyes were fixed on her closed lids. He forced himself to look at the four words she had written. In a choking voice he read aloud:

" 'I—come—in—peace.' "

We all looked quickly at the Martian. I suppose I smiled and nodded like an oaf. I was so relieved, I couldn't help it.

The President stepped out in front of us and gravely spoke into the sound detector. "We welcome you in peace. Is there anything you need?"

Bette's nimble pencil took down the unheard reply, and Ted translated. "Badly need oxygen, water, earth, solar energy."

The Chief passed that one to Zweistein, who promptly said into the Martian's hearing aid, "The air around you is twenty-one per cent oxygen. Can you breathe it, or do you need pure oxygen in a cylinder?"

The General watched suspiciously as the reply came back.

"Can extract oxygen from your air, if permitted. May I take a little, please?"

"Take all you want," the Chief said quickly. "We've got free air." His eyes were beginning to glow with appreciation of the ethical kind of mind that we were up against, for a change.

With a soulful sigh, two ventilators opened on each side of the huge pink egg. The man from Mars took grateful gasps of our fresh air, fragrant with the scent of Easter flowers. I caught myself drawing a deep breath in sympathy. I hadn't realized how very sweet our Earth's free air could be.

The big glass eye beamed with gratitude. Bette wrote, THANK YOU in capital letters. On second thought she added an exclamation point.

The President bent down beside her. "Are you all right?" he asked.

She scribbled on the margin of her pad, *I'm okay thanks. He thinks he's thirsty.*

"Thirsty, is he?" The Chief reached down and turned

on the lawn sprinkler. Cool water fountained on the grass. The Martian goggled at it in amazement. Bette recorded what was in his mind.

"Will give you a diamond for every drop that you will give me to drink."

"Help yourself," said the President. "We have oceans of it. There's no charge."

A drinking-tube uncoiled like the proboscis of a giant bee. The creature from an arid planet, where it never rains, drank humbly of the Earth's pure water.

"Enjoy our sunshine, too," the Chief said hospitably, edging closer to the Martian all the time. We sensed deep earnestness beneath his simple words and casual manner. More than any of the rest of us, the Chief knew what he was doing. But then, consider the experience an accessible president acquires in sizing strangers up and handling outlandish callers who make weird demands. The Martian's needs were simple compared to the patronage problems of Turtle County.

The President went on, smiling, gesturing with the half-eaten apple in his hand.

"You wanted earth, you say? Then have some, friend. Take on a load of dirt, if it will please you. This place belongs to the people of the country, and I don't think they'll mind. Come, help yourself. We've got plenty of everything here."

Windowlike plastic panels slid open on the space ship's southern exposure. The blessed Easter sun streamed in like benediction upon the unimaginable being from a have-not planet where their warmest summer noon would seem a wintery twilight to us, who had the good luck to be born on Earth.

A hand-shaped scoop dropped out and timidly spaded up a little of the White House lawn. The Martian fondled the rich southern soil like a miser gloating over gold. He let our good earth trickle through his metal fingers, musing:

"Beautiful, wonderful Terra— The Garden of Eden of

our solar system."

"We like it here," the President agreed. "Make yourself at home. You must be hungry, after your long trip. What would you like to eat?"

"May I have a bite of the exotic red fruit you are eating? It smells so good." The Chief took the second apple from his pocket and held it out in his open hand. The spidery long arm snaked out through the wall of force, hooked the apple off, and swung it back inside through the mouth-like door.

A little later a ruby of about the same size as the apple came rolling out across the grass. The President fielded it like a grounder and said, "Thanks. Do you have a name that I can call you by?"

"My name is One. It is I who must thank you. I will eat the apple."

(Today that ruby was placed in the Smithsonian Institution, but not without a struggle.)

We waited while the hidden something enjoyed the second most important apple ever eaten. It must have tasted sweet to him. Where he came from, such fruit could never grow. Their oxygen is almost gone, there is no liquid water, the distant sun is dim, and living conditions generally are believed to be as distressing as on the summit of a 50,000-foot mountain, here on Terra. Had we such a super-mountain, nearly twice the height of man-killing Mount Everest, about the only plant life that could conceivably survive would be some very tough variety of reindeer moss.

Bette began to write again. The grateful Martian transmitted, "Thank you very much. That was delicious. Are there any more of those on Earth? Will gladly give a ruby for each one you can spare."

"We pick at least five hundred million apples every fall," replied the Chief, who is something of a farmer, as you know.

"Fantastic!" sighed the man from Mars. "So many apples. No one back home will believe me."

The President beckoned to a frock-coated authority on protocol who was hovering anxiously in the background disapproving of the Chief Executive's coveralls. "Lug up a bushel of our best from the cellar, and give them to our company," he said. The frock coat tottered off.

Bette wrote, and Ted relayed the Martian's perplexity. "I have nothing valuable enough to repay you for the priceless treasures you are giving me."

"Oh yes you have!" the General boomed heartily, and for the first time I saw him smile. "Just tell us how you make that air armor that surrounds you, and in exchange we will present you with all the apples and dirt and water you can take aboard." It sounded like a bargain, the way he put it. "And fresh air, too," he generously added.

We waited tensely while Bette's darting pencil recorded the Martian's reply.

"Gladly. I agree. Here is the formula."

Bette wrote slowly and carefully for several minutes, seeming to photograph symbols in her mind and then draw what she saw. Ted bent down beside her, watching, but he did not read. At length he straightened up and said, "This isn't shorthand that she's writing. It's all Greek to me."

I looked over her shoulder. It was mostly Greek, with Arabic and Roman numerals, the polyglot of higher mathematics. Ted tore the pages out of Bette's notebook and handed them to Zweistein.

The father of modern physics read it through and shrugged. His shrugs are as eloquent as Bette's smiles. They mean much in little, without saying what they mean. He sank down in his chair, looking old and tired, and yet very much at peace, as if he had reached a journey's end. "Well, they've got it," he said.

"Got what?" barked the General. "Our atomic bomb?"

The physicist winced, as if hearing the same sour joke for the hundredth time. "Please, General," he said wearily. "This formula makes me feel like a backward schoolboy. They seem to have mastered the basic equation for the electromagnetic forces of life itself. I must go off by myself for a while and study this. Maybe I'll be gone a long, long time." He wandered off and sat down on a bench beneath a tree with the pages of Martian formula in his hand. He took out his pocket slide rule, and a pad and pencil. He looked like a little old white-haired professor, with baggy pants, harmless and rather helpless. Then he began to make marks on paper, and to use his brain, and he became potentially more dangerous than all the fire-eating generals in the world. He turned into a wizard who invoked the twin spirits of the spinning stars, Energy and Mass.

The General was standing at parade rest, by Ted. "Ask him who the other one is, in the Kremlin," he commanded.

"He heard you," said Ted shortly. "No channels here." Bette was growing pale with strain, and Ted was growing grim.

The Martian replied with childlike candor through Bette's open mind.

"He is my twin brother. His name is Two."

The President queried, "Can you communicate with him?"

"Yes, constantly. We of Mars are all one mind."

"Then what is he doing in Moscow?" the General shot back.

There came a painful pause. Bette tried very hard to put into shorthand English the ideas that were entering her mind, but she could not find the words. Her pencil faltered, crossed out, stopped. Abruptly she tore off the helmet and covered her face with her hands. Ted put his arm protectingly around her shoulders.

"I can't," she said.

"Can't what?" the General snapped. "We were just starting to get somewhere with this fellow."

"He *hears* you," Ted whispered. "Can't you get that through your head?"

Bette said, "I'm sorry, but I can't take his dictation any more. He's sending pictures now. In streaky strange old colors. They're like picture post cards of some foreign place I've never seen. Church domes like purple onions— Foreign-looking people are walking around. Oh, I can't describe the scene I see. I wish I could." Her slim shoulders began silently to shake.

Ted asked, "Can't we try someone else on this receiving job? She's not very strong, you know."

"I am *too* strong," Bette protested. "Besides, no one else can understand him." There may have been a trace of professional jealousy in her secretarial manner. "He's very hard to take." She began to pull herself together. "He says, I mean he thinks, we're *en rapport*. Whatever that means. He won't talk to you through anyone but me, because I was the first to give him flowers." She put on her thinking cap again. "Oh, these pictures he is sending! If I could somehow make you see—" All at once she brightened, and began to laugh. "My paints!" she cried. "Teddy, run up to my office and bring me down my water colors. They're in the bottom drawer."

Ted was back in a flash (as he would never write it). Bette began to splash down shapes and colors with her clever brush. "This doesn't make any sense," she apologized, painting very rapidly, "but this is what he makes me see in my mind's eye."

As the scene took shape on paper, the General turned a richer purple than any of the church domes. "You can't imagine how much sense you're making, child!" he bayed. "Wait till Intelligence sees this! You are painting a picture of the hidden inner courtyard of the Kremlin at Moscow. No foreigner has seen it since the Bolsheviks took over. The Premier's bedroom windows overlook it, we are told. Yes, there he is now." It was like looking at television to watch Bette pencil in the familiar mustached visage on a figure in the foreground.

Surrounded by men with scientific instruments, the Premier faced an egg-shaped pink space ship identical to ours with the same symbol on it. I don't know what a pale pink was doing in the Kremlin, but there he was, and they were giving him the works. There were tables of fruit and flowers, and fountains playing in the old palace courtyard of the Czars of Muscovy.

Bette became her own commentator and critic as she swiftly sketched. "This round thing—I can't draw a circle —is supposed to be a big globe of the world. The one that Ribbentrop gave Molotov, somebody's thinking. The Russians are marking it up with red crayon, like this." Bette carved it like a melon. "So much for you, so much for us, they're saying. They welcome him with bread and salt, and vodka, which he's never tasted; and a tub of caviar. He likes it. They have no caviar on Mars. Now the Premier is offering him—I can't get the Russian words but I get the general idea, here on the map—offering all the water in the Volga River, all the black earth of the Ukraine, all the fruits and flowers of the Caucasus, all the winds of Siberia and the sunshine of Turkestan, if the men from Mars will agree to establish their proposed colony on Soviet soil."

"Colonies!" the General groaned. "I knew they wanted something from us. Everybody else does."

"Wonder why our Martian hasn't mentioned the purpose of his visit?" the President thought aloud.

"Maybe because nobody asked him," Bette whispered. "In some ways he's rather bashful." Then she dropped her paints and grabbed her notebook, for the Martian had heard what both men said. She wrote, and Ted deciphered.

" 'Yes. We beg one little colony, a place in the sun with water flowing, and earth to grow sweet fruit and flowers. My brother Two and I were sent here to find a refuge for our people. Our ancient race is dying for lack of the four priceless elements you have here in such abundance. Only a hundred of us are left alive. We are a peaceful species, unlike you. We will make no trouble, and we will pay you well for a little garden somewhere here on this Promised Planet.' "

The President took it in his stride. "We will give you refuge. We have taken in the needy from every land on Earth, and we will take you, too. You can have your pick of Government land in any state you choose." He said in an aside to the Secretary of State, "Do you think Congress will ratify this treaty?"

"I'll go now and start explaining," said the Secretary. "I rather dread it." He asked the Martian, "How long can you wait?"

"Until twilight," said One. "We must return at the setting of the Sun. Our planets are passing closer to each other now than they will again for the next three years. That is how we came across, and why we must go back, tonight. We will do anything we can for those who save us from the growing cold of outer darkness, from hunger, thirst, and suffocation on our worn-out, dying world."

"We will save you," said the President. "Now let me ask a question. You seem to know something of this Earth of ours."

I heard the General mutter, "Yes, we've been scouted out— Those Flying Saucers—"

The President went on. "You must have noticed that our Western Hemisphere is younger, richer, less crowded, and better in every way for your colony. Why, then, did your brother go to the Eastern Hemisphere at all? It complicates our conversation, Mr. One."

"We are making an impartial survey," said the man from Mars. "We are authorized to take the better of two offers. Between us we decide for all our race."

"And if you disagree?"

"For ten thousand years, no one has disagreed on Mars. Wait. Something is wrong. I can feel my brother being tempted. He disagrees with me."

"In that case," said the President, "let me recommend to both of you a fifth essential element of life, which he has overlooked. Its name is Liberty. We can promise it to you, but they cannot. Or do you know what freedom means?"

The Martian pondered, blinking his big eye.

"All Martians are one happy family. As you will be, some day. We have lived in harmony so long we have forgotten what these prehistoric concepts meant."

"With us, freedom is historic," said the Chief. "Your colony needs freedom to survive. All this you see around you here began with one small colony of refugees who came here from the Old World to be free."

"What difference does it make?" the Martian wondered. "Free or not free, one still breathes, eats, drinks, feels the sun."

"It makes all the difference in the world," the Chief persisted. "Without our precious element of Liberty, you could not freely breathe our fine fresh air you love. You could not own an acre of the earth that grows these flowers, or claim its fruits. You would not be free to think your own thoughts, practice your beliefs, or even be a happy family, as you say you are. Think our proposition over, Mr. One. Our priceless fifth ingredient of life is worth more than the four natural elements you prize. Only our side can guarantee to supply it in unlimited amounts."

The Martian thought it over, and grew troubled. He shifted uneasily from foot to foot. "But this is what those other men are now promising my brother. They say you have no freedom here, they claim to have it all."

"That's not true. Without our kind of Liberty, I warn you, the good things of this Earth are not worth having because they cannot be enjoyed."

The steam valve sputtered in confusion. "But this is the same warning as they are giving to my brother. They tell him, 'Pick the winning side. We have more land, more people.' Now he has agreed. Brother is too easily influenced, I fear. He thinks that we must choose between you. Now he lets me know that Mars must support *his* side in a final war of global unity for your planet, as we had for ours."

We stood rigidly, feeling time run out and bleed away. To our surprise, the Chief shifted his attack, and quietly inquired, "Do you have wars on Mars?"

"Not since our final war of unity, ten thousand years ago. We lost half our race and most of our natural resources, but the survivors learned to live in peace. So it was worth it."

"We are now where you were then," the President said gravely. "We want one world, but we have two. Both sides dread the war no one can win. Nothing could be worth that much slaughter and destruction!"

"It is our duty to prevent that war."

"That is my duty, too. Why is it yours?"

"Because your heavenly planet is too precious to be destroyed in a nursery quarrel between spoiled children. You are too young to be playing with atoms. You are too lovable to become extinct. And how rich you are! Twenty-one per cent oxygen in every breath you take. It taxes my imagination!" said the man from Mars.

The President bent down and peered at Bette's notebook, filling rapidly with shorthand symbols. "Does he really think we're lovable? Are you sure you got that right?" She nodded, and began to write again, for the Martian had heard the question.

"Yes, lovable. You are all beautiful and young. Not many of you look much over a hundred years old. And you are the kindest creatures I have met in many a light-year. You gave me food and drink when I was thirsty. You let me warm myself by your fire, gave me the breath of life, and sweet flowers to smell. And this young female through whom we communicate has the most lovely mind that I have ever read." Ted paused and gave the Martian a searching glance; but the message was continuing with increasing agitation, and he had to resume his reading aloud.

"Wait— What is this? My brother interrupts my thoughts. He warns me to escape from you and fly over where he is, on the free side of the globe. He has begun to think that you are bad men who will enslave our colony. Is this true?"

"No! Extend my invitation to him to fly over here to our side of the world and see for himself what kind of men we are. Tell him not to take their word for it."

Martian Number One shook all over with the intensity

of his telepathic communion with his brother in Moscow. Then, gradually, to our despair, we could see him begin to get un-American ideas. Soon he started to throw his weight around on all three legs, to huff and puff like the big bad wolf. He blew off steam and cast his thought waves arrogantly at us, to this effect:

"The other species of man across the earth from you has made Brother and me a more attractive offer. They promise us one million human beings, men and women, to do with as we please. We knew we would need helpers in our colony, but to do with as we please— This primitive concept could be interesting. We had forgotten it was possible. What a savage little island you have here in the tropics of the solar system! It must be the heat. How many bodies do you bid?"

"Not one," replied the President.

"Why not? You have so many. Surely you could spare a few. Some specimens are more beautiful than your flowers." The big eye gleamed eagerly at Bette, but she was absorbed in taking shorthand swiftly, and did not look up. She did not seem to be aware of the meaning of the dictation she was taking, but, on the other hand, no man, not even a man from Mars, will ever know what his secretary is thinking about as she sits passively, her pencil poised.

The President was as patient with the mighty Martian monster as if he were a small boy who had brought home his first nasty words from kindergarten. "You see, Mr. One, ours are all free men and women. They are not for sale by me. They belong to themselves. We had a war that settled this question on our half of the world about ninety years ago. Our half-finished war of unity. If you want helpers in your colony, you can hire them, the same as I have to do. We have many people here in Washington who would gladly work for Martians. Incidentally, as one employer to another, I advise you that our free men and women work much better than the other kind."

"I believe you," impulsively decided One. "It stands to reason. I must now convince my foolish brother you are ight and they are wrong."

The big eye closed in concentrated thought. Bette took off the platinum-and-crystal helmet. "No signal," she said wearily. "The line is dead." She put down her pencil and stretched her cramped fingers. She laid her head back on Ted's shoulder and closed her eyes. She did look like a flower, I thought; a white hyacinth— Ted held her close as if to shield her from some nameless danger.

That was the day the Monday papers came out twice on Sunday afternoon. You're probably keeping those extras to show your grandchildren. At last editors got to use that "second coming" headline type they talk about.

Late Sunday risers with Saturday-night heads squinted at the front page, fell back in bed, and took the pledge. Others ran for the nearest bar only to see the same horrors on television. Those who fainted could not fall, so dense-packed were the crowds before the television screens.

The churches were crowded, too. Many a quick-witted preacher quoted verse and chapter prophesying what had now occurred. Missionaries volunteered to go to Mars in rockets.

The United Nations hastily whipped up a Committee on Extra-Terrestrial Control, so that our planet could deal with our neighbor planet as a whole; but this was vetoed.

Americans thirtyish and over laughed heartily at the first reports, and said patronizingly to their excited youngsters, "I bit on this same gag myself once years ago. Don't believe a word of it. You'll find out tomorrow it's just a play. That's what the other big scare was, 'way back in 38. Science fiction." Then, with a slightly worried look, "Wonder where they got an actor who looks so much like the President? Isn't there a law against that?"

Because "Wolf, wolf!" had been cried at us before, when the men from Mars *really* came, most Americans took it very calmly. Only here and there within our vast and varied land did we display, if not a lunatic fringe, perhaps a few loose linters on the frayed cuffs of sanity. By one p.m., rival Martians had been reported stunting over Naples, Florida; Killeen, Texas; and Glorieta, New Mexico. By two, in Burbank, California, you could buy a Martian Sundae with pink passion-fruit ice cream and two lady fingers.

Only a few people lost their minds and they probably would have, anyway, if not on interplanetary intervention, then over the astronomic price of meat. Rush newsreels of Bette reading the Martian's mind inspired a divorcing couple in Boston to accuse each other of "simultaneous and reciprocal thought-transference." (The judge is still thinking that one over.) In Loveland, Louisiana, a one-eyed taxidermist named Svoloch conked his wife with an elephant tusk, claiming that "invisible Martian voices" egged him on. (By last reports, Mrs. Svoloch has recovered sufficiently to swing a mean tusk herself.)

By three p.m., the frenzied radio industry had interviewed the redheaded fighter pilot nineteen times about his battle with what he still stubbornly called "the meat ball." No one could get him to say "Martian." The epithet caught the public fancy, the sound cameras recorded it, and wires began to hum with new accounts of the political crisis confronting "the Meat Ball on the White House Lawn." The nickname was just goofy enough to take the raw edge off the growing suspense and apprehension our nation felt as the truth of the news began to sink in. No matter how comical it looked, the sobering fact remained that this childlike brain possessed superhuman weapons that could destroy or save the human race, according to its whim or fancy.

The Soviet press did not call their Martian "the Meat Ball," due possibly to the meat famine, or "the Easter Egg," since it wasn't Easter over there. Instead, they dubbed theirs the *Krasnaya Sphera*, the "Red Sphere." Of influence, no doubt. *Izvestia* said Comrade Two asked the Premier's advice on Sovietizing Mars. In the inimitable gobbledygook of Soviet officialdom, *Pravda* stated, and we translate:

The great Lenin-like intellect within the Red Sphere is rapidly acquiring a broadly democratic orientation toward political realities. He has expressed admiration for our victorious Socialist culture, especially our tangerines. He has extended diplomatic recognition to the new, free, Peoples' Democracies of the liberated areas. He is swiftly mastering dialectic materialism, linked with an organized study of Stalinism."

I'll bet he was, at that.

Our own inimitable Tin Pan Alley, not to be outdone, had a new song writhing on the tortured airways by four p.m. We managed to keep our Martian from hearing it. Will you ever forget that maddening tune, that inane doggerel, with a major political or scientific error in every line:

> *He's got hot atomic ha-cha;*
> *He's our interstellar papa;*
> *He's the answer to our Uncle Sammy's prayer.*
> *He's on our side because*
> *He's a super Santa Claus.*
> *He's the funny little man who's really there!**

It wasn't funny for us, waiting on the White House lawn like prisoners awaiting the verdict. We may have been seeing things by this time, but it seemed to us that our cogitating Martian was slowly turning a deeper red.

Professor Zweistein rejoined us. His pad was full of calculations. His face was full of perplexity. "No scientists on earth, Russian or American, can apply this formula without the Martian's help," the physicist said flatly. "Their engineering skill is based on principles far beyond our present knowledge. They will have to teach us as patiently as I teach my youngest students."

"Or teach the Russians!" the General exploded. "Mili-

---

* Printed without permission, in defiance of the copyright owners.

tary Intelligence got you the secret. Now build it."

Zweistein smiled sadly.

The Chief said anxiously, "I'd hoped that you of all men could understand how this air armor is produced. Whoever gets it first— Well, no use saying that again."

"Theoretically, I understand," said the scientist, scanning the pages of figures as if they were pin-up girls. "It's a beautiful formulation. Somehow the Martian scientists have learned to curve the space-time continuum around us."

"What the hell does that mean?" the General grunted.

Zweistein picked up a slender branch that had been clipped off by a shell fragment earlier in the day. He flexed it and let it spring back. "Like that. The way some smart ancestor of yours, General, learned to bend a stick and make a bow and arrow. The Martians create magnetic fields that bend the cosmic rays into taut spheres of energy impervious to matter of any velocity or mass. Our cities could be roofed by these invisible umbrellas, just as your bombing planes could be made more horrible, dear General. I had always hoped that man's final guarantee of peace would not be some more terrible new offensive weapon, but a harmless method of total defense. This is it: Mother Nature simply saying *No* to naughty boys who want to throw things at each other. But a formula is not a machine."

The President asked, in a low voice, "And if you had one of the machines—"

Zweistein nodded. "It might make the difference between writing the equation $E = MC^2$ on this pad, and obtaining a real atomic bomb to take apart and study. Many years and many billions separated those two events, as you may both recall."

Bette seemed to awaken from a nap. Maybe she had really dozed off. Anyway, she opened her eyes, and they were very bright. She said shyly, "Our friend has one of those machines inside his Easter Egg, a few steps from where we're sitting." She sounded very much the practical female as she added, "Let's get it and take it apart." She stood up and checked her lipstick in her pocket mirror. Her lips were very red against the whiteness of her cheeks.

The ray of light streamed out from the big shell and looked her up and down. The man from Mars was not asleep, either.

"Where do you think you're going?" Ted asked.

As often happens, he did not get a direct answer to his question. Instead she said, "Well, hasn't he already offered to give us anything we want?"

Ted seized her hand and held it tightly. "How do you know what kind of thing may be in there?"

"He's nothing I'm afraid of now," she said, suppressing a faint smile. "After all, remember this: I can read his mind." She looked reproachfully at Ted, whose face was hard and bitter. "I'm glad I can't read your mind just now, Mr. Bonifield. I'd probably have to slap your face."

She walked over and stood in front of the President with her hands folded like a schoolgirl. "He's already invited me to come in," she said. "I didn't write that down."

"I wish you wouldn't," said the Chief. "We have trained operatives in Military Intelligence whose business it is to take risks like this. Maybe one of them—"

She shook her head firmly. "He thinks only of me, because I understand him."

She turned to the General for support. His purple face went ashen gray. "You said this was a military matter," she reminded him. "I hereby volunteer for Military Intelligence." She waited. "Orders, sir?"

"Do what you can," the General said weakly. "Take no unnecessary risks. Er, let's see. You have a pocket mirror. Flash it from a porthole every minute, on the dot. If you don't keep signaling that you're all right, we're coming in and get you. God bless you, child. Got a watch?"

"I've got everything I need." She laughed, and winked at us, and started off across the grass. "I'll find out what makes him tick."

Ted stepped out and stopped her a few feet from where

we stood. He swung her around so that her back was to the Martian.

"Please let me go," she begged. "Can't you see I'm the only one small enough to get in through that little door?"

He released her wrists and tried to plead with her. They were facing each other, about a foot apart. When he reached up to take her by her shoulders and shake some sense into her, his hands could not go through the air. The invisible air armor had been extended silently and stealthily. It dropped between them like a pane of glass.

He grappled at the empty air, like a man fighting with a phantom.

Bette walked to the space ship and knocked politely on the door. Two liplike panels split in an inhuman leer. Eagerly assisted by the spidery steel arm, she stepped inside.

The mouth clamped shut. Behind was a thud. A cop had fainted. They carried him away.

The General took out his watch and laid it on the table. The second hand seemed to be engraved upon the dial. Finally it crawled a little. So did my skin. A minute passed.

Bette's pocket mirror flashed cheerily from a porthole. We dimly saw her face inside, veiled as though in cellophane. Then she disappeared.

A minute and a half later, we saw her hand hold up the mirror and flash it briefly, once; but this time her face did not appear.

Two minutes and thirteen seconds later, no third signal flash had yet been seen. We looked at each other like murderers.

The red shell began to tick in a strange new way. Ticktock, tick-tock. The eye closed. The ear twitched. The mechanical hand clutched at the grass.

"Let's go get her," said Ted dully. "I don't care what happens to me now." He and the General advanced across the lawn like a suicide mission.

Suddenly the ticking stopped. The steam valve let out

a long sigh.

"The air armor is gone!" Zweistein cried, pointing. In the ghastly stillness of that wait, a sparrow had hopped across the invisible boundary line, pecking at the grass.

Ted and the General flung themselves ahead. Before they reached the space ship's hull, the panel opened, and Bette stepped out backward, waving good-by.

She moved slowly, carrying something big and round, rather like a plastic beach ball. We could not see what it was she had obtained. All we looked at was her transformed face.

She did not wear her glasses. On her lips she wore a smile—and what a mysterious little smile it was. I wish Leonardo da Vinci had been there. He could have brushed up his famous Mona Lisa, with Bette for his model.

She did not look at us. Perhaps she could not see us, with her glasses off.

Ted held out his arms to her, speechless with relief.

She put the shining globe into his arms, instead of herself, and passed him by. She walked straight past us all, without a word, but with that tantalizing little smile. Everything that girls since Eve had ever known was there on her curving lips, the mystery of the eternal feminine, the answer to the riddle of the Sphinx, the inner glow of Joan of Arc, and Woman's ageless laughter at the race of Man. She yawned and stretched luxuriously and went into the house.

The White House, that is. I had forgotten where I was.

Ted came toward us slowly, like a sleepwalker, holding the big round bubble in his arms.

Trying to be paternal, I said to Ted, "Give me that thing. You'd better go to her."

"He'd better not," the General said roughly. "He's the last man on Earth she wants to see just now."

Moving numbly, Ted put the round thing on the table and went in through the side door.

Zweistein reached out and touched the pinkish globe. It burst like a soap bubble, and there stood a most magnificent machine. We stared at it as cavemen might gape stupidly at the inside of a radio set. It was about the size of a basketball. The surface was a sphere of wires woven in open mesh that let us look inside. The interior was mostly empty space, but here and there were little round things like marbles, of some unknown substance, spaced on shining rings of strange alloys that circled and crossed like intersecting orbits. At the center was a core of baffling complexity. Disconnected from its source of power, the instrument was motionless and dead; but even my unpracticed eye could see that the machine was built to be a mass of moving parts, interacting with exquisite precision.

"Well, the Army got you your model," the General told Zweistein. "How soon can you have it in mass production?"

"If we did it in a thousand years, we would be working ten times as fast as the Martians," said Zweistein. "Imagine the progress they must have made in ten thousand years of peaceful scientific research, with no wasteful wars to destroy the best brains and laboratories of every generation. Makes me almost wish I were a Martian—but I'm glad I'm not. Mr. President, and General, we shall do our best. We didn't let you down on that other job, did we? Please send your fastest planes for Berkley, Jameson, Capri—"

"They should be here now," said the Chief. "I phoned the Council to assemble while I was cooling my heels in that bomb shelter this morning."

"Ach, good! And we shall need a workshop—"

"Use the Oval Room. Let's not get spread out all over town. Things may happen quickly now." The Chief was growing gruff. He, too, had Bette on his conscience. Every time we looked at that exquisite little machine we thought of her, and saw her mysterious smile. She had been laughing at us.

"I wish my wife was home," the Chief went on, pacing up and down. "She'd know what to do. Somebody ought to be sitting with that poor little girl."

"She's going to get the Congressional Medal of Honor if I have anything to say about it," said the General, his leathery lips quivering.

Allen came out of the White House. He was pale and shaky, but so were we all. "Admiral Sarver sent me to report that he is with Miss Pringle in the guest room," he said huskily. "She asked for her lunch. Says she feels fine, but hungry. Ready to make her Intelligence report, she says, Mr. President."

"Where's Bonifield?" the Chief asked.

"Mr. Bonifield is in the pressroom sending out his story. It is about Miss Pringle being a heroine, he says."

Zweistein had been examining the air armor device closely, turning it around and around in his delicate hands. An official car roared into the driveway and some billions of dollars' worth of scientific brains got out.

The President met them and explained the situation. Zweistein joined them, carrying the model, and they all went inside. The General brought up the rear. I sat down alone and looked at the Martian. He was thinking hard about the International Situation, rocking slowly from side to side and moaning softly, as we often do.

Ted came out. I think he was glad to find me sitting alone at the folding table on the grass. Alone, that is, except for the watchful ring of aides, secretaries, reporters, photographers, and guards who had surrounded us all day. Cabinet members were beginning to arrive, and soon they were all there, except the Secretary of State. He had his hands full, poor man. Imagine trying to explain a treaty with Mars to the Honorable Gentleman from— Well, anywhere.

Ted sat down beside me and lit a cigarette. "Any news?" he asked in a brittle voice.

I could not meet his haunted eyes. Not looking at him, I said, pointing to the motionless Martian, "They're still arguing back and forth about the future of the human species. I'd give anything to listen in on their thought waves."

"I wouldn't," said Ted. He flipped his half-smoked cigarette away. "I'm not interested in said species any more."

"Hello," said a little voice behind us. Bette was standing there. She had her glasses on. Some new kind of fancy frames.

Ted stood up and held a chair for her. "Is there anything I can get you?" he inquired. "Besides the Congressional Medal of Honor?"

"You might give me a little smile," she said.

"I'll do anything in this world for you, but that," he said.

"Hello," I croaked, looking very hard at her. She seemed about the same. She looked all right. Quite all right. In fact, I had not noticed before how completely all right a girl can look.

Bette drew some ticktacktoe squares on her notebook, filled them in. Somebody won. I don't know who. After a while she asked us brightly, "Isn't anybody interested in what it's like inside an Easter egg? Cat got your tongue, Ted? Then I'll tell you anyway—"

"Wait," I said. "Every word you speak is of great scientific value. There will have to be a transcript." I beckoned to a husky veteran court reporter who records secret sessions of the Supreme Scientific Council. "Take down every word she says," I told him as he sat down.

"Goody, I get to give dictation to a man instead of taking it," she said. "Ted, don't look at me like that. Right inside the door, I stepped into a big plastic bubble he had ready for me. He kept me in it all the time, like a goldfish in a bowl. He explained that my blood pressure—no, it was my *air* pressure—I didn't know I *had* air pressure, like a tire— Well, anyway, whatever it was, it had to be nine times higher than his was, or I would pop. Just like that." She showed us with her hands how she would pop. It looked like something to avoid.

We began to relax. Ted more than me, because I was conscious of my scientific responsibility in interrogating the only Tellurian who had ever seen a Martian in the flesh. I said, "Miss Pringle, are those protruding limbs we see out here organic parts of the Martian?"

"Don't be silly," she said. "They're not him at all. What you see are just gadgets he controls by pushing buttons. He sits at the cutest little silver desk you ever saw. Puts his feet up on it. All of 'em."

Ted asked, "Why doesn't he come out of his shell where all of us can see him?"

She said sweetly, "He asked me to offer his regrets. He says he isn't properly attired for a public appearance. He says to tell you that on his next trip he'll know what to bring. Without a pressure suit of some kind, he would be smashed flat."

"He may still be," said Ted. "He hasn't got his air armor to protect him now. A bubble, did you say? But bubbles break."

"This bubble didn't or I wouldn't be here, dear. Let's not say bubble any more."

"Excuse me," I said. "I am attempting to take testimony which may change the entire science of biology. Miss Pringle, please describe the Martian."

"Well," she said, "he's kind of cute."

I mopped my streaming brow. "Thank you. Now could you be a little more specific concerning his anatomical characteristics?"

"I don't know what you mean," she said indignantly.

Ted interposed. "He means, dear, what the hell does the guy look like?"

A knot of curious aides and guards clustered around us, listening. Bette looked thoughtfully from man to man, with a faraway look in her eyes, and said, "Well, all I can say is, he's not the least bit like any of you. He's most unusual."

The General emerged from the White House. His cheeks were burning. "Can you imagine that?" he grumbled as he approached. "They asked me to leave. Said my questions bothered them." Then he saw Bette and gave what is known technically as "a double take." He looked and he looked again. "Hrmph!" he said. "You. Well, which side is the Meat Ball—Brr, I mean the Martian —going to be on? Ours or theirs?"

"We didn't talk politics," she said, demurely.

The General smote his brow and sank down in a chair.

"I think you'd better go and rest," said Ted to Bette. "You're all confused."

"Not any more," she said, very seriously. "I used to be confused sometimes, before today. But that's all over now. I know exactly what I want."

"A cute, unusual Martian?"

"Not on a bet," she said. "I want to live in a small town in the United States of America, planet Earth, right now, married to the editor of a country weekly, preferably you, Mr. Bonifield." She squeezed his arm and tweaked his nose simultaneously; and he loved it. "You're much nicer," she assured him, with growing enthusiasm. She had apparently come back to Earth. She held his arm very tightly. "I love you more now than before I went in there," she said. "Why, you're *human*, Teddy boy!" She made it sound like a scientific discovery of the first magnitude. "That makes all the difference in the world to me. You're real flesh and blood. Poor old Mister One, in there, is just a brain wrapped in cellophane." Whereupon she stood up on tiptoes and kissed Ted, right in front of the President and everybody; and the big glass eye of the man from Mars gazed wistfully upon the scene.

Abruptly Ted held her at arm's length and said, "You have different glasses on, young lady. Scotch plaid."

"Have I?" she asked innocently. "I have several pairs."

"Where are the golden frames you were wearing when you went inside that space ship?" he demanded.

"Oh dear, I don't know. I must have left them some place. You know how girls are, Ted dear. Scatterbrained."

"I'll scatter his brains," Ted said. "Why did you need to take your glasses off, if you were inside a plastic bubble?"

"When people yell at me," she said, "my mind goes blank."

Suddenly the Martian's whistle let off a screech, like a locomotive gone berserk. He began to wave his steel arm wildly. He seized the platinum and crystal receiving set, put it on Bette's head, and thrust the pencil into her hand. She began to take dictation.

Ted had to stand by her and read her shorthand aloud to us no matter how he felt or what he thought. In a little while his hand unconsciously had slipped down off the back of the chair to her shoulder; and she was smiling unconsciously as she wrote. They had been in love so long, I guess, that it had got to be a habit.

There was turmoil in the Martian's mind. "My twin brother is enraged at me, and I at him. No one has been mad at anyone on Mars for centuries. Now he is sending me a challenge. My own brother wants to fight against me to the death. This is what your Earth has done to him. The other species of man has convinced him that your world cannot long endure half slave, half free."

The President walked up to the defenseless egg shell and put his hand on it in a friendly gesture. "Listen. Those words were spoken by an American president ninety years ago. Those other men had no right to say them to your brother. They mean the opposite of what he thinks they mean. You tell him to fly over here to us where it is free, while he still can, as so many of their people try to do."

We moved our chairs and tables closer. I touched the space ship. It was not like any metal I had ever felt. It was somehow alive, like human skin. I could feel it growing warm and warmer as the Martian agonized, "But my brother says yours is the slave half of the world, and theirs the free!"

"The truth is the opposite of that. Kindly tell him so for me. And tell them I said so."

"Your planet is a crazy place," the Martian complained. "How can this same word freedom mean two entirely different things?"

"It can't," the Chief said bluntly. "Somebody's lying. My friend, do you know what a lie is?"

"Let me think. Yes, I remember this barbaric concept, from an ancient book. But no Martian has told a lie in many centuries. We live in the peace of truth."

The President put both hands on the Martian's metal chest and leaned close. "Someone's lying now," he said, "and I don't mean Martian. Now get this straight." He spoke confidentially into the hearing aid for some minutes.

The Secretary of State burst in. He was haggard and disheveled but elated. "I put it through," he gasped. "Even the Senators who still think this is all a funny radio program have agreed to vote for it. And, luckily, the new Chairman of the Foreign Relations Committee is a science fiction fan. He assures me that the Mars Colonization Treaty will be ratified at a Special Session one minute after midnight."

"There, you hear that, Mr. One?" the Chief said jubilantly. "You have found your free colony for your people, as we once found for ours. No dictators gave it to you. Our whole free country, with perhaps a few die-hard exceptions, cordially invites you to enjoy the benefits of Earth."

The Martian vibrated all over and tootled with joy. "What can I ever do to repay you, Man?"

"One thing. Teach us your scientific knowledge."

"Gladly. But why do you peculiar organisms wish to study science in laboratories when you could be outdoors in the fresh air, playing in the green grass with beautiful young females, basking in the sun, and swimming in liquid water? It seems so unintelligent, if you will pardon me for thinking that about you. If I were one of you, on lovely Planet Three, I would never do anything else but enjoy the beauties of nature, in the broad sense of the word."

The President laughed. "You know, I like you," he confided. "The only reason why we ask your help in science is

to guarantee that our bright sun will not be blackened by
the smoke of burning cities, anywhere in the world. To
make certain that the air, the earth, the water will not be
poisoned, anywhere in the world, to be forever sure that
your peace on Earth, and ours, will never be disturbed
again!"

"I like you," said the Martian. "I promise to teach you
everything we know. Speaking on behalf of Mars, I officially accept your offer. Subject to my brother's agreement,
naturally."

They shook hands on it, the hand of flesh in the claw
of steel.

A breathless runner handed the Secretary of State a Tass
release, hot off the wire:

*An exclusive treaty of colonization and mutual aid be-
tween the USSR and Mars has just been signed in the
Kremlin by Comrade Two, the sole official envoy of the
Red Planet. The working model of a military invention
of decisive value has been given to Soviet scientists as
proof of good faith. Comrade Two denounces the rene-
gade Martian, falsely claiming to be his brother, who is
now being held captive by the FBI in Washington and
may be forced to sign anything.*

In the midst of our consternation, Bette tugged at Ted's
sleeve. The Chief held up his hand for silence. The Martian was wishing, "Would someone please read aloud the
thoughts written on the paper? I cannot read it from in
here."

The Secretary of State read the Tass statement to the
man from Mars.

Things began to hum. Slowly the Martian monster rose
out of the earth on his mighty metal legs. In thought waves
so violent that Bette winced with pain, the Martian con-
veyed, "This is the first time in ten thousand years that
one Martian has deceived another. My brother did not
tell me any of this that he has said and done. Now I grow

very angry for the first time in my life." A heavy clanking of machinery began. We smelled ozone.

The President tried to hold him back, but it was like trying to restrain a battleship. "Don't blame your brother!" he called up to the rising shape. "It may not be he who is deceiving you, and us. Here on Earth you mustn't believe everything that's printed. Can't you read his mind, and learn the truth?"

"The truth is that my twin has shut me from his mind and heart." Steam began to pant through the valve like heavy breathing. "No Martian has ever done so horrible a thing to another since our race came of age, a hundred centuries ago."

The clanking changed to a wild moaning, dreadful as a giant's funeral dirge. "Now I do the same to him. I shut my brother from my mind, my heart. His last message was, 'I come to kill you. There is not room enough on this earth for both of us.' And I replied, 'I accept your challenge. One of us must die. Our happy family must not know disunion. The survivor shall report the other lost in space.' "

With terrifying power the huge legs rose up and up like trees. The ground trembled like an earthquake. With scorching brilliance a great light began to swing its searing ray from side to side. The crowds in the streets fell back, and began to run. Marines and soldiers and White House guards shielded their faces with their arms as the fearsome beam passed over them.

At treetop height the Martian stood, looked down upon us in awful majesty, and left us with this thought:

"Man's Fate must be decided in man's cruel way, this one last time, as ours was. I go now to kill my brother. When on Earth we shall do as earthlings do. It will be our first murder in ten thousand years. But it is necessary. My brother has challenged me to a duel to the death. The winner will return with a hundred ships to enforce peace on Earth forevermore, for the side that he has chosen. I choose liberty. Your tragically divided planet must be united, as is ours, before your good green Earth is fit for Men or Martians to inhabit. Farewell. *I shall return!*"

Bette sprang up and screamed. Her voice was drowned in a dreadful roar. A torrent of blue flame crashed down, and the space ship shot into the sky. Blasted earth and smoking sod was flung into our faces, and many of us fell, from the concussion and from fright. Dazed and half blinded by the flash, we stumbled to our feet and watched it go.

The man from Mars did not vanish into azure depths of ether, whence he had come to us that morning when the church bells rang for One who had risen some nineteen hundred years before.

The man from Mars was now a man of Earth, sick with Earth's old sorrow. Searching the sky with a beam of light, the Martian groped northward across America, zigzagging like a fierce bird seeking prey.

Bette sobbed and hid her face against Ted's chest. The fragile helmet had fallen to the ground and broken.

Zweistein and his colleagues hurried outdoors just in time to see the space ship vanishing over Baltimore.

We stood helplessly on the scorched earth between the burned flower beds. It became surprisingly quiet.

A presidential secretary came outdoors looking for the Chief. She found him sitting on the grass looking at the sky. His hair and eyelashes were singed. He had been closest to the pillar of fire. She bent down and said, "Mr. President, the Ambassador at Moscow is on the radio-phone."

He nodded, stood up, and brushed blackened earth from his zipper suit. "Let's all go inside now," he said in a calm, clear voice to the whole group. "We must stay near our communications."

As we trooped solemnly inside, still badly shaken, the shadows of the afternoon began to sift across the White House lawn like phantom fingers.

We sat in the room where the Supreme Scientific Council meets. Ted and Bette went into the pressroom. He had to file his story. It was his last story as a White House correspondent, although he did not know it then. Men seldom do. Perhaps it's better that way.

The radiophone operator reported that the Ambassador's call had become inaudible. Electromagnetic storms were disturbing radio frequencies all over the world. Sounds more gruesome than any horror show came from our radios that night. Remember?

"All frequencies are jammed," reported the Naval Monitor.

"I'm not surprised," said the President. "We are all in quite a jam, I fear." He did not smile. His face was deeply lined by the strain he had been under for many hours. He looked around at each of us in turn, and stopped on Professor Zweistein. He said, "I realize that you have had only a very short time in which to examine the model we obtained, but I was hoping that perhaps— No, that's impossible, of course, I apologize."

Zweistein said, "Doctor Berkley can answer you better than I can, Mr. President. I am an old dreamer. It is these young scientists who do the real work." He smiled proudly at the keen young faces around him.

Dr. Berkley reported crisply, in his nasal New England twang. "We took it apart. It wasn't hard. We have done it before."

The General's bushy eyebrows went up like flags. "You've been meeting Martians secretly? This is treason!"

"Well, not exactly," said Dr. Berkley, and for the first time I saw his dry smile. "The Martian machine is a working model of a uranium atom, magnified some billion, billion times. The synthetic atom is the ultimate in physics. When you have that, you have everything."

"How soon will we have it?" the General demanded.

"In three or four years, if we drop everything else, we can probably build you a duplicate. But it won't work, because we do not know its source of power. Its circuits all terminate in a heavy cable that plugged in somewhere else. Until they show us how to build that unknown power source, the machine is useless. We have a strong suspicion it harnesses the cosmic rays, of which we know practically nothing. But it's a beautiful job of engineering, that synthetic atom. It's going to be a real privilege to work with those brains when they come back."

"Come back where?" the General said gloomily. "To Washington or Moscow?"

"Moscow is on the wire, Mr. President," said the radiophone operator.

Our Ambassador said in his soft Southern voice, "Well, that thing is gone. It shot up out of the Kremlin across the street from us a few minutes ago in a cloud of fire. It left Moscow headed due east, and was last reported over Lake Baikal, in Siberia."

"Yes, ours is gone, too," said the President.

The faraway voice hesitated. "Mr. President, were those things really from Mars, or is all this some kind of joke?"

"I wish it were a joke," said the Chief. "I'd feel better than I do now. Thanks for calling. Good night."

Then came an NBC radio monitor's "catch" of a badly garbled broadcast in Russian from Radio Moscow. We translated the audible phrases:

"Mighty Red Sphere risen over Red Square . . . defense from unprovoked treacherous attack . . . craven lackey traitor Martian . . . victim of lying warmongering propaganda . . ."

At this point we gave up trying to make sense out of it. The yellow fringe of our own press was nothing to be proud of, either. I have before me a copy of a tabloid displaying this headline:

RED MEAT BALL TO BE HASH, OUR GOOD EGG VOWS

At 5 p.m. our Martian was sighted over Philadelphia. Two minutes later he passed Denver, narrowly missing

Pike's Peak in his haste.

At 5:03, the U. S. Army headquarters in Tokyo reported Martian Number Two "crossing Japan at a speed estimated to be in excess of one thousand miles a minute, soon disappearing over the Pacific."

At the same minute, Martian Number One streaked over Santa Barbara and lost itself against the sun.

For five minutes there was no news. A watching world held its breath. Even the most dogged soap sponsors had stopped trying to sing their commercials. All radio stations were on the air, but silent. Sometimes you could hear excited announcers breathing heavily as they clutched their microphones and waited for the next news flash.

At 5:06 they all spoke in unison, a Greek chorus chanting a global tragedy, stern, relentless, fore-ordained.

"From Honolulu comes this report: The two Martian space ships have sighted each other over the Hawaiian Islands and are maneuvering for position. Sounds like human cries are coming from the sky. People are fleeing from their homes and running wildly in all directions. Sparring and feinting like boxers, the huge aircraft are moving eastward, out of sight."

They joined battle over San Francisco at 5:09. Thousands of eyewitnesses have described it as the most awe-inspiring spectacle that the eyes of mortal men have ever beheld. The view from the Top of the Mark was said to be especially good, a ringside seat. From a hundred pages of verbatim testimony, some of it hysterical, these representative phrases are culled from the accounts of housewives, taxi drivers, farmers:

Sheets of blue and violet flame waved like window curtains. . . . They dove and whirled and dodged across the sky like devils dancing. . . . It was like this, see? Take all the fireworks out of Hell and sling them into Heaven, see? . . . I thought it was the end of the world for sure. I looked at my poor babies all unbaptized and one of them not even my husband's. . . . Damn if them two crazy silos weren't a-throwing pitchforks of lightning at each other.

At 5:11, one Martian chased the other up across Canada and Newfoundland. At 5:15 they were over England, from where they fought their way across France and Germany, then veered south over Italy to Africa. By 5:30 they had fought their way completely around the world and were back over St. Louis, Missouri, in a blaze of infernal flames and peals of thunder.

By this time the whole world was standing in the streets, straining for a glimpse of the conflict whose outcome would decide our fate. Even Chinese coolies seemed to sense that something was being decided by the dreadful battle in the sky. Russians and Americans stood helplessly and watched their political proxies slug it out for the planetary purse. Many must have hoped in their secret hearts that this duel of giants in the sky would settle things one way or the other, without war, so that John or Ivan could come home from the army and marry Mary or Maria. Others were minded of the olden days, when a fencing match between two princes settled international disputes.

The clash over Alabama was especially severe. Drops of molten metal fell from the sky, and several spectators in Mobile were blinded. Then like blood-crazed eagles the Martians closed in to short range and began to fight their way northward.

Although thousands of binoculars were trained on the fight, and hundreds of amateur movie cameras were whirring from rooftops, it was impossible to determine then or now which Martian was which, or who was winning. Stripped of their magic armor by man's craft and woman's guile, brother fought brother with the clanging of celestial anvils. The primitive aggressions that had slumbered in their blood for ten thousand peaceful years burst forth in atavistic fury. They lashed savagely at each other with mile-long whips of blazing solar energy, degrading the peaceful science of a tranquil planet in the fratricidal strife of jungle beasts.

That was the night we had a preview, in thrilling Technicolor, of the Armageddon that is in store for us, or for somebody, depending upon which Martian won, and which men said what to the survivor. For this was a battle to the death. Maddened by the fire-water ideologies of partisan politics, the twins asked and gave no quarter. Only one of them would return to Mars, with his side of our story.

At 5:33, they began to spin together in a fiery dance of death at a point thirty-six miles northeast of Columbus, Ohio, in Delaware County. At 5:34, as the sun was setting on brown fields softly green with tender corn, the awful battle of the space ships reached its crashing climax.

With the shrieking of a million demons, with the flames of all Hades spewing out in every color of the rainbow, the two Martians flung themselves headlong against one another, at supersonic speed, in a two-way suicide crash.

The explosion in the sky has been likened to a volcanic eruption, to Krakatau, to Hiroshima. It broke windows from Cleveland to Cincinnati. The dazzling flash of crimson light was visible from Indianapolis to Pittsburgh.

Then, with an ear-splitting shriek of anguish, one Martian space ship fell slowly to the Earth streaming green and yellow flames. Eyewitnesses at Woolley Park stated that it was almost entirely consumed by weird spectral flames before it reached the ground.

The other Martian, whoever he was, was completely unharmed. He followed his brother down in circles to make sure he died, and delivered a sizzling fireball of pure energy as the *coup-de-grâce*.

The dead Martian crashed in a cornfield one mile northeast of Ashley, Ohio, between the old tile mill and the high school. (As I write, my radio announces that this field has just been proclaimed a National Monument. Tourists are streaming there by thousands.)

The winning Martian, either to show us he was safe, or as a gesture of hostility, flew three low circles completely around America, humming triumphantly, clearly seen by millions of reliable eyewitnesses, including me; and at six sharp took off for home.

Yes, he soared into space as the sun went down, and on the horizon a red planet rose. Whether he was Mister One, or Comrade Two, he was last seen by the Mount Palomar telescope leaving the Earth's gravitational field at meteoric speed.

And that's that. For a while—

I wish I could record that conditions quickly returned to normal, but conditions did nothing of the kind. The world isn't back to normal yet. If the condition we were in, before the Martians came, was normality, then you can have my share of it. Everybody seems to like it better this way. There are outbreaks of spontaneous laughter, singing and dancing in the streets, all over the world, and nobody knows why. Maybe Bette Pringle knows, but she's not saying.

She wasn't much help to us that night. Her testimony would have stupefied Solomon. Of course, we all piled into airplanes and flew to Ashley, Ohio. The presidential pilot landed the Sacred Cow in the fair grounds. The mayor had cars waiting. We reached the cornfield about ten. Maybe eleven. I can't keep those time changes straight when I fly. The Ohio National Guard already had floodlights set up, and was doing a fine job of keeping souvenir hunters off the field.

There weren't many pieces to pick up. A few shimmering fragments of broken wreckage strewn among the first tiny pale green blades that would have grown up to be tall corn, if they had been in some other cornfield. This field, of course, was trampled into total ruin by our searching parties, combing the wreckage for some clue to the maddening mystery that confronted the whole world: *Which Martian got away?* That was the 64-ruble question. We never did find out what made him tick. If Bette knows, she hasn't said so.

We poked around all night, out there in the cornfield. The dazzle of the searchlights hid the watching stars above. Early next morning Allen captured a grizzled little old man in a printer's ink-stained apron. He had forced his way into the guarded area without permission and was loudly demanding to see the President of the United States.

Ted ran over to where they were holding him. It looked like a story. He might even be a Martian, for all we knew now. Nothing would ever look quite the same again.

Ted and the other two wire service men were there with us, as a matter of course. It is a White House S.O.P. for these three regulars to accompany the President almost everywhere he goes. Other newspapermen were arriving, too, from all directions.

Firmly gripped by two husky Secret Service men, the little old man addressed himself to Ted in a voice that rang with fearless indignation. "What in tarnation is everybody doing trampling down my cornfield?"

"Who are you?" Allen demanded.

"I'm the editor and publisher of the *Tri-County Star*, and furthermore, I own this cornfield."

"Release him," said Ted grandly, with a wink to Allen. "This gentleman is a member of the Fourth Estate."

Allen took the wink and set him free.

"Thanks, young fella," said the old man, adjusting his ruffled dignity and shaking Ted's hand. "I'm suing you—"

"I'm not the President," Ted interrupted. "That's him over there in overalls leading the searching party."

"What's he searching for in my cornfield?"

"Haven't you heard?" Bette asked, coming up quietly behind us, as she has a way of doing.

"Heard nothing. Been printing this week's issue. Can't even hear my radio when my presses start to roar. Why, what's up?"

"Oh, just men from Mars," she said, beginning to get a calculating look in her eye and sidling closer.

"I don't take no stock in it. Young fella, I see you wear a press card in your hat, and you look fairly bright. How does a citizen sue the government for damages?"

"I'll explain it to you," said Ted, and took him by the

arm. "In fact, I'll help you draw up the papers. You'll win your suit, too, if they don't buy your field outright, by Act of Congress, for a national monument."

Bette took the old printer by the other arm. "What are you going to do with so much money?" she asked sweetly, smiling.

"Do? Do nothing. I've done enough. I'll retire."

"Then you wouldn't be wanting too much for the *Tri-County Star,* would you?" asked Bette innocently. She opened her capacious shoulder bag and took out a small folded newspaper. "I've been reading this. Found it at the fairgrounds." She unfolded the paper.

"That's last week's issue," said the editor. "That news is cold. You should see this week's issue. Hot. Got everything in up to Friday noon."

"It looks good to me," said Ted, scanning the front page. "What's the circulation?"

I missed hearing the rest of that historic conversation. I was called into conference. The Chief had found a little blob of organic matter spattered on an unburned bit of wreckage.

Zweistein asked me to analyze it, and at last biochemistry had its shining hour. I scraped the remains into a paper cup, dreading the long flight back to my laboratory in Washington. Then a bell began to ring, and looking up I saw Ashley High School, a large modern building. School busses were arriving.

Instead of flying to Washington, I walked over there. I felt confident that in a good American high school I would find a well-equipped science room, turning out the boys and girls who have put us up in front and who will keep us up in front in science.

I found it. With the science teacher and the 4-H club, we tested, analyzed, and examined the substance the Chief had found. I gave each of them a peek through the microscope, explaining carefully, "The characteristic structure of the cerebral cortex tissues is unmistakable in this specimen."

A small boy gave me a dirty look. The science teacher translated. "It's brains."

I lumbered back across the baseball diamond to the cornfield with a military escort. I held that paper cup in both hands like a funeral urn. I took the science teacher's cue in rendering my official report. I said, "Gray matter, same as ours."

The National Guard formed a hollow square, and we buried the spoonful in the paper cup with full military honors.

We went over that field with a fine-toothed comb, but that's all we ever found of the man from Mars. Perhaps Miss Pringle's biologic studies were more accurate than we believed. Maybe that's all there was of him. A brain. Or maybe not. No man will ever know, until the Martians come back and move in with us. Or with somebody.

"I think he would have chosen to be buried in a place like this," said Bette, as she stood beside the little mound. It was no bigger than the grave of a newborn baby, and quite as difficult to look at.

It may be that Bette was crying a little, but it is risky for a man to speculate upon what Miss Pringle does or does not do, because of those confusing glasses that she wears, all gold and ivory and rhinestones.

The sun rose higher. Her frames sparkled. Ted's eyes flashed. "And where did you get those glasses?" he asked her.

"I've had them on all along," she said. "Surely you must recognize these frames."

"That's just the trouble," he said, with a deadly quietness creeping into his voice. "I do recognize them. This is the pair you left inside the space ship. You picked them up last night in this field when no one was looking."

"I did not," she said pleasantly. "I had them in my handbag all the time. You know how keys and purses and stuff eventually turn up, if you don't scare them off by hunting for them. Well, glasses are like that. They have minds of their own. Mine have, anyway. And so have I.

I hate being questioned."

"I am quietly losing mine," said Ted. "If I can't ask questions, will you make a statement for the press? You are the only person on this earth who can give us any hint as to which Martian got away. A trivial question that may already have crossed your mind lightly."

"It crosses mine like a Sherman tank about once every three seconds," said the General grimly. He was marching nervously up and down the field trampling the hopeful sprouts.

The other two press association correspondents were waiting for Bette's answer, as was the Foreign Editor of *The Columbus Citizen*.

Bette said, "If I knew the wrong one got away, I wouldn't be so happy, would I?" She smiled that cryptic little smile.

The General executed an about-face and asked eagerly, "Then can you positively state as a Military Intelligence report that this wreckage is not part of the one who was on the White House lawn?"

"I positively refuse to make any such positive statement," she said. "After all, they were twin brothers, and I was in a plastic bubble. Besides, I'm dreadfully near-sighted."

"With your glasses off," Ted corrected. "With your glasses on, you see more than anyone I've ever known."

"Let's not say glasses any more," she said softly, and turned away, and arranged a handful of spring wild flowers on the pitifully small grave. She had picked anemones and violets. Then, with a woman's wordless insight, she added a sprig of those dainty and mysterious blooms called shooting stars.

We gazed in bafflement upon her flowerlike little face. She seemed so guileless and so wise, so candid and so inscrutable. I suppose we will never know what really goes on inside their minds. They may all be in telepathic communion with those unusual men from Mars. Maybe that is what girls are thinking about when they get that faraway, starry look in their eyes and then say, "I wasn't thinking about anything." How can cerebral cortex be thinking but not about anything?

Bette took Ted's arm and turned her back upon the grave. "Please take me over to the town," she said. "We have business to attend to. I'm so glad you're *you*, and not—somebody else."

They walked toward Main Street, where I saw them joined by the editor and the publisher of the *Tri-County Star*, accompanied by a character who was obviously, even at that distance, a lawyer.

The newsreel moguls who had meanwhile arrived in chartered planes captured Professor Zweistein and induced him to say a few words about the great occasion. You may have seen the films of that bizarre service the morning after Easter, how the old prophet's fluffy white hair blew in the wind like an autumn dandelion, how simply he spoke in his halting German accent, beside the Martian's grave.

"I hope he's happy now, whatever his name was. He lies in the tender mercy of the four elements he prized above jewels. Elements we take for granted. Our air, our sun, our rain, our Mother Earth. I suppose this Martian thinks he got to Heaven. Who am I to say that he did not? Perhaps we have a Heaven here on Earth, unnoticed all around us, except when a few men turn it into Hell on Earth. My hope is that this strange adventure may somehow end in greater happiness for all mankind."

What you didn't hear on the newsreel was the voice that then yelled cheerfully, "Okay, Mac. Cut. Now shoot that spiel all over again, and put more zip in it!"

That brought me back to Earth with a jolt.

It is still too early—this happened just last week, you know—to say more than that the man from Mars, whichever one he was, has already brought happiness to at least two human beings. Ted and Bette now make their home in the pleasant village near where the space ship fell. Through his death they found the life they dreamed o having. Which is the only way any of us get life, if we stop to think it through, biologically.

I said good-by to Mr. and Mrs. Theodore Bonifield last night on their front porch. It was a spacious corner porch, overlooking Main Street's single business block. Such porches make convenient offices for editors, who have to keep an eye on the most important news events in the world, for their readers. Ted and Bette beamed like proud parents as they told me the purchase price. "That includes two setting hens in the city desk," said Bette. "Their names are Caps and Lower Case."

After the Justice of the Peace had kissed the bride and gone home, we sat and rocked awhile. We let the cool breeze blow on us, and sniffed the clean wet smell of the freshly watered lawn. We had a frugal wedding supper of cider, apples, and a six-pound sirloin steak that a friendly neighbor named Jennie brought over when she saw newly-weds moving in.

For once, I knew when to leave. I kissed the bride, and left immediately, walking west on Main Street to the Big Four depot to catch the evening local down to Columbus. I was tired of traveling fast.

Yet even on Main Street, which is as down-to-earth a place as you could ask, I sensed an electric difference in the air, noticed the changed way people looked and spoke to one another, the new atmosphere of hope, since those men from Mars had come and gone. The crackling action was over—for a while—but people all around the world were thinking crackling thoughts. An idea can be more genuinely exciting than killing somebody on every page.

For instance, those three great circles that the winning Martian flew above America. Were they threats, or promises?

Mr. Tvordyznak, the Soviet Ambassador, insists they were three cheers for the U.S.S.R. Sir Jules Jameson, as nearly as anyone can make out what he's saying, seems to think the three circuits were the Martian's intellectual way of telling us they would return to America—not Russia—on Mars' third solar cycle. Could be. Or were the three ten-thousand mile rings a skywritten testimonial to a beverage, as a certain advertising agency now claims? I just can't imagine what it meant. Have you any theories?

Or have you taken a good look at Mars lately? Millions have. Observatories are more crowded than the bars. Watch how significantly it swings across our sky, the red planet of peace, misnamed for the pagan god of war. Tonight it's not just another "star" to millions of Johnnies and Vanyas, walking their Mollies and Marussias home across the same good earth, breathing the same wind that blows around the world to make all mankind literally blood brothers by the oxygen it carries. Now Mars is our companion ship on the high seas of space, a ship we passed in the night. Now Mars bids good-by to its brief encounter with our Earth, and sets sail alone, swinging off into majestic deeps upon its annual grand circle cruise around our central lighthouse Sun. But Mars comes back around, as all things do. We two shall pass again, and that is when our friends or foes will sail across to us.

Who can look into the sky tonight and not think to himself, *Somewhere out there in the aching cold and awful loneliness of interplanetary space an agitated brain inside a pink egg shell is streaking home with great good news. The deal he got here is certain to delight his happy family, where no one ever disagrees, everyone believes what he is told, and no one ever tells a lie.*

Whether the surviving Martian envoy was our Mister One or their Tovarisch Two, we may all be sure that they are busy up there now on Mars preparing their Exodus to Terra, their promised land of milk and honey. There may be Martian agnostics who doubt that Earth exists, but these skeptics can easily be left behind to go down with the ship. There may be last-minute conversions as the Martian Armada prepares to sail, as our Mayflower sailed from the Old World to the New three centuries ago, to shores more dangerously distant then, than Mars is from the Earth today.

Those Men From Mars

You may rest assured, if you can rest at all, that the Martians—red, or red-white-and-blue—will return "in force," as the General would say. And does. Frequently. In his sleep. Yet all that those men from Mars will do, when they return with their invincible machines, is to enforce without bloodshed one of the two fates which Man has already prepared for himself. The *deus ex machina* did not create Man's problem; but they will solve it. Whichever side they take, we will be spared the fratricidal holocaust that would lay waste to God's green earth and make both sides the losers, evermore.

Naturally there's no sense in fighting now, when it may start raining pink Easter eggs. The Premier is reported to be spending most of his time looking through the right end of a telescope at Mars, instead of through the wrong end of his telescope at Terra, not so firma. The Politburo is busy trying to decide whether the Martian Soviet should be placed at Omsk, or Tomsk, or Minsk, or Pinsk, thus giving themselves a splitting headache, for a change. Mr. Tvordyznak, the hard ambassador, has been replaced by Madame Myakyznak, a softer sort.

Letters are arriving at the White House by the sackful offering suggestions on where we should proclaim the Sovereign State of Marsiana, should we be needing one. For some diabolic reason, probably my beard, I have been assigned to sift the facts and recommend the spot that best its their biologic needs. Have you any suggestions?

In the strangely happy, slightly wacky peace that has descended from above, bewildered little men on both sides of Earth's iron curtains have begun, ever so slightly and all in fun, to suspect their parentage—for they realize now that in their hearts they have always been men from Mars. They find themselves in the same space ship with One or Two, dropped impartially into a partial world, asked to take sides on burning issues which, whatever their undoubted patriotic merits, have sad results for nature lovers who would very much prefer to sit and smell the flowers. What more does anybody really want from life beyond our four commonest elements, which the Martians told us were precious beyond price? A place in the sun with a flowing brook and the good earth underfoot. Or even an apartment. Do you know where I can find one? As a biologist, I must officially confirm that our Martian made excellent suggestions on how biped mammals should spend their time, playing in the grass with young females, basking in the sun, smelling flowers, and swimming in the liquid water. That's what they did in Eden. For a while I suppose that's what Ted and Bette Bonifield are doing now.

Well, whichever Martian got away, the Kremlin's *Krasnaya Sphera* or the Meat Ball on the White House lawn, it won't be long now until we know the worst. Or best. Every three years or so, according to my almanac, Mars and Earth come into conjunction. Any planetarium will be glad to show you what this means, with pretty models. Maybe not too glad, if they find out what you've been reading.

Every fifteen or twenty years, Earth and Mars enjoy the intimacy of an extra-close conjunction. I hope we enjoy the next one. Our Earth will practically brush shoulders with Mars, at a mere 35,000,000 miles.

That's just a sleeper-jump, in science fiction.

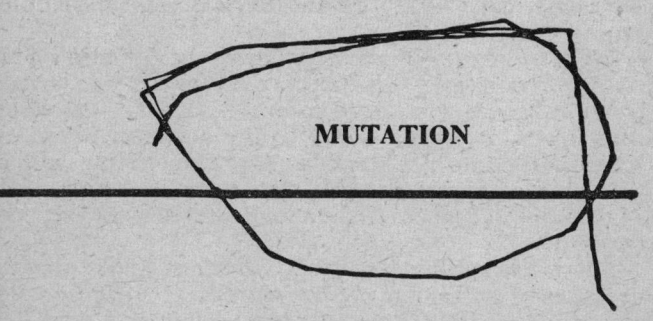

MUTATION

UNDER THE PINES, beside the mountain brook, where the bearded man lay reading and fishing, it was almost as if nothing had changed. The air was fresh, the water clear and merry.

The book he read was badly scorched. Reading it made the Reverend Adam Jones heartsick. What bright promises this book had made to man. Promises Adam had preached, pleading for belief. Promises that had come to nothing, now. To worse than nothing.

Yet he read the book, when he could spare the time from grubbing to stay alive. It was the only book left, and he did not want to forget how to read. It was terribly easy to forget, to revert to the primitive, as his son had done.

The Reverend Jones was barefoot, his loins wrapped in a goatskin. He read, *And a troop of shining angels appeared and ministered unto the newborn babe; and men's hearts were uplifted.*

With a sigh he closed the charred pages. Shining angels, indeed. He could use a couple now, to minister unto him. For two days he had eaten only wild berries. His heart was badly in need of uplifting. Mary was not well. She was hiding something from him.

The fishline tugged. Adam seized it with both hands. He could guess, from the ugly way it pulled, what he had caught. One of the new fish. He did not like their looks, but they were good to eat. Their meat was rich and white, like lobster.

He hauled the thing to shore, clubbed it to death, and

carried it home.

He hurried. He was hungry. They were always hungry.

Mary was standing in the mouth of the cave, drying the wooden dishes she had made.

He called, "Look, dear. I've caught another of the queer fish."

She waved cheerfully to him. She was a large, strong woman, capable and calm. She wore her doeskin apron with dignity. Like her husband, she was barefoot and sun-burned and half starved. In marrying a minister, years ago, she had chosen a life of privation to be spared from the flames. She had not expected either to come true quite so dramatically as they had, but she did not complain. At least the Joneses were alive. That was more than anyone they had known could say.

Mary took the monstrous fish from Adam's hand and held it up to admire. "I wouldn't call them queer," she said thoughtfully. "They're rather beautiful, in their strange new way. And so nourishing! We couldn't have lived on trout, you know. No calories. Isn't it miraculous, Adam, the way this new species simply appeared in the streams after—"

She changed the subject. By tacit agreement, they never mentioned what had happened. Yet it was so hard to talk about anything in their small ruined world without leading back to that blinding instant of universal catastrophe, years ago. The Joneses did not know what year it was now. Who cared?

Their son swaggered up from the spring. He was a shaggy brute, brown as an Indian. A stone knife dangled from the belt of his buckskin loincloth. He remembered nothing of the other life, except that one night when he was a child there had been pretty lights in the sky. Awfully pretty. "Gimme the fish," he growled. Under his matted hair his eyes were hard and dull.

Mary said, "No, Kane. This is for all of us. Mother will cook it and divide it equally, dear."

Kane seized the fish by the tail and began to pull,

screaming. His father stepped between them and twisted the wiry fingers off, one by one, gently. Kane whipped the knife from his belt and lunged. His father slapped the hand aside. The brittle flint blade fell to the cave floor and broke in two.

Backing away, Kane threatened, "I'll make me another knife. A bigger knife! Then you'll see!"

Grief in their faces, Adam and Mary watched their savage son slink into the forest. Mary said, "I don't know what's come over him since he's grown up. He was such a sweet child, when he had other children to play with. When he was four—" She broke off again, and concentrated upon cleaning the freakish fish.

Adam said, "Lately he acts as if he was a throwback to some race of devils."

Mary shook her head. "Throwback or throw-ahead, it's all in you and me. Locked in the cells of our flesh like a will to be opened and read, when the time comes. If our son has gone savage it's because we were all savages once. Look, Adam. This fish was ready to bear young."

He blinked at what he saw. "I thought fish laid eggs," he said weakly.

She laughed. "That's because you haven't cleaned any of these new ones. Incidentally, my dear, I have a little news for you myself." She smiled and hummed as she worked.

Adam Jones staggered back against the cave wall, white-faced. After a while he gasped, "Mary, how could you?"

She leaned over and kissed him. "How could *you*, Adam? Don't look so terrified. Everything is going to be all right. It will be fun, having a baby to love, after all these years. It's lonesome in this cave, Adam, with you out hunting, and Kane gone wild—and no neighbors."

The man pulled himself together. "Maybe there's a doctor left, somewhere. Will you be all right for a couple of months, while I go out on a scouting trip? I've wanted to for years. Now I've *got* to."

Fear clouded her bright, calm face. "No, Adam. Promise

me, no matter what happens, you won't leave our valley. There's food and unspoiled water here, enough for three or four of us—but no more. Don't take any chances on our heaven-sent sanctuary being discovered. Remember what we saw, a year after, the day we climbed up to the ridge and looked at the city through your field glasses."

He shuddered. It had not been a pretty sight, what the few maddened survivors were doing, in the ruins of Los Angeles.

Kane appeared at the cave door and said sullenly, "If I brung you somethin', would you lemme eat?"

Adam started to correct his son's uncouth speech, then stopped. It was no use. Kane was losing the language, along with other human attributes. Already he growled and barked oftener than he spoke.

Mary said gently, "Son, we want you to eat with us. It's just that you can't have all of it. We're just as hungry as you are."

Adam asked, "Kane Jones, what are you hiding behind your back?"

One grimy paw disclosed the charred stump of a leather-bound volume. Kane grumbled, "You're always stickin' your nose in that little one you got. Thought you might swap me your spear for this big one. It's got pitchers in it. Of funny fish."

Mary cried, "Kane, you haven't been—*outside?*"

The young man's brutal face hardened. He said craftily, "It's safe if you go at night—and carry a club. Few people, and them mostly blind or crippled or silly. Easy pickin'— what's left."

Adam said, his voice shaking, "Kane, I've warned you that anything you touch down there in the ruins may be poisoned. By radioactivity, and bacteria."

Mary asked curiously, a strange look in her eyes, "Son, did you notice—any *babies* down there?"

Kane scowled. "Seen one." He dropped his eyes and squirmed uneasily.

Mary turned and went quickly into the cave.

Adam said, "I forbid you to leave our hiding-place again. Coming back, you might be followed. Think what that would mean to us!"

Kane bared his teeth at his father. "One of these nights I'm gonna find me a shootin' gun," he snarled. "Then we'll see who's givin' orders and who ain't." He snatched a slab of raw fish from the table by the door and ran into the woods wolfing it, and growling.

Adam picked up the blackened book where his son had dropped it. It was a volume on ichthyology, from the Los Angeles Public Library, lost now as utterly as the Great Library at Alexandria, Egypt, whose burning a thousand years earlier had drawn the veil across the secrets of two millennia of civilization, blinding men's eyes forever when they turned to look back beyond that tragic event. The Reverend Jones had always felt a pang of intense personal loss at the destruction of the Alexandrian Library, because the original manuscripts of the New Testament were there, and probably documents in Christ's own handwriting. Take away the books, and mankind had little left, he thought. Like Kane.

A tear ran down Adam's cheek. Distracted by his despair, he turned the illustrated pages. *A baby,* he thought, *in a cave, in a dead world. God help us!*

Suddenly he stiffened. His eye had caught something familiar, lost it. He turned back a few pages, found what he had seen. It was a picture of the fish he had just caught. Described and named—by an archeologist. It had been extinct for fifty million years.

Cold awe crept through his veins. To think that locked away in the microscopic genes and chromosomes of the common brook trout the image of this prehistoric monster had slept implicit. To realize that this extinct species could be sprung loose again by a freak dice fall of shaken life germs, split and scrambled by radiations that had sterilized all but a few living things upon the sickened earth.

Then Adam thought of his pregnant wife, and stumbled

out of the cave, and threw the book away. Tried to pretend, as the months grew, that he had never seen the book. Hunted and fished as never before, to feed Mary. Her appetite was enormous. She grew very thoughtful.

Spring came, the gentle California spring, carpeting the mountain meadows with bizarre wild flowers Adam had never seen before. There were daisies shaped like orchids, white violets big as sunflowers, and all the clover had four leaves.

Mary tucked a spray of them under the strap of Adam's goatskin, at about the spot where the buttonhole used to be, on his pastoral frock coat. "Good luck fishing today, darling," she whispered. "Don't look so worried. Most of the babies in the world used to be born at home, without doctors. Many of them in hovels worse than our nice cave. It wasn't a good world—remember? Let's not grieve because it's gone. The holocaust was God's will. A blow that big, that awful, *must* be purposeful. Nature will take care of me, as she does the animals."

Adam forced a smile he did not feel. Her reference to the animals was unfortunate. Mother Nature was on a spree. That morning Adam had found, abandoned in a thicket on the mountain, something that was apparently intended to be a bear cub. Adam did what the mother bear had done—left hastily.

To hide his growing panic, he took down his spear, and his bow and arrow, and told Mary, "You need fresh meat to keep up your strength. I'm going out and try to kill a deer."

"Wait a minute," she said. She stood with her hands pressed to her sides, her eyes closed, her face grave. When she opened her eyes they were bright and wet. "I want to tell you something, while I can, Adam. First, this baby is no accident. It was deliberate, on my part. I prayed to God for him."

Adam fingered a flint arrowhead. "Why? Under the circumstances—"

"That is why. The circumstances. It was as if I *had* to—

before I was too old. And another thing. I don't feel like I did when I had Kane. I feel—different. Not bad. *Good*—Adam—don't stay away too long today."

"I won't," he promised. They walked to the cave door with their arms around each other.

Kane sprang out of the bushes in front of them brandishing a rusty rifle with a bayonet. Mary gasped and turned white as the trigger snapped. Adam wrenched the rifle away, examined it, handed it back. Kane hooted with cruel laughter. "Ain't found no bullets yet—but I will." He gave his mother a knowing grin. "Gonna catch me a girl, too, tonight, and haul her up here to cook for me." A troubled look crossed his face. "I seen a girl last night, out where the town usta be. It was dark, but—" He hesitated, and eyed his father. Adam could see that his son wanted to ask a question, but he had the barbarian's reluctance to admit there was anything he did not already know. How long it would take to build again if the other survivors were like Kane! Centuries of agonizing upward climb from savagery to civilization—*for what?* Another deafening guffaw of Homeric laughter?

Adam saw fear in his son's stony eyes, and he said encouragingly, "Yes, son, you saw a girl in the dark. Did she have a light?"

Kane moved uneasily. "She didn't need none," he muttered. He turned abruptly and loped into the woods, dragging his rifle by its bayonet.

Mary stared after him. "What do you suppose he meant?"

Adam said, "He must have seen some poor child dying of radium poisoning. Toward the last, their hair might glow. Oh dear Lord, I've frightened you, Mary!"

He ran to her and helped her lie down on the bed. She smiled and pushed him away. "You're the one who's frightened, poor Adam. I never felt better in my life. Run along now, and try to bring home enough meat for a week ahead. We may need it." Gaily she waved him away, and anxiously he went.

He climbed to the head of the canyon to the salt lick and lay in the blind of boughs he had built beside the deer trail. He did not know that for at least a million years men had hidden by salt to kill their meat, picturing their ambushes on cave walls. So far as Reverend Jones knew, the idea was original with him, and he was rather proud of his cunning.

Fitting an arrow to his bowstring, he thought what a splendid woman his wife was. How bravely she had adapted herself to the stunned reality of survival. How gladly she accepted the miracle of life, like a lone tree left standing after a universal forest fire. Women had things to cling to even after the world ended. The familiar drudgery of housework became a sacrament. And there had been a child to rear, the food to cook, love to give.

For Adam it had been harder. He had never done a day's physical labor in his life. He had had to teach himself to hunt without a gun, to fish without store tackle, to sow and reap the wild grains by hand, to kindle fire without a match. Yet from some hidden reservoir within him the ancient arts of prehistoric man welled up in the gentle little preacher, as if forgotten secrets slumbered in his marrow, needing only a sufficient shock to set them free.

The shock had been sufficient.

They had been lucky, the Joneses. On that fatal Monday, when the new peace pact had just been solemnly signed before the television cameras, when half the world heaved a sigh of relief while the other half sneaked to its hidden rocket launchers, Mary had a sudden impulse to go camping. As tenderfeet will do, they loaded their big old sedan with practically everything they owned, and took the baby. Exuberant with the general joy of peace in our time, Adam drove up the Angeles Crest Highway far beyond the usual picnic grounds to the highest canyon in the Sierra Madre Mountains, as far as their car could go. Shifting into low, he said, "You know, dear, I feel a little ashamed now of my sermon yesterday. About the war danger. Now that everything's all right, we'll make